Praise for Randy Ryan's *Perspectives*

"I really enjoyed reading this book. The concept was original, and I have never read anything like it. I don't think it's easy to go into detail without spoiling, but I thought it was quite innovative how the story unfolded."

Amazon Reader Review (First Edition)

HAUNTED FARM

RANDY RYAN

HAUNTED FARM

Pokeberry books may be purchased for book club, educational, business, and promotional use. For information, email editor@pokeberryexchange.com

ISBN 978–0–9972276–7–3

FIRST EDITION

Printed in the United States of America

Book Design by Stephen V. Ramey

Cover Design by Stephen V. Ramey

Prologue

It was October the 31, 1998. A full moon hung low in the sky, blazing harvest orange, its craters holding a deep, rustic copper–like hue. On a narrow, backwoods path walked four young men, ranging from their late teens to early twenties. They were drunk, slurring their speech, but not obnoxious or belligerent. Just kids. Harmless and having fun. They even displayed sense enough not to get behind the wheel of a car as they headed back to their dorm after the party. The road they traveled was long and narrow and dark. Very dark, indeed.

As barren as the woods seemed, they teemed with life. The chirping of crickets, the croaking of frogs and toads, the occasional hoot of an owl, made for some eerily sweet music. Wind gusts stirred up swarms of flaming red, gold, orange, yellow, brown, and purple leaves.

The oldest of the four young men, also somewhat of their leader, was starting to second–guess his cohorts' idea of taking this shortcut home. He looked toward his buddy. "I'm beginning to wonder whether you know where you're taking us."

His buddy, distracted by a dizzy spell, was tempted not to answer, but this was their guy, his pal, the *alpha*. He tried to sound reassuring. "Have I ever steered you wrong?"

"Are you sure you really want to get into that?" the leader said. That drew a snicker and for just a moment the disease of this place was cured.

The heaviness returned, a thick, dark fog. His buddy went quiet. Perhaps he was trying to conjure a good comeback. Or maybe he was trying to overcome the sick feeling beginning to churn through his soul.

A dozen steps later, he managed a response. "Have a little faith, brother. I've walked this path many a time."

The leader reluctantly concurred. They kept walking and talking and laughing—nervously—but it was only a matter of minutes before they came across something that would change the course of their lives.

A sign, crudely constructed from splintery old wood and faded white paint. In runny red letters, like melting candle wax or blood, were two simple words:

Haunted House

Below that, an arrow pointing north.

"No way, man," said the boy who initially spotted the sign. He pulled it from the soft ground, twirling the post in his hands like a baton. "We have to check this out."

The others weren't so sure. What kind of haunted attraction would be located along the side of this dirt road? And that's exactly what his friend asked.

The one whose idea it was to embark on this trek answered. "No, no, no. There's a house back here."

The kid spinning the sign suddenly stopped. "You've got to be kidding, right?"

Shaking his head with his eyes closed as if to indicate he couldn't be more serious, the other continued, "It's an old two–story farmhouse. The man who owns it lives there with his son."

This comment got him a laugh. "Well, of course the man who owns it lives there."

"You're missing the point. He must have set his house up. Made his own personal haunted attraction."

Another chuckle. "Maybe, but can you imagine what kind of dinky operation he has to be running?"

The sign–holder jammed the sign down. "That doesn't matter. I think it would be worth checking out."

At long last, they reached their destination. Not their original destination, but the new one, and they were no less than taken by it. On their left a long dirt drive led to a two–story farmhouse, complete with a chimney and weather vane. A small set of stairs led up to the porch, which wrapped around the sides of the house. At the base of the porch, tangled masses of old growth huddled in shadow. Two square beams supported the roof. Between them was the front door, a window to either side. Smaller beams were spaced along the front and side. Above the porch roof were three more windows—one on the left, one on the right, and one in the middle. One of the friends made a joke, "What is this, the house of Usher?"

They walked down the long driveway, rocks grinding beneath their feet. The house itself was no more or less than a typical Pennsylvania farmhouse, but as they drew close they truly got to appreciate the beauty of the decor. If not beauty *per se*, then the craftsmanship that had gone into the process. Professional or unprofessional, there was no denying it looked legitimate. A fog machine, unseen of course, spewed a blanket of fog across the front yard. From this snow–white smoke, tombstones protruded haphazardly. They were of all different shapes and sizes and designs. Gargoyles and Grim Reaper architectures. Many were cracked, others showed splotches of what was supposed to be moss. A very nice touch. The dates on the stones ranged through the eighteenth and nineteenth centuries. Some were intended to suggest the tombs of revolutionary or civil war soldiers. Blue coats and red coats and confederates. Even the names were cool. Some funny, like Harry Wood Booger; others creepy in a fun, neat way, like Igor von Greenwich. That was just the front yard. The best part was the house itself.

Light bulbs had been strung under the front porch eaves, not noticeable from the road, but impossible to miss as they neared the house. These lights were not big bulbous ones, but small twinklers. Sparkling reds and blues and greens and yellows and oranges. Another unseen contraption cast a dim light upon the whole front of the house. Light that would change color, giving a chameleonic aura. Props inhabited all five windows, the two framing the door and the three above the front porch roof, were props, humanoid figures but decidedly inhuman. The lead young man thought that the one in the window left of the front door resembled the crypt keeper from the horrible, bloody EC Comics, while the one in the right–hand window looked like Frankenstein. Peering down from the upper story, were Dracula, the mummy, and the wolf man. Very traditional of the farmer using classic universal monster props. It was comfortable, a good old-fashioned haunting. But all the young men could see at this point was the outside. What was going on indoors was anything but traditional.

There was a booth set up near the porch. More like a stand. It made the boys think of a lemonade stand. The kind you couldn't walk but two blocks in Willow Falls during the summer and not run into. Sitting in shadow was a young boy perhaps eight years of age, certainly no more than nine. He was too busy interlocking the tusks of his triceratops with the short arms of a tyrannosaurus rex figurine to notice the four young men. Even the sound of their footsteps was drowned by the boy's growling sound effects.

The leader cleared his throat, "Excuse me, bud. Is this where we get in?" The sound effects and clashing ceased abruptly. The young boy looked up. He was bright-eyed and seemingly shy. His response was meek as a mouse. "Yes, it is."

The four boys exchanged glances. "How much does it cost to get in?"

The boy didn't answer right away but studied the four older boys standing before him. "Five dollars for grown-ups, four for kids."

That sounded fair enough. Hell, what did it cost to get into a popular haunted house attraction? Fifty bucks? A hundred? Anyway, there was no problem there. The house looked simple but cool enough from the outside; the young men figured it would only get cooler on the inside.

"Okay," said their leader. "You guys each have five bucks?"

Three began searching their pockets. The other, the one who had twirled the sign, thought of something. "We're actually students at the university, so would it still be five dollars for us?"

The boy's eyes flashed. He wasn't sure. "Wait here while I go get my dad."

They stopped him as he was getting up. "Don't worry about it, kid. We'll pay the adult fee."

"Are you sure because I can run and get him. He's only right around in the back."

The leader spoke for them all. "You don't have to get him, my man. We have enough. It's only one dollar difference."

The little boy between the age of eight and nine nodded his tiny head. "Okay. That will be twenty dollars please." The four students shared a smile and thought to themselves what a cute little guy they were dealing with.

So, they paid, each scrounging up the last bit of cash they had on them.

"We just go in through the front, then?"

The little boy snapped a glance at the front door and nodded very fast. "Yup. Once you're inside, you can go to any room in whatever order you want. But when you're done, make sure you leave out of the back door."

The student who had asked looked to the front door and then back to the child. He gulped. There was something about the way the kid said it.

The boy flashed a missing–tooth grin. "Go ahead. Don't be scared."

He watched the four of them inside, then went back to clashing his titans of terror. He was too engaged to notice a shadowy figure emerge from the woods. "Roar," snarled the little boy as his miniature models collided. He didn't hear the heavy, crunching footsteps until they were nearly right on top of him. A withered hand with hideously long fingers and unkempt yellow fingernails fell upon the child's shoulder.

The boy jumped in his chair and uttered a startled "Huh," before twisting around. A grin spread across his face, revealing prominent dimples. "Dad."

The farmer was in his mid–to–late fifties and towered above his son. He stood a good six–and–a–half feet tall in his bare feet, the scuffed steel–toed work boots he wore only boosting the effect. The way the son was looking up at his father created a close–up shot with a low angle, making the man seem even larger than life, the sky and surroundings within the child's vision barely large enough to contain him. He wore midnight–blue denim overalls and a long–sleeved red, black, and green plaid button–down shirt. He was bald on top, with wiry white hair growing in patches from the back and sides. The top of his skull resembled a spectacled egg.

He flashed a reciprocal grin at his child. "Just came to check on you, son. Had to take care of something. Anybody else come by?"

"They sure did. Four guys from the school just walked in."

"They go to school? You mean they go to school with you?"

The boy laughed. "No, they're older. They go to the big university."

He got a chuckle and a pat on the head for that. "Oh, I see. Well, you just wait here, little man, and I'll be right back. After this, I think we'll close shop for the night. If anybody else comes by, tell them we're closed. Halloween's just about over. The rest of the night it's just you and me. You okay staying out here a few more minutes?"

Still looking up in awe of his huge father, who most people would have guessed was his grandfather, the boy nodded animatedly. "Sure." Very fast, cute, and reassuring.

As the college boys closed the door, three or four bat props dropped down. The victims jumped, and then shared a good laugh. "Rats with wings," one of them whispered. That description could not have been more befitting. The *bats* were verminous, virulent creatures, with patchy gray hair and mangy skin. Membranous wings laced with red and blue blood veins spread from their emaciated bodies. Their faces featured yellowish teeth and bulging red eyes. Very good props indeed.

A staircase led upstairs. To the right was a long hallway with several doors.

"Should we go up?"

They had to think about that one for a moment. "Let's check out the downstairs first," the leader suggested. "That sound cool with everybody? If you guys want to do it different just say so."

The other three didn't want to do it different. Of course not.

They approached the first door. "Shall we go in here first?" the one in front asked.

"Sure, may as well," another said. The others nodded.

The young man slowly gripped the door knob.

"Are you going to open it or just stand there with your thumb up your ass?"

He looked back at his taunting friend and laughed. "Have to admit I'm a little nervous after the bats. I don't think I can handle any more jump scares, ha."

The natural teasing ensued. His friends called him lady parts and what–not.

"I just wanted to make sure you guys weren't sneaking out on me, that's all." He twisted the knob. Hinges creaked as the door swung in.

It was the dining room. No surprises, no scares from anything popping up in their faces, but a rather cool display. A beautiful crystal chandelier hung above the dining room table. In the corner of the room stood a wooden cabinet with glass doors. The shelves inside displayed some of the finest china you'd ever want to see. Paintings, primarily portraits, lined the room's walls. Two faces were very recognizable: George Washington and William Shakespeare. On the table, silver platters held prop human body parts: a limbless torso, a severed head with wild white hair and crazed eyes, a hand, a foot with ankle and calf complete with protruding muscle and artery. Smaller trays held glistening organs and entrails like succulent sausages. Hunched in chairs around the table were various zombies and cannibals with blood–red lips. Some wore wigs and powdered white faces with horrible wooden teeth, others dressed like British red coats. A few might have been early Pennsylvanian settlers. Then Indians and pilgrims. Each mannequin leaned in toward the feast or had their arms propped to look as if they were reaching for a delicacy.

"Some Thanksgiving," one of the young men mumbled.

Placed in front of these life–sized figures were plates and silverware as well as tea cups and wine glasses, some filled, not with real tea or wine, but solid dark matter that would not drip or spill. There was a fake pot of English tea, coupled with several bottles of wine. Blackberry and Blueberry Marlowe to name a few. Candles with running wax burned along the table's spine. Above their heads, set up so that it appeared to be crawling on the chandelier, was a giant, black spider, massive and hairy. Its jet–black torso and abdomen were swollen, contrasted by two solid, sanguine eyes like large rubies. The room itself featured similar contrasts, with harsh shades of black and gold patterned into the wallpaper, chair rail and trim. The scene looked like the work of a professional cinematographer. It was quite impressive.

"Man, that was some setup," the one who had left first said. He was bringing up the rear now and feeling a need to speak.

"*Halloween 4*," another offered.

"More like *Ghost Brigade*," a third said.

"*Ghost Brigade?*" the rearmost retorted. "What a wuss you are." The laughter than ensued broke their mood.

They strode forward for several steps, the old, wooden floorboards creaking. A loud, mournful groan sounded as the old house settled into its foundation. The young men laughed again.

"Where next?"

"It looks like there are a couple more doors. The kitchen is ahead. We won't go there obviously, since that's probably the way out."

"Obviously," someone echoed. "Obviously," from a third. Each repetition brought a new tremor of doubt.

The next door was locked. It must a storage closet. The one on the end, however, opened easily. This room was much smaller than the dining room.

"It appears to be a study," their leader, who was actually in the lead this time, said. His friend agreed. "I think you could call it that. Looks more like a miniature library to me though." Three walls were lined with solid oak shelves full of classic, leather–bound volumes. A work desk abutted the fourth wall. It held an old manual typewriter and vibrantly colored Tiffany lamp next to a stuffed bard owl. Did the farmer write on the side? The space above the desk held laminated newspaper clippings and the mounted head of a fox.

"Why not a buck?" one of the young men said. Real hunters showed off their hunting trophies, not a mangy scavenger.

The mounted head was scary, but the glassy eyes that appeared to look right through you was enough to send a chill down their spines. Imitation cobwebs decorated the corners of the room. Black cats, fake of course, glared down from the topmost shelves, needle–like fangs bared as if hissing.

"Spooooky," one of the young men whispered.

A light flickered to life, revealing a rotund black pot. A fan came on and paper flame—red, yellow, orange—licked up from the pot's base. Encircling the pot was a trio of witches, old, scraggly hags mechanically stirring a boiling, green goop, which shone like radioactive waste. Small bones floated atop the goop amid silhouettes of spiders and centipedes. A grainy recording started of high–pitched crackling laughter.

"Must be voice–activated," the leader said uncertainly. *At least I hope so.* As unreal as the scene looked, there was an uncomfortable *realness* to it as well. These weren't just taxidermy witches like the fox head above the desk, but misshapen, albeit tiny, women with crooked noses, puss–infested warts, and rotten teeth set in the gums at all different angles like funhouse mirrors. He couldn't help but think of the three witches that corrupted Macbeth, and wonder if they worshipped Hecate, the queen witch and goddess of the moon.

As the four college boys made their way back toward the stairs, one of them wondered, "Maybe we were supposed to go upstairs first."

"I don't think it really matters," one of the others said. "Let's finish checking out the downstairs first." At least downstairs, they were close to the back door. Upstairs the only way to quickly escape would be to jump out a window. They walked around the stairs to what looked like the living room.

From this room, you could look out the front window, which was comforting somehow. Above a bricked–in fireplace a shelf held framed photographs of a one–room schoolhouse, of men donning trousers, white button–downs, suits from ages past. Catty–corner from the fireplace stood a grand piano. As if on cue, the piano started playing Beethoven's *Moonlight Sonata*. Sitting on the piano bench was the shadowy form of a deranged pianist. This prop's face and hands were covered with matted hair. The fingers ended in talons, and its face showed the dull gleam of protruding canines that seemed distinctly vulpine. It sported a pair of pointing ears, also matted with fur. "Werewolf?" one of the young men suggested. The leader moved closer, but not too close. The prop's features were more catlike. "Werecat," he said. It was a clever little deviation that brought him some comfort. Werewolves tore jugulars. . Werecats played with their tails and groomed each other senseless.

As their eyes adjusted, it was clear that the room was rife with sophisticated werecats. One group sat on the sofa facing away from the window, dressed in fancy attire with ruffles at the wrists and around the neck. The leader thought of the classic black–and–white picture *The Cat People*, a film with its own brand of violence. The leader backed away, and nearly tripped over a glass table. The table held a sparkling glass candy holder, cup holder, and ceramic elephant. Sitting in a chair across from the table was yet another fancily dressed werecat. In a chair closer to him was a trio of deliciously evil teddy bears, with glassy black eyes, and razor fangs. Another table; this one wooden with a glass inset, bore a lamp, antique telephone, and bifocals, as well as an old book laying open.

One of the young men picked the book up and realized it was the *Necronomicon*, or book of the dead. "Way cool," he muttered under his breath. As they left the family room, the same young man noticed a wooden dummy on top of the dresser to their right. A cryptic passage coursed through his mind. *That is not dead which can eternal lie. But with strange aeons, even death may die.*

The kitchen came next. Not much to see there but a stand of fake autumn leaves laced with orange and black lights across the window sill above the sink, a block of wood painted orange with a black face in the middle, and a couple of pumpkin men made from stacked jack–o'–lanterns. Each had a different face. It was a fine country kitchen, with beautiful plates, vases, and bottles displayed in a simple hutch, and a refrigerator, stove, oven, and solid oak cupboards. And a small table draped in checkered cloth.

One of the young men imagined piping hot pies, apple and cherry and blueberry, being taken out of the oven to cool. On the checkered tablecloth was a tiny wagon hauling a cargo of autumnal flowers. From the window at the head of the table hung a mini frame constructed of branches in which sat a bear dressed in farmer's clothes, complete with coveralls and a straw hat and chewing a piece of wheat. Block letters spelled "Happy Fall."

What *wasn't* in the kitchen was the back door. That was unsettling. *Maybe there's no way out*, one of the young men thought. But, of course, there must be. Hadn't the boy, that charming, innocent boy, told them to leave through the back door?

They came to a louver door, which was closed. "It must be through there," the buddy who had led them to this haunted house said. No one had to ask what he meant. *The back door.*

He opened the louvered doors and they walked together, bunched like kittens or baby ducks, into the living room. Two long shelves along the back wall held more picture frames, a book of memories, encyclopedias, a row of paperbacks pressed between gargoyle bookends and several stacks of VHS tapes. A small banner hung from the highest shelf. Bold block letters spelled:

FALL

A set of sliding glass doors were inset into the wall opposite them. Its blinds were closed, but a silhouette of an imposing figure, at least six feet tall, waving something, presumably a knife, showed through. The young men stopped in their tracks and stared.

Outside, wind chimes sounded an odd cadence, quite unsettling, but it reinforced the mood. Even the leader jumped when a grandfather clock went off. Whether or not it was meant to be part of the act was uncertain, but it sure as hell helped matters–all four hearts were racing. A squeaky, *scritching* sound started. Suddenly, the blind thrust open, revealing the knife–wielding maniac scraping the outer glass.

"Wow," someone whispered. The lunatic prop appeared to be constructed of wood and was unlike any the young men had seen. It wore a drama mask, but holographic, changing from happy to sad as the head turned from side to side.

One of the boys edged closer, mesmerized by the awesome mask. His breath, still tinged with alcohol after all these hours and adrenalin rushes, fogged the inner glass. "How'd the curtain open?" He was too transfixed on the being staring back at him to notice the Igor–like mad scientist display whose arms were designed to open and close the blinds. As it pulled down on the ropes to close them, the boy didn't move. He couldn't take his eyes off the freaky visage separated from him by a thin layer of glass.

"Man, that little hunchback of Notre Dame dude is creepy," another said. The others agreed. "Yeah, what was his name, Quasimodo?" The young man turned from the closed blinds. "Yeah, he's freaky but not like that dude that on the other side. Did you guys see that mask? The way it was changing from face to face, man…"

"Let's go," one of the young men suggested. "I've seen enough."

"Yeah," the buddy agreed. "We should get back to the dorm before lockdown."

"Whatever you guys want," the leader said. He was ready too.

Outside, the farmer was poised. He had come prepared with his burlap sack and his chainsaw. Initially, he was going to wave a pitchfork, but a chainsaw would be much more effective for the final scare. He could hear the boys talking inside in hushed, almost reverent tones. They had embraced the haunted house, and that made him rather happy. He pulled the burlap sack with one eye hole over his face. He was now in role as Leather Face due to his choice in weaponry, though he more closely resembled Jason from *Friday the 13th Part 2*. Didn't matter. A good scare was a good scare. As soon as they opened that door, he would fire up the old saw and make sure to hold it high above his head, away from the boys just to be safe. Give them a little thanks for coming. Send them out with one final jolt to complete the tour.

The door opened, and just as he'd ruminated, he fired up the ole buzz saw and raised it high, taking several lurching steps forward. Startled, and with reflexes that may have been described as preternaturally quick, one of the boys let fly. His fist connected burlapped jaw with a solid thump. The farmer wobbled and stumbled back. He tripped over a stump, and went crashing to earth, smacking his head in the process. The chainsaw landed on his thigh, severing the femoral artery. Deep sanguine blood seeped at first, before gushing in quantities that would have filled buckets.

The four young men sprinted to the man and ripped the sack from his face. "Oh my god, what did I do?" cried the boy who had punched him.

"Just help me stop the bleeding," their leader said. "We have to get a compress on the cut."

The problem was the cut was huge. One of the boys ripped his sweater off to simulate a compression suit, but it did no good. "There has to be a phone inside. Somebody go call an ambulance!" But it was too late for that. It wasn't the blood loss so much as it was the farmer's heart condition. Unbeknownst to the four college students he had a heart murmur and had at one point suffered a mild heart attack. Now, due to shock and blood loss, it was giving out. It was only a matter of seconds before he was gone.

After they checked every body part possible for a pulse, their worst fears were confirmed. They were mortified, petrified, stupefied, and in utter shock, crying, tearing at their hair, pacing in circles, asking how anything even remotely close to this could have happened.

"Man, what were you thinking? Why did you hit him?"

"Be quiet. Keep your voice down," the leader said.

"I don't know, man, I don't know. It just—he caught me off guard. I wasn't expecting it. I just reacted. Oh, man, oh, man, what the hell are we gonna do now?"

One of the others bent over, violently throwing up. Initially, they had the impulse to do the right thing, as expressed by their leader. They should go to the police and be totally straightforward. There should be nothing to fear as it was a complete and utter accident. His friends didn't agree.

"Hell no. Manslaughter. They'll rack us up on manslaughter charges. Think about it, man. Regardless of whether it was intentional, we killed the freaking guy. They'll string us up on involuntary manslaughter charges, and when that happens forget about it. Everything is over for us." He took a step closer to their leader and grabbed him by the shoulders, looking him directly in the eyes. "Everything."

"So what do we do?" the one who had punched the man asked.

They thought about it long and hard, or for what seemed like long and hard, before deciding that they had to dispose of the body. One was repulsed, thinking they were going to chop it up, put it through the wood chipper, burn it, but the idea was simply to take the man out in the woods and bury him. Their leader was reluctant; he was too upstanding, too moral, but his friends convinced him that being convicted of this atrocity would spell doom for him, his academic career, his relationship with his girlfriend. *Everything.*

"What about the boy? We can't just leave him without a father. He won't know where to go or what to do." They were thinking about this as they lifted the body. A thought occurred to one of them. The boy. Where was the boy? What if he saw? He let go. The body tore itself from the others' fingers and fell, *thud*, to the ground.

The one who had the thought ran around front to check, but there was just an abandoned stand and two abandoned dinosaur figurines, no one to make them growl, bite, and claw. "He's not there."

"Where is he?"

"How in the Sam Hill am I supposed to know? Maybe he went inside."

They searched the entire house from top to bottom, even the attic and basement, which weren't part of the attraction. He wasn't there. They told each other that they thought it would be cool if the boy had left before the accident. Maybe he had a friend in the woods. Maybe he lived with his mother. One young man stood guard outside with the massive body while the others searched the property's perimeter. No sign of anybody. The boy was gone. The coast was clear. Whatever.

As they lifted the enormous heap of dead weight, a recurring thought came to the one who had inspected the Necronomicon inside. It was a line. It kept playing over and over in his mind.

That is not dead which can eternal lie.

He blinked heavily, trying to shake the dreadful sentence, but it wouldn't stop.

That is not dead which can eternal lie.

That is not dead which can eternal lie.

As they disappeared into the brush, as they vowed to each other that they would never speak of this night again, much less think about it, they were unaware that they were being watched, oblivious to the pair of hateful eyes now gazing upon them from the shadows. Not only did the four young men not notice the eyes, but they neglected to see that the costume worn by the knife–wielding maniac prop was missing. Every article of clothing from head to toe, including the holographic mask and hunting knife were gone.

Clouds half–covered the moon, turning it into glowering sickle in the pitch–dark sky. At last, the God–awful sentence ceased playing in a young man's mind, only to be replaced by another, even worse.

But with strange aeons, even death may die.

.

1

It was that time of year again. The time when students and teachers alike had to bid good–bye to summer. When the lush, green foliage of warm and sunny seasons started behaving like a chameleon–snake hybrid and shedding its colorful skin to dance upon sidewalks and streets with the assistance of a chilly evening breeze. To most people, the unofficial official first day of this beautiful season was the first of September; to others it was the first day of fall classes. In the case of an institution of higher learning such as Westminster in the borough of Willow Falls, Pennsylvania, that date was the twenty–fifth of August this year.

Twenty–one–year–old Jack Sayer from Pittsburgh, Pennsylvania had just gone through his third go–around of packing and unpacking his bags into a dormitory room. Willow Falls was approximately forty–five minutes north of Pittsburgh. Not terribly far, but far enough. Jack didn't think a quaint horse–and–buggy town like Willoughby, a township of Willow Falls, was superior to his hometown of Pittsburgh in any way, but any option was better than living out a four–year prison sentence at home. The moment he became a legal adult, he'd done a disappearing act that would make an illusionist envious.

It wasn't that he didn't love his parents and siblings. He did with all his heart, but he'd had to "leave the nest," as one of his friends so eloquently put it. Had to get out and experience, be an individual, be independent. Even so, he probably would not have selected an institution such as Westminster—ranked number one in the world for women in the fields of science and engineering—had his high school sweetheart, Julia Wrightson, not been a biology major. She wasn't domineering. She didn't force him to go there, but the thought of only seeing her on fall, winter, spring, and summer breaks was too much to bear. Maybe more so for her than for him, but there you have it. Jack was an accounting major.

He didn't necessarily regret the decision to sign on with Westminster. He'd made new friends, met some really cool professors, learned quite a bit more than he'd expected, and even grown accustomed to the small campus and town despite it being a dry community. Oh, well, that's why frat houses existed.

Jack stood in line holding his girlfriend's hand. It was Friday, September 26, opening day for a haunted attraction known as Blood Moon Farm in Canterbury, Ohio, about a half–hour drive from Willow Falls. The time was 6:30 p.m., and the brilliant, opal sky hung over them like Michelangelo's Sistine ceiling. Jack was becoming a little fidgety; there was a nip in the air, and they had been waiting in line for quite some time.

"I told you to dress warm," Julia said. "I don't understand why you never listen."

Jack rolled his eyes. His internal reaction was a cross between annoyance and wanting to chuckle. "You're starting to sound like my mother."

Julia laughed. "Oh, very typical, Jacky boy."

Julia had discovered the haunted house and hayride called Blood Moon Farm thanks to a billboard in downtown Willow Falls while she and "Jacky boy" were carousing the streets between classes. Its tagline read "We Grow Fear," and the event ran from September 26 to November 1. The desire to check it out defeated the likelihood that it would be as cheesy as she expected, and she set about coercing Jack into coming. Jack was semi into haunted attractions and hayrides and such, but like most kids his age was more into the partying aspect of the season. Pumpkin ale, seasonal lagers, and dressing up, which constituted hanging out with skimpily clad women that he could secretly eye–screw.

He rubbed his cheek and rotated his neck. "Are you sure you wanna go in the house first? The line for the hayride seems shorter."

Julia shot a look. He was right that the hayride line, but that didn't change her thinking. "When we bought the tickets, they said we were to go through the *barn* first." She emphasized the word barn in deference to Jacks' earlier sarcastic observation that a haunted barn wasn't technically a haunted house. Technically this wasn't even a farm. But then again, a barn was part of a farm, so yes, it was. She loved correcting Jack. "After we exit the first part of the tour, then we can get in line for the hayride. I think it will be more fun that way. We'll have something to look forward to after we get outta the barn." She pulled her hand from Jack's and wrapped her arm around his, which was quite solid and muscular. Jack was a starting middle linebacker for the Westminster Titans and one of the team's captains. "Just be patient, sweetie. It will be worth it in the end." She ran her finger across his lips. Jack pulled his head back as if caught off guard, which made her laugh and rest her head against his shoulder.

Jack wanted to remind her that it was her idea to come here, but then he remembered that he was the only one complaining, albeit not very much. Waiting in line was tedious and the bite in the air was beginning to develop real teeth, but having Julia close by made up for a lot.

"Oh, and don't forget the slaughterhouse," Julia said, "We bought tickets to both the barn and the hayride, so we get to go through the slaughterhouse too if you want."

Jack thought about it for a moment. "Yeah, what the hell. Might as well get our moneys' worth."

The line was getting shorter. They were getting closer.

"Hey, what's the legend behind this place?" Jack said. Julia was good at researching that stuff.

She smirked. "I don't wanna tell you. I think it'll scare you too much."

Jack all but ignored his girlfriend's attempt at humor. "Seriously, tell me. Didn't you read about this place in the *Vindicator*?"

Julia shook her head. "No, not in the *Vindicator*. On the organizer's personal website, though it did show an article from the *Vindicator*. Apparently, in the early nineteenth century, there weren't facilities for the criminally insane like we have today. In urban areas, they were confined to private sections of prisons, while in more rural areas like the Canterbury scare grounds, they were committed to prison farms. Buildings were built to house them." Now she really had Jack's attention. "These patients were ignored and locked up until they wasted away. Legend has it the Canterbury scare grounds was such a farm. One day the prisoners revolted and freed themselves. They attempted to escape beneath the guise of darkness, but there was a full blood moon in the sky. The 'blood–filled moon,' the article called it. Guards saw them, but this only fueled the lunatics, and the night became known as the 'night of blood' as these insane inmates embarked on a slaughter of everyone in the prison, including the remaining inmates and farm animals. The carnage only ended when state police were called in and shot eight escaped inmates. Although two hundred years have passed, and the evidence has long since been washed away, locals have forever nicknamed the site of the Canterbury murders as Blood Moon Farm."

Thoroughly impressed, Jack told her that she sounded like a novelist narrating their own audiobook and asked if she'd remembered what she'd read verbatim. Julia chuckled and informed him that she did. Then the thoughts really started coursing through Jack's mind. "You don't think any of that's true, do you?"

She gave him a look that said, *you can't possibly be serious.* "Jack, I read it on a personal website that featured a picture of a fake newspaper article. Of course, it isn't true. You can't be that gullible."

"Yeah, it's not like they would set up a haunted attraction on the site of a real multiple murder. I mean, that would be pretty distasteful, don't ya think?"

Julia did. It was yet another reason why the story was fake, "simply a fictional backstory to give the site a sense of mystique and mythology," which was what she figured the actors inside would be drawing upon for inspiration. Whether this assessment was correct, they were about to find out. It was time to go in.

As they approached the barn doors, Julia gripped Jack's arm tighter, which made him think that when it came down to it, that was what this was all about. Jump scares and nightmarish imagery brought couples like him and Julia closer. At the end of the day, people loved to be scared. There must be a psychological reason behind it, but Jack wasn't a psych major, and, in fact, found the field dreadfully boring. It must be the same as watching a horror film or riding a roller coaster. Flirting with mortal danger, knowing all the while that you'll exit safely. Maybe that temporary reprise was the only victory that humans could hope for over death. *People take what we can get,* he thought. Right now, he was going to have to take what he could get, as Julia dug her nails into his bicep and told him how nervous she was getting.

The people who entered before them should be well ahead by now. That was one good reason for the lengthy delay. He always hated running into people when he went through these things.

"Does this door swing or slide open?" he asked, admiring the chipped and faded red paint bedecking the barn door. The people running the place should have told them it wasn't paint but blood, as part of the act. That would be a cool detail, even cooler since he knew he was the one who thought it up, even if nobody else knew. Maybe he would tell Julia later.

"I'm pretty sure it swings," she said, testing her theory. It was correct. Hinges creaked as she slowly pulled the door open with her free arm. To Jack, it felt suddenly as if the leviathan were opening its gaping mouth, the entrance to hell. He pressed his hand over Julia's and held it even tighter to his arm.

Dark. Very dark. But it looked like a typical barn house. Golden straws of hay scattered across the floor, leading to walls of massive bales that Jack estimated must be upwards of a half–ton each. The barn door closed with a squeal and a bump. Darkness crowded around them.

"Where are we supposed to go?" Julia asked.

Jack wasn't sure. There had been no signs. "I guess we just walk straight until we come to something, then we can figure it out from there. You'd at least think they'd tell ya where you're supposed to go."

Julia shook her head. "No, no, you're right. We'll just go ahead." Jesus, she thought, we're only trying to find our way through a haunted barn, not disprove the theory of relativity.

Only a few steps were taken before they met the first big boo. A massive and powerful snort blew past Jack's ankle and made him leap toward Julia, nearly knocking her over.

"Jeez, are you trying to kill me or what?" she asked with a nervous laugh.

"What the hell was that?"

They looked down and saw exactly what it was. A small trench ran beneath the side wall boards like a tunnel something had been digging. The couple stood arm in arm, waiting for the inevitable jack–in–the–box scare they knew was coming.

Another snort kicked up dust and straw. Then, whatever it was began grunting before its head and snout burst through beneath the boards. Julia's nails dug into Jack's skin, drawing a grunt of his own.

The creature's wet nose twitched like a schizophrenic sniffing the air. Gleaming tusks protruded from its upper and lower jaws, ivory, the tusks of a miniature mammoth or mastodon. Or the extinct wooly rhino *Elasmotherium*, Julia thought. The ginormous robotic head thrashed from side to side. The maw snapped shut. Tusks clicked as they interlocked. Then the grunting, squealing monstrosity ceased its commotion and receded back to wherever it had come from.

Jack and Julia walked away, laughing and feeling relieved.

"I wasn't expecting that," Jack said.

"Neither was I. How do you think they did it?"

As Jack was explaining it had to be a mechanical head operated by some dude outside the barn, they were surprised again by a moaning sound. A light came on, revealing one of the prisoners. Not exactly unexpected, but the prisoner wasn't alone. He was accompanied by a mad doctor.

The sickly, sad–looking prisoner was strapped into a chair. The moaning sounded too real to be a recording. Must be a live actor. It was at this point that Jack and Julia decided that whoever had made up these actors did a stellar job. The shackled and chained mental patient had the top of his skull removed, exposing a portion of his brain. His plaintive wails evoked ultimate misery, really selling the act.

This disturbed Julia slightly. She didn't tell Jack, but it reminded her of one of her friends who had been engaged to a tall, dark, and strapping young man. About a year ago, around this very time and two months before their planned wedding, he was in a terrible car accident, plowing into the back of a tractor trailer while texting. They had to Life Flight him and remove the top of his skull to alleviate the pressure in his head. He was still comatose as far as she knew.

The employers couldn't have selected a better actor for the scalpel–wielding mad scientist. He was extremely tall and lanky, features emaciated and skeletal. He looked withered, old and tired. His pale complexion and prominent cheekbones were sharply contrasted by his sunken, purple eyes, which looked as if he wore too much mascara. The top of his head was bald and egg–shaped and accessorized with tufts of wiry white hair that jutted from its sides. He wore a long, tattered medical coat, and his nametag read, **Dr. Ernest Blackwell**. A toothless smile spread across his scruffy cheeks as he cackled an ear–splitting peel of laughter and scraped gray matter from the despicable patient.

As they passed, Jack thought he heard the insane doctor taunting him. "Leaving so soon?" or "Don't you want to be next?" but he didn't stop to listen. Jack was beginning to approve of Julia's decision to come here. He'd had his doubts, no doubt, but after only two surprises, he was really coming to appreciate what the Canterbury scare grounds had going on here.

The scares didn't stop. There was all manner of what looked like medieval torture displays or rudimentary scientific procedures you might see in the late seventeenth century when ignorance was bliss and murderers, cannibals, rapists, and sadists were indeed classified as mad victims of witchcraft, demonic possession or even lycanthropy. Jack was reminded of the Salem witch trials in Massachusetts and the multiple cases of so–called possession that inspired *The Exorcist*. Or what he had learned in French 101 when a man–eating wolf, dog, or wolf–dog hybrid terrorized the former province of Givaudan between 1764 and 1767. Many theories had been advanced concerning the monster's identity, ranging from werewolf to a punishment from God, a red–colored bull mastiff bearing the armored hide of a young boar, or even an Asian hyena. The film *Brotherhood of the Wolf* was inspired by that horrific incident. Today the creature was known as the Beast of Givaudan.

Julia tugged him past a series of animated displays, a macabre variation of shock therapy, solitary confinement, patients strapped in chairs or being dunked in ice water. Jack guessed that their screams when they emerged probably weren't acting. If they were, they were selling it extremely well. Jack couldn't imagine an actor agreeing to be subjected repeatedly to that kind of torture. He thought that was taking it a little far, before he realized that the players alternated, never going into the freezing water more than once or twice. Some film actors were all about realism. Hell, it was probably one of the performers who suggested they be dunked in forty–degree water.

Not all the characters being subjected to torture were patients. In many cases the tables were turned, and it was the escaped madmen dishing out a little punishment to doctors, nurses, orderlies, and guards. Amputations pantomimed with rusty hacksaws and hatchets were perhaps the grossest and coolest effect Jack had ever seen in person. Judging by Julia's rapt stare, she agreed.

"That's how they did surgery in Gettysburg," Jack said. "When soldiers needed an arm or a leg amputated, they gave them something to bite down on and hacked it off. No anesthetic or anything. A lot of people who visit Gettysburg claim to see ghosts of confederate soldiers walking the streets."

His mini–lecture was cut short when they came to a ladder.

"Should we climb up?" Julia asked.

Jack hesitated. He wasn't sure the ladder would support the both, maybe not even one, but he it must be okay if people had been using it all evening.

"After you, my lady," he said, trying to sound knightly.

Julia snickered. Sure, Jack would claim he wanted her to go first so he could catch her if she slipped, but a proper gentleman would go first to make sure it was safe. Either way, she didn't consider it a big deal. Jack hadn't put that much thought into it. He just wanted a good view. She whispered playfully, "Just don't get caught looking at my tight little butt, mister."

Jack didn't, but he gave it a playful smack on the way up, causing Julia to look back over her shoulder and hiss his name, almost tipping the ladder in the process. After they steadied, she laughed and continued to the top, which was just a couple more steps. She leaned out from the hayloft and took his hand. "Are you sure we're supposed to be up here?"

Jack shrugged. "I don't see why not. I can't imagine a haunted house only having one floor. Besides, the ladder wouldn't be here if we aren't supposed to climb up." With her help, he pulled himself over the lip and plopped onto the loft's edge, legs dangling.

"There has to be a way down other than that ladder," Julia said. "I mean, why would they make us backtrack? That wouldn't be very creative."

Jack agreed wholeheartedly. They searched around. Not only did they not find an exit other than the ladder and a low rectangular opening where hay was apparently brought into or out of the loft. The yard outside was empty. There didn't seem to be any displays on this floor at all.

"I was sure this was a two-floor attraction," Jack said. "I guess not." He scanned the area. It was nothing but an abandoned hayloft, dark, musty, and small. A single bale of hay lay on end in one shadowy corner where wall met wall. Someone could hide behind that, but it didn't seem likely. "Maybe we're supposed to go *down*stairs. You know? To the floor below the one we came into."

"You mean, there's a basement?"

Jack nodded. "There must be, unless they consider the slaughterhouse the second part of the tour."

That sounded about right. They weren't supposed to be here after all. But why was the ladder there? The organizers seemed to thorough to miss a detail like that.

"Oh well," Jack said. "Let's head back down."

The ladder was no longer there.

"What the hell?" Julia said.

Jack peered over the edge. "I don't see it." A realization came over him. "Oh, this must be part of the act. There's something going on up here after all. Let's just walk around and see if we run into anybody."

"I don't know," Julia said. "There's nobody here."

"Maybe they're hiding."

"Where? There's nowhere to hide."

"We'll have to find the ladder," Jack said. "We must've knocked it over."

"Well, this is just great, Jack. How in the hell are we supposed to get down?" She sounded frustrated and more than a little scared.

Jack didn't admit it, but the feeling was becoming mutual. He shot her a somewhat disgusted glance. "Are you forgetting that there's dozens of people working in the barn? We just have to get their attention."

As Julia was agreeing with him, she heard something. It sounded like shuffling feet. She even saw a shadow out of the corner of her eye. She tapped Jack's arm. "There's someone up here."

Jack's grin flashed. "Well, I guess this is part of the act after all."

Julia wasn't so sure.

"Where?" Jack asked.

She pointed a shaky finger towards the bale. *God*, she thought, *why is my finger shaking?*

Jack started creeping in that direction. Step by step, he progressed toward the rotund bale with Julia hovering in close pursuit. He latched onto one side and whipped his head around with a scream to surprise the actor before he surprised them. Nobody was there.

"I'm scared," Julia whimpered. The shadow, the ladder, it was all too *real*. She stopped herself. It had to be part of the act. But why play it out so long? Wouldn't they want to set the ladder up for the next group? The other actors didn't take their sweet time trying to scare you. They were bold and in your face. "Let's go," she whispered. "I want to get out of here."

"All right," Jack said. "We'll call for help."

As they approached the loft's edge, neither of them noticed the silent, shadow looming behind them, a broad, mocking grin consuming the breadth of its sickening mask below upward–slanting eyes. The being slowly and carefully approached as Jack hollered for help, moving gingerly as if walking on eggshells or hot coals. A gloved hand removed the razor–sharp hunting knife tucked behind its belt. The blade all but glowed when moonlight hit it.

The figure reached for Jack just as he saw another young couple approaching. "Hey!" he said as its fingers descended across his shoulder.

Jack's eyes widened. He started to turn, and the grip on his shoulder tightened, fingers digging into his trapezius muscle. Jack gasped upon seeing the hideously smiling visage.

It was the last thing he would ever see. The blade crushed through his ribcage, creating a cringe–inducing screech as it scraped bone on its way to his right atria.

Death was nearly instantaneous. Before the cloudy blackness completely consumed his vision, Jack thought he saw the expression on the mask change from happy to sad, an upside–down horseshoe and downward–slanting eyes. It was strangely fascinating.

Julia's scream split the crisp night air as Jack's body crumpled. She ran for the rectangular opening, her long, flowing hair just eluding the attacker's reach. She stumbled and barely managed to brace herself. It was a long way down. Certainly far enough to kill her if she landed the wrong way. Or the right way.

She glanced back to see her attacker approaching at a brisk pace, still clutching the bloodied knife. Once again, she looked down. It was her only hope. The fall might not kill her. This psycho surely would. No time to spare. Any moment, she would feel that blade pierce her flesh and sever her spine.

She didn't count to three or even breathe. She just jumped. It seemed she was free–falling for quite some time, but the ground closed in quickly enough.

She landed on her feet and rolled. Pain shot through her ankle like a bolt of electricity. Looking up, she saw her assailant loom over the edge, casting his taunting eyes and smile down upon her before disappearing.

Teeth gritted, she struggled to her feet and hobbled for the nearest building. *Lucky*, she thought. *I'm lucky, lucky, lucky.* The ankle must not be broken, only badly sprained.

"Help," she gasped. "Help me." Her pleas went totally unheeded. There was nobody in sight on this side of the barn. How convenient for her stalker. "Help? Please help."

Her ankle gave out. She cried out and rolled into a ball on the ground. An urge to stay there washed over her. The pain was too much, the effort too great. And, Jack... Jacky–boy... She wiped her steaming eyes with the back of a sleeve. A sob pulsed through her.

No. She couldn't give up. There was a light at the end of the tunnel. The slaughter house was up ahead. She remembered from the map where they'd come in. There would be people in the slaughterhouse. Yes, this was good. Salvation ahead. She pushed to her knees, then her feet. Only a few more steps. A building appeared from the shadows. She found it odd that there wasn't a line.

At last she reached the door and pushed through. The interior was filled with white smoke. It was impossible to see more than a few feet. She'd read something about that on the Blood Moon website, how the slaughterhouse was a maze and the night of the escape had been thick with fog.

"Help," she called. "I'm hurt." Hand thrown forward, she limped into the smoke and its myriad obstacles. Walls, tables, a square post. A sadistic butcher in a blood–stained apron wavered into view, meat cleaver extending from his fist. Others flashed past, some wearing pig masks, others with fangs like pointed needles, bulging fish eyes, necks rolled with fat. Choice cuts of meats dangled from hooks.

No once paid any mind to Julia. Perhaps they thought she was trying to pull one over on them, or that she was fellow performer. This continued for what seemed like an eternity. She continued blindly, fueled by adrenaline and fear. Finally, somebody ahead, seemed to notice her. A dark figure, turning in the fog as she lurched toward him. She extended her arm.

"Please. Please help me. My boyfriend." She broke down sobbing. "He's dead. Someone, someone murdered him."

As her shaky hand was about to grasp the individual, it moved with a quickness that can only be described as supernatural, or so it seemed.

Julia's blood ran cold. She recognized that dreadful smiling mask, the theater face. Her boyfriend's killer whipped its arm across its body, slashing her hand wide open.

Shock swept through Julia. The sight of the gash made her lightheaded as she pulled her arm to her body. She clenched her fist as hard as she could. Tendons stood from her lean forearm as blood seeped through her fingers and splattered down. Feeling drained from her face. Nausea overpowered her senses. Her vision closed in, turned gray, edged black.

The glowing mask would forever be etched into her memory and materialize in her nightmares if she survived. She blinked and blinked again. The figure appeared to be levitating now, attached to some immaterial wraith or shadow.

The next Julia knew, every inch of the blade plunged into her stomach. She coughed and gurgled as blood drizzled down her chin. Her lower jaw went slack, as if unhinged, revealing blood–stained teeth and lolling tongue. Her eyes fixed on the mask, which moved from side to side. As it moved, it changed from the happy drama face to the sad drama face. The knife twisted in her stomach and pulled out. Julia frowned as intestines spilled and landed at her feet with a sound like a water–logged towel thrown onto the floor. A shiny heap of innards, a massive coil of mating serpents. Julia fell to her knees. Her eyes rolled back in her head. She collapsed.

Forevermore would she be in the dark. Outside, perched on a scarecrow's shoulder, a crow gazed upon unsuspecting visitors. Its beak cracked open and raucous cawing resonated through the night.

2

Laurie Williams opened her eyes. Not so much opened them wide as opened them to the point where she was simply squinting at the morning sun slipping through her blinds. It was early Saturday morning, and Laurie had slept in. Even if it was early, like nine o'clock she guessed, Laurie still considered that sleeping in. She didn't want to waste her entire weekend, especially considering it was one of those rare weekends off from the lifeguard job she had gotten as part of a work study program. It wasn't a particularly well–paying job, but then again, that's all in how you perceive it. Bookish girls like Laurie tended to be good with their money. She didn't *need* to make as much money as someone less frugal. She didn't do drugs or drink, except for that one time when she did two double shots of Jack back–to–back to impress her girlfriends. She'd been sicker than a dog, which put a stop to that. For the most part anyway.

Rarely did she go out as she tended to preoccupy herself with studies and work. And she was single. She had been single for most of her life except for a brief fling with Jake, cut short by several extenuating circumstances despite the potent chemistry between them. Laurie would never let her friends on to the fact that Jake was the first and only man in her life. Her two best friends were true and good, but she didn't want them to tease her. Not that they would, but they *would* probably try to help her out, hook her up, push her to go out and talk to more boys. She didn't want to deal with the headache.

Laurie yawned and stretched before rolling to her back. She sat up, pulled the covers open, and ran her hands through her shoulder length, sandy–blonde hair. Every morning consisted of routine. Laurie assumed that everybody's morning centered on routine to some degree, but she stuck to hers stringently. She would make her bed, put in her contacts, take a hot bath, brush her teeth, and fix her hair. Depending how she felt, she would grab something to eat and be on her way to do whatever it was that needed doing that day. Nothing out of the ordinary.

She was excited today, however. Not only did she not have a project due at school for a change, but she didn't have to work either. Her job was okay, but it did get boring perched on her chair watching swimmers splash and frolic in the water. In theory it was an ideal job for her since she was on the swim team, but she longed to breathe some crisp, cool Saturday air instead of the moist, muggy, chlorine–laden air of the pool room. There was enough chlorine in that pool to kill a donkey. Open your eyes under that water and you'd pay for it with interest. Laurie often told her friends jokingly, that she wondered if the pool was more chlorine than water.

She stretched again and stood. No school work, no work–work, no swim meets or training or lifting—this was shaping up to be a fine day, indeed.

The smell of French toast wafted up the stairs. Certainly, very pleasing. What was equally pleasing to Laurie was the sound of it sizzling in the pan. *Ah*, she thought. *September sun shining like a big orange basketball, the air crisp and cool, birds singing sweet melodies. House fills with sounds and smells. A great morning to start anew.* Laurie was a poet in her free time, so yes, that is how she tended to think. She enjoyed employing the creative side of her brain, not letting it go to waste like 99 percent of the population. Her poetic impulse even followed her into the dream realm. It led to some bizarre dreams, but she wasn't concerned. She had read somewhere that if your dreams are out of the ordinary, it simply means you are a normal person. Whereas if you had normal dreams, you may need an injection of Thorazine. Her mother was an RN and claimed that any drug that ended with –zine was typically administered to mentally deranged patients. *Z is for the zanies.*

Laurie was happy to know that she was normal. But what was normal? How could anyone define 'normal'? She supposed that as long as you weren't a rapist, thief, or some type of criminal, perhaps a violent misanthrope or sociopath who liked to butcher people, normal was a pretty big tent and most people would fall into the category.

Sometimes, though, Laurie would experience a macabre fantasy that seemingly came from nowhere, popping into her head and back out before she even fully knew it was there. Sometimes they would follow her into her dreams, turning them into nightmares.

A Nightmare on Elm Street, she thought, making her arms break out in gooseflesh. The idea of that deformed boogeyman Freddy Krueger invading her dreams was ugly. She pushed the image down and thought of the carefree day ahead. She always tried her best to erase the ugly and channel the good into something creative, fruitful, and productive. To rid herself of the yin and concentrate on the yang. And it worked quite well. Laurie had placed several poems and short stories in Westminster's on–campus literary magazine, *Scrawl*, which published photography and art as well. Last semester she had a poem entitled "the way of The Mind," in the spring edition of *Scrawl*, and her Poe–like short story and poem was in the recently released Halloween/Fall semester edition.

She hoped to one day become a renowned poet and short story writer, perhaps an occasional novelist. Her two favorite authors were Edgar Allen Poe and Ray Bradbury. She had read their works multiple times. In fact, she had just begun to reread *Something Wicked This Way Comes*, which she liked to read every year at the start of the fall season. When she finished that, she planned to reread *The Halloween Tree*. Of course, she would mix in a few classics from Mr. Edgar Poe, as Jules Verne like to refer to him. But where to begin? God, there were so many to choose from—*The Tell-Tale Heart*, *The Black Cat*, *The Murders in the Rue Morgue*. Maybe she would keep it simple and just read them all. One of her favorites was *The Cask of Amontillado*. For one thing it was set on Halloween, which really helped get her in the mood, and, like all of Poe's tales, was rich with atmospheric imagery. In this case, the catacombs beneath Paris—which the recent film *As Above So Below* also used—and the ill–fated Fortunato dressed as a jester, lured into a trap by Montresor who was quite fittingly dressed as death. Just thinking about it made Laurie's stomach flutter. To get a glimpse into the psyche of a killer—not just any killer, but a killer that feels wronged or cheated—discover what makes them tick, see if they ever second guess their motives. It was all very exciting to a literary nerd like Laurie.

The Cask of Amontillado was a tale of revenge. Perfect revenge. The victim knew who was enacting their vengeance upon them, and they knew why. Moreover, they knew that their assailant would get away with the crime. *Fifty long years since Montresor had walled up Fortunato in that tomb, and it hadn't been disturbed since.* That was a lot different than putting a thumb tack on someone's chair and watching them sit on it while rubbing your hands together and laughing menacingly, confident that your victim will never knew who engineered the implement of torture.

Laurie had started as a creative writing major before she decided her true passion was teaching. She could always read and write and make herself better in the process. A teaching degree would be more marketable. A few classes in primary education had convinced her that she wanted to work with older kids, so she quickly opted to focus on secondary grades, seven through twelve. Once she did her student–teaching and completed her BA, she'd sub for a while, land a full–time position, and go back to school for her masters and doctorate degrees. She had so many interests and wanted to have deep intellectual conversations with her students rather than handing out detentions or sending them off to suspension. Although it was a lot of work, it was still a few years down the road. She'd cross those bridges when she came to them. Until then she would enjoy the life she had. After all, she had just turned twenty–one earlier this month.

Her mother greeted her as she walked into the kitchen.

"Morning, mum." Laurie debated what she wanted to drink with her mother's famous French toast, thick slices of Texas toast fried in a pan with butter and eggs, infused with brown sugar, and—the icing on the cake—drizzled in maple syrup, sprinkled with powdered sugar, and complemented by a couple slices of fruit on the side.

"Sleep well, hon?" her mother asked.

Laurie sighed. *Ovaltine or orange juice?* "Yeah, not bad. I was up kind of late, though. But I got to bed eventually." Ovaltine seemed the right choice today. She fixed a glass—three scoops—the spoon clinking as she stirred.

She sat at the table. If Mom had made anything but French toast today, she probably would have passed on breakfast. Maybe she'd've made an exception for a pumpkin–spiced English muffin, but that was about it.

Her mom was a breakfast enthusiast. How many times had she informed Laurie that if she didn't eat breakfast, her metabolism would slow down? Their doctor—possibly in cahoots with Mom—even recommended she eat seven meals a day. Laurie couldn't see that happening. One or two was enough. She'd read that the body will think its starving and begin to feed off fat if you eat just one big meal a day, but she worked out quite a bit—lifting weights and swimming, which was just about the best cardio you could do—so having a little cheat meal wasn't going to hurt her.

"Where's Dad?" Laurie asked as her mom set a plate in front of her.

"Oh," her mother sighed. "He's not up yet. Had a long hard week and all, you know how that goes."

Laurie nodded and poured thick golden-brown syrup over two slices of toast, careful not to contaminate the strawberries and blueberries on the side. She had just gotten off antibiotics and was eating a lot of dark fruits such as strawberries, blueberries, raspberries, and cherries for their antioxidants.

She glanced at the TV on the counter and saw that her mother had been watching the news. That was surprising. News made Mom nervous, all the shootings and robberies. Then there were the sickos that shook their babies to get them to stop crying and killed them. Or boyfriends who killed their girlfriend's kids because they were someone else's. It made Laurie nervous too, now that she thought of it. How primal people could be.

Things like that happened in the animal kingdom. A bigger, stronger, younger male lion defeats the smaller, weaker, older male and kills his children by closing his jaws around their windpipes, or a male grizzly mauls a mother's cubs for succession, carrying on their better genes. Natural selection fascinated Laurie. But getting back to the news, she remembered her dad saying that if the news was all good, people wouldn't watch it. Laurie aspired not to be the world's ultimate pessimist, but she guessed her dad was probably at least somewhat right.

Her mother joined her. "So, what do you have planned today?"

Laurie shook her head. "Not sure." She swallowed a forkful of syrup-drenched toast and chased it with a swig of Ovaltine. "I haven't talked to Darian and Margaret yet."

Although the TV's volume was low, anchorwoman Jean Burnett's statement about a tragedy at Blood Moon Farm caught Laurie's attention.

She looked up from her plate. **Haunted House Horror** appeared on the screen.

"Do you have to work at the pool today?"

"Hold on, Mom," Laurie politely commanded as she stood from her seat to get the remote.

"I'll get that for you, hon." He mother wiped her hands on a dishcloth and leaned toward the counter to retrieve the device. The volume bar appeared onscreen and increased.

"Thanks, Mom."

"Two Westminster students found dead at Blood Moon Farm in an apparent double homicide."

The words struck Laurie hard. Blood Moon Farm was just a few miles away, over at the Canterbury scare grounds. Two Westminster students? That really hit close to home. A horrifying sensation swept over Laurie. Did she know them? What if it was Darian and Margaret? No. It couldn't be. She'd talked to Darian last night and she didn't mention anything about going to a haunted house.

Her mother's head snapped around. "Oh my god, Laurie."

"Mom, shush, I want to hear."

Jean Burnett's carefully worried face filled the screen. "After multiple frantic 911 calls, police made the grisly discovery of two bodies, one male, one female, on the Blood Moon Farm grounds."

Her mother's hand went to her mouth. Laurie fumbled for her phone. It wasn't Darian and Margaret then, but could be Darian and Rick, or Margaret and Billy.

"We're going to take you to Patricia Cornwall who is at the scene. Patricia." The scene cut to an area outside of Blood Moon Farm. The farmhouse and the slaughter house had been sectioned off with yellow police tape.

"Thanks, Jean. Police haven't yet revealed the identity of the two students but have described their deaths as more brutal and horrific than anything they have seen. Like something straight out of a horror film."

Laurie dialed Darian's number. It rang and rang and rang. Laurie grew antsy, shifting in her seat. *Come on, Darian, pick up.* There was a click.

"Hey, babe."

Laurie closed her eyes. "Darian are you all right?"

A moment of confused silence. "Of course I'm all right. Why wouldn't I be?"

"Didn't you hear about the murders?"

"Laurie, it's too early for you to be messing with me like this."

"Is Maggie okay?"

"Sure. Laurie, why are you acting so—"

"Turn on the news."

"Why, what's on the—"

"Just turn it on, hurry."

Darian did as Laurie said, but not without telling her that she didn't understand why she was acting so weird.

Now Patricia Cornwell was interviewing Sheriff Gram, a big man standing a good six–foot–two and weighing upward of 220 pounds, Laurie guessed. He sported a trim, jet–black moustache. "It's indescribable, Patricia," he said in a deep baritone. "Twenty–five years on the force and I can't say I've seen anything like it. I'm not sure my men will ever be the same after witnessing what we witnessed here today."

"Darian, was Maggie and Billy—"

Darian cut her off. "Maggie was with me at the frat house last night."

Laurie breathed a sigh of relief. "What about Rick?"

"Rick was with Maggie, and Billy stayed home. They're fine."

Laurie told her she'd call her later and hung up. She felt as if a weight had been lifted off her shoulders, but not completely. Darian and Maggie were her only truly close friends, but she knew other kids on campus. It was a small, private college, a liberal arts school, a close–knit campus consisting of fifteen–hundred students. The odds were good she knew the victims, at least in passing.

Laurie had been through too many instances of classmates committing suicide or overdosing in high school. College was supposed to be a new beginning.

"—have no suspects at this time. Just two dead kids, and it looks as though Blood Moon Farm will die along with them."

Mrs. William's looked to Laurie. "You're good with words. Don't you think that was a little tasteless? He could just as easily have said the event place was going to be closed indefinitely, couldn't he have?"

Laurie nodded absently. "Yeah, that sounds like something kids around a campfire say, not something you say publicly while the families of the victims are grieving."

"Well, there you have it, Jean," said Patricia Cornwall. "A community rocked over the gruesome deaths of two college students, and not a single lead."

3

Sheriff Gram had to cover his mouth as the crime scene reporters snapped photos of Julia Wrightson. Or what had been Julia Wrightson.

"I don't know, Sheriff," said Deputy Flynn. "I've never seen anything quite like it. I think if Deputy Swart knew what he was going to be getting into, he may have second–guessed joining the force. Hell of a thing for a rookie to have to see."

"What's the girl's name?" Sheriff Gram sympathized with his men, and he sympathized with the victims.

Deputy Flynn scratched the side of his head, "Julia something or other. Oh, Julia Wrightson."

"And the boy?"

"Jack. Jack Sayer."

"Hmm. And he was put on display, as well."

Deputy Flynn nodded. "Yes, sir." He wasn't sure why the sheriff was asking him. It wasn't as if he hadn't seen the body himself. They had determined that the boy had been killed by a stab wound to the chest, but his throat had been slashed, nearly decapitating him, and his eyes were gouged out.

All of this seemed to fall into a realm of its own, Sheriff Gram thought. A realm known as overt homicidal violence. Did the killer have some type of vendetta against the victims? This had to be a personal crime. A hate crime, although Gram despised the term. Weren't all crimes born out of hate? Anyway, this seemed very, very personal.

"They found these stuffed in the boy's eye sockets." Deputy Flynn held up a small plastic bag containing two rolls of film. Sheriff Gram inspected the bag thoroughly. It was almost as if he'd never seen a roll of film, but Deputy Flynn understood why the sheriff was curious.

Sheriff Gram sighed. "What's the significance, Deputy?"

Deputy Flynn was at a loss. The sheriff's guess was as good as anyone's.

The Sheriff returned the bag. "Take this back to the lab, see what you can find out."

"Yes, sir."

Sheriff Gram rubbed his face. He had put his daughter through mortuary school. Was this a case of a mortuary student gone awry? It seemed so random, so senseless, yet personal. Both victims had been stabbed multiple times in the face and chest postmortem. Julia's blood–drained face, open mouth, and blank eyes would forever haunt the manly sheriff, as he assumed it would his deputies. Especially the poor rookie Swart, who very nearly became ill when he saw their killer's handiwork. And that was another thing. How could the killer have pulled this off?

The bodies had been found in different locations. One in the farmhouse, the other in the slaughterhouse, a good walking distance away. The killer had murdered the boy, chased the girl to the slaughterhouse, murdered her, did the rest of his work on her body, and set up his satanic display, before returning to the farmhouse to put the finishing touches on the boy's body. It just didn't add up. How could he have pulled all that off before anyone saw him? He must have worked fast. Or he had an accomplice. Accomplices? The sheriff's gut said these Blood Moon Farm performers knew more than they were letting on, but he didn't want to rush to judgement. He'd had wrong hunches before.

So many thoughts and questions, so few answers. How weren't there more witnesses until after the fact? How was it that there wasn't one single shred of physical evidence? No DNA, fingerprints, footprints. No skin beneath the victims' fingernails. Nothing. And, the ultimate question: Why? Would this killer, or killers, strike again? It seemed too likely. Time would tell. In the meantime, maybe those rolls of film would yield some answers. They could be a calling card. Sheriff Gram only hoped he could put a stop to this terror before it spread like a pandemic.

Monday rolled around fast. The second–to–last day of September had arrived. Laurie's alarm was set for twenty after eight. Her first class, Mathematical Perspectives, began at 9:20 and ended at 10:20, and her second class, Spanish 201, began at 10:30, and ended at 11:30, giving her ten minutes to get from Patterson Hall down over the hill to the field house, a five–minute walk on a good day. She loved her Mathematical Perspectives class because it applied toward education majors, and she loved Spanish 201 because she loved language.

"*Me gusta lengua*," she said. Her Tuesday/Thursday courses included Film Criticism from 9:20 to 10:50 in the McCelvey Campus Center, and Shakespeare with her favorite professor and renowned playwright, Dr. Abe, from 11:00 to 12:30 in Old Main. Darian and Margaret, also English majors and the same year as Laurie, were in most of her classes this year. Just a few of the many things these best friends had in common. They had even graduated from the same school, Willow Falls Junior/Senior High School. The only difference was that Laurie was a homebody. Darian and Margaret moved away after graduating senior year. They now shared a dorm over at Hillside. Laurie had stayed right at home. She often joked that while Darian and Margaret lived in Hillside, she lived on the North Hillside of good ole Willow Falls. North Hill bounded the northern end of Willow Falls, and it was rich with history. One of the most famous landmarks it housed was the Hoyt Institute, which had been robbed by two petty thieves this past Christmas Eve.

How low, Laurie thought. *To commit a crime on such a holy night.* The crooks had been captured when they plowed into the back of a police cruiser. Very stupid of them. What had they been doing returning to the scene of their crime so soon? And how hadn't they seen the police cruisers from a mile away let alone slam right into one? Laurie hoped the criminal behind the atrocious acts at Blood Moon Farm was as stupid as those others and would slip up soon, before anything else happened. But it was unlikely. From what she had read so far, the killer was way more intelligent than your common criminal scumbag. He wouldn't return to the crime scene. It seemed far more likely he would start a new one.

She couldn't let that stop her life or get in the way of what was important to her. She rolled out of bed, did her morning routine, and was soon out the door. Her commute wasn't bad. Fifteen minutes at most, ten on a good day. Westminster College wasn't in Willow Falls, but was part of Lawrence County, in a little Dutch/Amish town called Willoughby. There were many small communities in the area—Willow Falls, Ellwood City—each a little different, each with its own personality. That was what Laurie liked about Western Pennsylvania. It was very scenic too, especially in the fall.

Laurie often applied her teachings to the real world. She remembered her professor in her Introduction to Literary Studies: British course, Dr. Hitchcock, saying that driving through rural Pennsylvania on an autumn day is an example of sublimity. Dr. Hitchcock. Laurie just loved that name, associating it with Alfred Hitchcock.

Before Laurie transferred to Westminster, she had taken an introduction to film course at Butler County Community College, where she was assigned to write bios for two directors. The filmmakers she chose were Alfred Hitchcock and Roger Corman, king of the B movies. The quality of education between Westminster and Butler County Community College was drastic. At first, Laurie couldn't understand why her Westminster advisor told her to take Film Criticism and Shakespeare, as she had already taken them at BC3. But just because the titles were the same, the content wasn't. And that was something she found out first hand.

She enjoyed explaining to people what a film class had to do with her English major. Film is as much a text as the printed page. The director is the author of a motion picture. Their pen is a camera they use to illustrate their point. Laurie enjoyed pursuing a broad scope; it made for a great quality of life. These were her thoughts as she drove through Neshannock Township on New Willoughby Road, past Giant Eagle, Get Go, Preston Motors, which was across the street.

Laurie loved this part of town. Arby's, Wendy's, a plaza with a bunch of different stores including Ollie's Bargain Outlet, Dollar General, Great Clips, JC Penny, and a beer distributor at the end. Opposite the plaza, tucked into the trees was a nursing home, Jameson Health Care Center. She tapped the brake as the car ahead of her slowed and turned into the Perkins where Laurie, Maggie, and Darian frequently ate dinner. Up ahead was a bank and a bar/restaurant called Tuscany Square, which Laurie despised.

She'd only been there once, but that was plenty. Last November, the Wednesday before Thanksgiving and biggest drinking night of the year. Laurie had been underage, but her friends, being ever so sly, concocted fake IDs. This made Laurie quite nervous. She wasn't a fan of the idea, but she figured the worst that would happen was the security guard would not let them in. Hopefully. She felt guilty at the prospect of presenting false identification. Fortunately, she didn't have to, as the bouncer didn't ID them. What did happen was a huge fight broke out. Fists flew, shirts came off, curse words dropped followed by threats of violence and death. It had left a bad taste in Laurie's mouth, along with the overpriced food, snobby Neshannock crowd, and over–the–top–sloppy–drunk Willoughby High students.

She drove by the restaurant without a look, passed Sheets, and entered Willoughby Township. She made a right onto Willoughby Park, a left at the next stop sign. Past the McGill library, she made another right onto South Market Street and the financial aid office. Laurie just loved the Amish wooden rocking chairs on the porch. Laurie's favorite building on campus was next, Old Main, a nineteenth–century stone church where she took most of her English and education courses. Vines covered much of the stonework, and an antique lantern above the door added a nice gothic touch.

She passed Thomson Clark, a building that housed many English professor and associate professor offices. Then came a dorm across from the McCelvey Campus Center where the campus bookstore, cafeteria known as the TUB, and Mueller Theatre film criticism course were housed. The Mueller Theatre was where Laurie took Film Criticism and where the English department held the Bleasby Colloquiums every Thursday evening at seven, in which professors gave presentations on their creative work and research.

Laurie especially enjoyed attending these. The first one she had gone to was required by Dr. Hitchcock for her Brit Lit class. Dr. David Sword gave readings from his two published books of poetry, *Bodies on Earth*, and *Small Holes in the Universe*, as well as various unpublished poems that he informed the gathered students and professors "lacked the singing," of his published work. He even read a sample from his working novel, *Television Man: An*

American Tragedy. The second Colloquium Laure experiences was Dr. Hitchcock giving a presentation on her favorite poet, Elizabeth Bishop. Her most recent Bleasby featured her former Inquiry professor, Dr. Jim Ashbrook Perkins, doing readings from his latest book, *Decembers*, which oddly enough, came out in October.

She pulled into the student parking lot. All students had received a mass e–mail from the dean over the weekend, informing them of the tragedy. The murder victims were identified as Jack Sayer and Julia Wrightson. Laurie knew them. Not personally, but she knew who they were. Jack Sayer a twenty–one–year–old bio major, had been in Laurie's Spanish 102 class. She had never had classes with Julia Wrightson but had seen her around campus with Jack. Their love for each other had been obvious and carefree. No bills, no family. Not yet anyway. They were getting ready to finish their degrees and enter the real world. But, it was not to be. Laurie just had to ask herself, why? She figured there were some questions she would never have an answer to.

The e–mail blast had read something like this:

Dear Students,

A terrible tragedy has befallen our small, peaceful campus. It has left our community heartbroken. I regret to inform you that two students here at our prestigious, private institute, Jack Sayer and Julia Wrightson, were found dead, the victims of an apparent double homicide at a haunted attraction a mere half hour away at the Canterbury scare grounds on the twenty–sixth of September of this year. The details of their deaths are not important. What is important is that our school spirit is not broken. We shall unite and persevere and get back on our feet after this horrific and senseless criminal act that has left us reeling. Not only will we stay strong for us, but for Jack and Julia, as well. In the meantime, we shall reflect, pray, and honor their memory. Jack and Julia, both twenty–one years of age, and less than a year to go, haven't even began their lives yet. Jack was a biology major and wanted to one day work in a laboratory, and Julia, a business major, aspired to one day become a successful businesswoman and own her own company. It hurts me to say that neither of these dreams shall be realized.

We here at Westminster are going to do what we do best. Students and faculty alike. We will pick ourselves up and keep pushing forward. It is my pleasure to inform you that the authorities indeed have leads, and there is nothing alarming. The suspect in question will be apprehended shortly. In short, justice will be served. In the meantime, however, we will try our best to have a good remainder to the semester. To those of you who knew Jack and Julia best, our thoughts and prayers are with you, as well as with their families. For the purposes of honoring their memory, a candle light vigil will be held on Monday, the twenty–ninth, at 6:00 p.m. on the courtyard in front of the Thompson Clark facility. All students and staff are welcome to attend. Until then, we are going to have to put it behind us and concentrate on the future. A bright future is ahead, indeed. Stay strong, all of you. After all, it's what Jack and Julia would want.

Sincerely;

Dean Anderson

The letter really hit home. At this stage in life, you didn't think you were as invincible as you did in high school but learning about this happening to two fellow students whose current situation was not so different from yours was mind numbing. Bone chilling. It could happen to you. *Would* it happen to you? Why would the killer choose to attack a haunted house rather than bringing an AK–47 to campus? Parkland Florida, the Virginia Tech massacre, Sandy Hook. Why did this feel like a whole different type of monster?

Walking into Patterson Hall, Laurie saw a promotional poster for one of Dr. Abe's plays that Westminster theater had been running for the Halloween season. It was a horror play entitled *Reports of a Home Invasion*. Would the university cancel it now? A glass case held a banner that read

"Theatre Westminster" beneath the two classic symbol for drama, two masks, one a grin, one a frown. Laurie made her way up a flight of steps where another poster advertised a play adaptation of Dr. Jim Ashbrook Perkins novel, *Snakes, Butterbeans, and the Advent of Electricity.* Laurie hadn't read the book, which she was pretty sure was non–fiction. From what she knew, it concerned running barefoot through meadows at midnight, gazing up at stars, and fishing in a basement. A girl named Rachel Addams who had been in Laurie's Romanticism class with Dr. Hitchcock supposedly played a dog in the play, wearing a pair of big, floppy dog ears.

Laurie entered a medium–sized classroom. *Mathematical Perspectives.* Dr. Sherri Lennox was very cool. Today they were probably going to continue their discussion of Euler circuits and get into standard deviation. For their final project, students had to write a three–to four–page paper, single spaced, with charts and graphs permitted sparingly, APA style, applying one of the methods used in class to the real world. Laurie was excited for this one. She had always loved dinosaurs, especially the meat–eaters, and that's what she wanted to focus her paper on. The topic would be the standard deviation between sizes of select Therapod, or lizard–hipped, dinosaurs, perhaps correlating that to African or Asian elephants. Rachel Addams, the girl playing the dog in Dr. Perkins play, had worn a shirt depicting various sauropod dinosaurs to a Romanticism class last spring, Sauropods were the ones with the long necks. They were herbivorous, and the largest animals ever to walk on land. She remembered Rachel saying that dinosaurs were her obsession growing up. Laurie didn't say anything, but she and Rachel shared similar childhoods. Funny, on that same day, Dr. Hitchcock had worn a pair of pterodactyl earrings.

Darian and Margaret were already seated. They were English majors, technically English majors with a Secondary Ed minor. Unlike Laurie, Margaret didn't aspire to one day becoming a professor, and Darian was going for Communications as well as English. There was a few good minutes before class began and not everybody was there yet. Dr. Lennox was, perched in her high chair and desk like usual. Normally, professors didn't arrive before their students, but Dr. Lennox taught a class here before this one.

She usually played funny YouTube videos before class, but not today. She usually greeted students with a warm and welcoming smile, but not today. This morning she seemed rather somber.

"It's going to be kind of hard to concentrate on Euler circuits," Darian said as Laurie took her usual seat nearest the window. It was eerie but befitting the mood on campus. Mellow, quiet, and pensive. "Tell me about it," Maggie whispered.

They let that settle before sharing some details about their weekend. Darian had stayed home with Rick, while Maggie had hung with Billy at his place. Laurie had spent the weekend alone with a good movie in bed Saturday night. She had always believed that people who had to constantly be on the go were insecure, running from something. Themselves?

Laurie had no qualms spending time with herself, even a Saturday evening. The murders probably had a thing or two to do with her girlfriends choosing to snuggle with their men. Darian and Maggie liked to go out and do their thing, more so than Laurie, but they weren't *all* that wild. Laurie could understand wanting to go out and have a good time, but she didn't prefer it, at least not too often. She was too busy thinking her own thoughts.

Dr. Lennox's shrill voice broke through the buzz. "I normally like to say happy Monday on beautiful Monday mornings like today, but I don't think that would be appropriate given the recent tragedy. As most of you know, something happened to two students on this campus, both of whom I've had in class at one time or another. Just a show of hands, did any of you know Jack Sayer or Julia Wrightson?"

Hands shot up. Darian and Maggie slowly raised theirs as well. Laurie hesitated. Neither of her friends knew the couple personally but would know them to see them. The same held true for her, which is why she decided to join the fray and half-raised her arm. One of the few who did not raise their hand was Marshall Matthews. That surprised her, though it probably shouldn't. She didn't know Marshall that well—they shared a class or two—but he didn't seem to have a lot of friends. Laurie was sure that he must, just not so much on campus. He was a commuter like her. Aside from that, she didn't know much. Not even his major. He looked to be about her age.

Maybe he was a tad bit introverted or sheltered, but he didn't seem like a meek little mouse. He was good–looking enough, with an athletic build. She would like to know him better, but she assumed that even if he felt the same way about her, he didn't seem like the type who would make a move. Laurie wondered why it was that the guy always had to make the move. Why couldn't the woman ask the man out? She sighed. That was just how society worked. Of course, there was always the option of flirting. There wasn't any law that said she couldn't send him signals.

Dr. Lennox continued. "If any of you haven't received Dean Anderson's e–mail, please know that there will be a candle light vigil this evening at six. Of course, you're all welcome to attend and should attend. It will be right out here in front of Thompson Clark." She pointed. "Terrible, terrible thing that I thought would never happen to anyone in our little community." Laurie glanced at Marshall. He looked a little despondent, but then he always did.

"We're going to have to try and piece ourselves together and keep our heads high," Dr. Lennox added. "In the meantime, we'll continue about our regular routine, so we don't fall behind on the syllabus. I understand it's going to be hard for a lot of you to focus, but just try and do your best. Believe me, I'm having difficulties of my own, but, like Dean Anderson said, we have to stay strong."

Indeed, they did. Laurie felt as though getting back on track and going about a normal routine would be best for everyone. It might be difficult but trying to better understand Euler circuits and the Spanish subjunctive seemed rather healthy. Who knows, maybe she would try and talk to Marshall at some point. She'd tried before. Actually, she didn't try, but wanted to try, thought about trying, but never got around to it. Always saying next day or next time. Maybe she would tell Darian and Maggie, that way they could help her out. At twenty–one, Laurie still liked for her friends to play matchmaker. Not so much to hook her up and do her work for her, but just to give her a little nudge, let the guy know she was interested, so that he would make a move. Of course, this wasn't very often, but Laurie figured it was time she began dating again. If not, there was always some other time.

Sheriff Gram and Deputy Flynn looked on in stunned silence. It wasn't so much what they were seeing as it was that they didn't know what to make of it, although it must have meant something. It had to mean something. The two rolls of 35 mm film that had been stuffed in Jack Sayer's eye sockets were being projected onto a screen. The two law enforcement officers sat alone in the dark room. Not a sound could be heard apart from the film feeding through an old–fashioned projector. Deputy Flynn hadn't taken a puff of his lit cigarette, the red-hot ashes falling into a tray on the table.

What they were watching was what they assumed to be old home videos. The quality of the footage was grainy and blotchy, like a seventies' grind house drive in pic or B exploitation film although they estimated the film to be much more recent. It showed a father, possibly a grandfather, with his son or grandson. They were standing out in front of a two–story farmhouse, waving at the camera. The pieces were edited together. "Spliced," as Deputy Flynn put it, with each clip showing something different, but all of them involving the old man and the little boy. One of them showed him pulling the child in a wagon on a bright fall day. It was evident that it was autumn based on the foliage of the surrounding trees, not to mention the fact that the boy was holding a pumpkin in his lap. The last clip they saw was of the boy reading what looked like comic books in what looked like the attic of the farmhouse.

"What do you make of it?" the deputy asked his commander in chief.

"That I can't tell you," was his response. He rubbed his unshaved chin. The stubble felt like sandpaper against his fingers.

Deputy Flynn's eyes widened as a sudden realization dawned on him. "Wait a minute, Sheriff. I recognize that house from somewhere." The sheriff looked at Flynn as he was lost in deep thought for a while. He clicked his fingers. "About sixteen or seventeen years ago, '98 I think it was. A father and his son from western PA went missing. I remember reading about it in the papers."

Thinking he may have been onto something, the sheriff asked him where he was going with this. "Willow Fall, I believe, is where it happened. The man, I can't remember his name, was a farmer, and every Halloween, he would set up his own personal haunted house." The sheriff didn't quite understand. "What do you mean he would set up his own personal haunted house?"

"His house. The house where he lived. The farmhouse. He would decorate it and set it up and let people go in for meager admission. Anyway, back in 1998, on Halloween, him and his son disappeared without a trace. I remember reading and hearing about their physical descriptions, and they match the two in the film. And the house, I'm certain that's the same house."

As much as the sheriff trusted his deputy's instinct, if that's what you would wanted to call it, he wasn't sure what this had to do with the murders of Jack Sayer and Julia Wrightson. "Do you think there's any correlation with the murders?"

Flynn shook his head no, not in a manner that would indicate no, but one that would indicate that he wasn't sure. Although he was leaning toward a yes. "How would the killer have gotten his hands on this film? And, more importantly, why this specific film?"

The sheriff couldn't deny, Flynn had a point. There had to be some type of significance. Had to be. "You think it's some kind of clue or calling card?"

Flynn was still pondering. "If it is a clue, it's cryptic, and, like all good clues, raises more questions than it answers, but I'm sure that's intentional."

Gram agreed whole–heartedly. "You think he's trying to mislead us?"

Flynn didn't think that. In fact, he thought the killer was trying to lead them. In what direction he wasn't sure, but he was sure that this was a piece to a much larger puzzle. Time would have to tell.

4

Ghoul Mansion in Sharon, Pennsylvania was by far the region's top haunted attraction. Featuring the demented jack in the box, the bat cave, the tormented baby doll, the REDRUM room and the body bag among others. It was the longest-running haunted attraction in western Pennsylvania, having been open since 1994. Originally located in a Wilson Furniture building, it was moved to the James Winner Art and Cultural Center. Since the building was not available as a permanent location, the owners sought out a permanent location that would suit their needs. After spending two years in a building on Pitt Street, which the people behind the scenes jokingly referred to as "the two years in the Pit," the current location was found at the Ivor J Lee building at 66 North Main Avenue. Dennis Hutchinson, who was good friends with the owner, Matt Reynolds, tried to come here every year. Dennis knew that Matt had invested a lot of money in this place, turning it into one of the best professional attractions in the tristate area. He even had a finalist from the Syfy channel reality competition, Face Off, working for him, on both the animatronics and the live actor's makeup.

Dennis, thirty-one, and his fiancée, Kaitlyn Jones, twenty-eight, had come here together for the past three or four years, making it somewhat of their Halloween tradition. It helped that Dennis was such good friends with Matt, but what didn't help, was the brutal murders that had taken place no more than a week before. The murders themselves, let alone their gruesome nature, was enough to stop even the most hardened haunted house fans in their tracks, and although it would be accurate to say that Dennis and Katy hadn't thought twice about not coming, they decided they weren't going to let some criminal act scare them off. Apparently, there were a lot of other people who felt the same way. They weren't about to stop having fun. Of course, security had been increased, which heightened everybody's sense of safety.

Before opening, the house had undergone a clean sweep before the actors set up. Even the actors had to provide proper ID. And everybody, man, woman, or child, would only be allowed admittance after they were wand down by the metal detectors. All tenants considered, there should be nothing to worry about. That's what Dennis had told Katy as he tried to convince her to come here. She wasn't so taken at first, but it did make sense to her. Still, was there anything foolproof? Anything guaranteed? There weren't many things in life that were.

The thrill of going to haunted houses was flirting with danger that wasn't real danger. It was the rush of coming face–to–face with death and coming out clean on the other end that compelled Dennis and Katy. But, when there was real danger involved, which Katy thought was a stretch, but at least possible, it sort of took the fun out of the experience. Nevertheless, they were here now, as were a number of other people, and, although it wasn't necessarily too late to turn back, Katy didn't want to "chicken" out, as her fiancé so eloquently put it. She did have to remind him that a real murder had taken place not very far from Ghoul Mansion, and it would make sense if he was telling her not to chicken out if she was just afraid to go to the haunted house, but considering she was afraid of being murdered, the phrase "chicken out" didn't seem to fit the context.

The moment of truth had arrived. It was their turn to go in. "You ready for this?" Dennis asked as Katy clung to him like a child.

"As ready as I'm going to be," she answered.

They walked inside. Once inside, neither Katy nor Dennis was surprised to find that it was dark, and they weren't sure which way they were going. "Oh my god, Dennis," Katy laughed as she groped for his hand. Finally, their fingers interlocked. Katy breathed a sigh of relief as she had found her safety net.

"Just follow me." He laughed.

"Oh, you lead the way, my knight in shining armor," his beloved fiancée jokingly replied.

They had been there before, but it didn't mean that they knew what they were in for. Matt liked to up the ante every year. More extreme, more intensity, just like Dennis liked it. The same couldn't be said for Katy.

The first thing they encountered was the demented Jack in the Box. This section of the mansion was demented indeed. It involved live actors, with a man in a jester's costume springing from an enormous colorful box. The meat cleaver–wielding jester happily waved the blood–stained murder instrument about, snickering all the while. There were actors dressed as clowns being sawed in half. Their big clown feet in their big clown shoes kicking from side to side, up and down, as they moaned and wailed. Dennis and Katy exchanged glances and smiles as the two evil clowns with the rusty two–man handsaw spilt the brilliantly colored boxes in half, separating the suffering sad clown's upper torso from his lower torso. But the effect didn't end there.

As the big awkward feet flailed about, a hideous, animatronic clown head attached to a long accordion–like neck, popped out of the top of the box containing the lower half of the clown's body. Covered with dripping, blood–red greasepaint, a huge, immutable grin spread the width of the repulsive clown head, revealing rows upon rows of jagged, yellow fangs as the round head bobbed up and down on the expanding and contracting red neck. While this was happening, the upper half of the clown's torso sprouted a pair of reptilian legs, with flat, duck–like feet, complete with webbed talons for toes.

Clowns that could regenerate lost body parts and limbs, just like worms, Dennis thought. It was more akin to the mythological Hydra. When Hercules would cut off one of its heads, two more would grow in its place.

"You two want to be next?" one of the clowns holding the saw hissed. Katy was genuinely freaked out by the clowns. Their frilled wrists and collars. The fluff balls bisecting their costumes. The actor that taunted them had his face painted, while the other was wearing a mask. The one with his face painted was sweating noticeably, causing his paint to be runny.

"God," Katy whispered to Dennis. "They remind me of *It*, the clown." Dennis chuckled.

"Hell yeah. Pennywise."

The bat cave was the next stop of the tour. "So, is this going to be like Batman's bat cave? The one where he keeps the life–sized tyrannosaurus?" Katy asked.

Dennis smiled. "I have a feeling that this is going to be something a little bit different."

Dark and cold, just as Katy and Dennis had expected. The cavern was alive with the sound of chirping. Shrill and rapid, the kind that a rat or bat or any other type of virulent vermin or rodent would make. Katy shrieked as something brushed up against her ankle, and Dennis nearly knocked her over as something flew past the top of his head, rubbing against his hair. It wasn't long until the giant bats with jet–black fur and leathery, membranous wings, spanning a full ten feet, made themselves known. They were animatronic, but very impressive. Something Dennis certainly believed would work on film.

He wondered if the former Face Off contestants designed them. There were ghastly, more humanoid bats, angels, demons, winged monstrosities. Some of them had long fangs and feminine features, while others had faces like that of a simian. The humanoid beasts were the performers all done up. Dennis remembered reading about sightings of such creatures around the world. Whether it be reports of soldiers being attacked in caves in Afghanistan, or the harrowing encounters of veterans being swooped down upon in the jungles of Vietnam. Oddly enough, the monsters that called the bat cave their home, strongly resembled these reports. Dennis wondered if that's where the makeup artists drew inspiration from. As scary as everything was, it was hard not to be in awe of all the talent it must have required to pull off such extraordinary effects.

When Dennis and Katy came to the tormented baby doll, they were surprised to find that it was the most unsettling room they had been in thus far. There was more to the room than creepy dolls. Of course, you had your ceramic and creepy Raggedy Ann dolls, which reminded Dennis and Katy of the case of the supposedly possessed doll Anabelle, whose case inspired the events of *The Conjuring*. But there was more to this room than that.

The axe–wielding manic with the doll face stitched over his, for instance. And the huge, man–boy, sporting a pair of overalls that had his teddy bear sewed to his face. The black button eye, as dull and lifeless as that of a Great White Shark, seemed to stare right through Dennis and Katy. The eyes of the inanimate beings seemed to watch them as they left, and the demented man–boy who was a little too in love with his teddy bear played with his yo–yo.

"Did you see that black button eye on the teddy bear man?" Katy asked. The reason she asked was because it reminded her of the film and novel *Coraline* where the beldam in her mock universe rocked a pair of black button eyes, as well as everyone else who lived there. Dennis didn't answer. He was too busy paying attention to something else.

"Here's Johnny!" he exclaimed as they approached the REDRUM room. This was the room Dennis really wanted to see. He held the door open for Katy. "After you, Wendy." Katy got both references and giggled, giving Dennis a playful push on the shoulder before walking in.

Dennis stepped in and closed the door behind him. It was a room of mirrors. Like a funhouse. Dennis and Katy looked around as they stepped inside. Written on the mirrors was the word REDRUM, in what appeared to be red lipstick. But the room wasn't only mirrors with REDRUM written on them. While the distorting mirrors were a big part of it, the main theme of the room was a hotel suite. The door was splintered, as if Jack Torrance himself had been trying to chop it down with an axe, like the big bad wolf blowing down the straw and hay houses of the three little pigs. Written on the door was the word REDRUM. As unsettling as the fake hotel suite was, Dennis was surprised that there wasn't more to it than that. The lighting really helped set the tone. There was fake blood splattered on the sofa and walls. "I guess this is supposed to be like a crime scene," he told his girlfriend, who soon nudged him, trying to get his attention. "Dennis, look!" Dennis turned his head. There was the performer. He smiled and was pleased to see that there was more to this room than he'd thought. After all, it was the one he was most looking forward to seeing.

The actor, who was dressed like a psychotic lumberjack, was pinned to the wall, his feet about six inches off the ground. He was being held up by a harpoon, which he had been impaled with through the neck. Gasping for air, and clutching the harpoon with both hands, he extended a shaky arm toward Dennis and Katy, and managed a choked plea for help, through a mouth and throat filled with blood. Dennis and Katy approached as the performer's gurgled pleas became more and more meek and muffled.

"Wow," said Dennis as they got close enough to see the blood spurting from the fresh wound. "That's some pretty neat prosthetics." When they were close enough to touch the man, a morbid realization dawned on Katy. Those were no prosthetics.

She screamed. "Dennis. Oh my god. Dennis. That's real."

Dennis leaned in closer for a better look. A sinking feeling hit him like a Mac Truck as he realized Katy was right. He looked around. There seemed to be no sign of anybody else in the room.

"Call for help!" Katy screamed as she reached for the instrument that had skewered this poor individual.

"No," Dennis shouted. "Don't pull it out otherwise he could bleed out."

Katy wasn't so sure Dennis was on point with that one. "Yeah, but if we leave it in he could suffocate."

Shaking his head, panic mode was beginning to set in. "So, what do we do?"

"Just call for help!" Katy shouted, as she began to ask the flailing young man if he could breathe or not. He was slipping away. Katy couldn't understand what he was trying to tell her. As she continued to try and get a coherent response from him, and Dennis fumbled for his phone, she felt a hard thump on the back of her head. She had been struck with some kind of blunt object. Her eyes rolled back into her head as the haziness and dizziness overcame her. She could feel something warm and wet trickle down the back of her neck as the darkness consumed her.

When Katy came to, she found that she was still in the REDRUM room. She was lying on the floor, but she did not know how long she'd been unconscious. Lying right beside her head was a bloody knife stick. Putting two and two together, she concluded that that's what she'd been knocked out with.

Dennis. Where was Dennis? She slowly sat up with what little strength she could muster. Her head throbbed, and a heavy nauseous feeling had settled in her stomach. Blinking several times, her fuzzy vision finally cleared. The man who had been impaled through the throat was still suspended from the wall, but he wasn't moving or begging for help. His arms hung limp, and his head slumped on his slouched shoulders.

Katy's ears were ringing, but that didn't stop her from hearing the muffled screams coming from somewhere in the room. She looked around rather quickly, making herself sick as the room began to spin. Slowing herself down, she pressed her hand tightly against her eyes and forehead. As she stopped to catch her breath, she realized that the muffled cries were coming from right in front of her. Looking up, she saw that the nightmare was only getting worse. In front of her was Dennis, bound and gagged to a chair, a creaky wooden chair that hadn't been in the room before. He was strapped there by the wrists and ankles, there was a leather strap running around the back of his head and mouth, with a big red ball attached to the front, stuffed in his mouth. Stumbling toward him, Katy unstrapped the leather belt around his face, and pulled the squishy red ball out of his mouth.

Coughing and gagging, Dennis spit repeatedly, as if trying to get the taste of the ball out of his mouth. As he gasped, trying to catch his breath, Katy murmured. Her speech was slurred and incoherent as she tried to formulate a sentence and ask Dennis if he was okay. She stopped immediately as she looked down and saw that Dennis's wrists were slashed open and gushing blood. The straps that held his arms down were applied at about mid–forearm. She could see the straight razor lying at his feet, ensanguined with his deep, scarlet blood. The cuts were wide and deep. Katy could see the tendons, which looked like choice cuts of meat, flexing in the wounds. The ones that connected through your hand, which contracted when you moved your fingers, were severed. Through the panic and terror, Katy couldn't help but be reminded of that bathroom scene in *The Terminator*.

The chair had been nailed to the ground, so there was no chance of Dennis tipping it over and breaking free. Even if it wasn't bolted, Katy wasn't sure that he would have been able to. He was noticeably weakening as he lost more and more blood. His lips drooped. Dennis rolled his eyes up as he noticed the figure approaching behind Katy, who was frantically trying to undo the straps as he bled out. "K–Katy," he gasped. "Look...look out."

She managed to catch that and turned around just in time to see the marauding figure dealing his death blow. Instinctively, Katy manage to get out of the path of the rusty, descending axe, which found a home as it was buried in Dennis's skull. Katy screamed. "No!"

Dennis's eyes rolled back into his head, and he violently twitched and went into spasms, seemingly going into a grand mal seizure. Blood ran in streamlets down his face. At last, the twitching and jerking ceased, and Dennis settled into the chair. He was dead. As grief stricken and terror ridden as Katy was, she realized she had to get out of there. Somehow someway. The killer put his booted foot on Dennis's chest, and ripped the axe from his head, which made a popping sound, like a vacuum tube being pushed up against the carpet. He spun the axe in his hands so that the pointed side was facing downward. Katy looked up in horror at her and her fiancée's, now her ex fiancée's, assailant as he approached her.

He wore a black cut–off vest. V–cut by the collar. On his chest was a big red cross with curved edges and pointed corners, outlined in thin gold rope. His skin–tight red sleeves covered the length of his arms, which ended abruptly at the wrists covered two black gloves. He wore a wide black belt with a large gold buckle. The bottom of his vest protruded from the bottom of his buckle for a short way, and he wore red tights and high black boots that weren't leather, but a soft, velvety material. They ended in a point by the toes. Katy thought to herself that her attacker resembled Peter Pan, not so much consciously though as she was thinking more important thoughts, the thought of survival, for instance.

But that other one just kind of popped into her mind uninvited. Completing his attire was a bear skin cloak. It was a black bear, maybe a juvenile, maybe an adult—Katy wasn't a bear aficionado. It was attached to his back. The snout began at the base of his neck, and the rump terminated at the back of his knees. But that wasn't what really completed the killer's Halloween costume. It was a mask. A mask that Katy had never seen before, and never wanted to see again. A mask unlike any other. The faces of theater. Happy and Sad. Grinning and frowning. Yin and Yang. One and then the other, and then both at the same time. It was holographic, changing every time Katy would look at it from a different angle, or depending upon how the light hit it.

He stepped forward. Katy noticed his grip tightening on the axe with each step he took. She screamed as he whipped it above his head and brought it down with lightning quickness. Again, whether it was her instinct or adrenaline, she managed to dodge the blow. The pointed end of the axe was planted into the ground where her shin had been only milliseconds before. She crawled backward on her rump, pushing herself back with her hands and feet as the axe—wielding psycho struggled to pull the axe out of the floor in which it had been embedded. At last she got to her feet and made haste toward the splintered door with the word REDRUM scrawled across it.

As Katy approached the door, she realized that the running red letters were in fact written in blood, the blood of the actor impaled through the throat, or maybe Dennis's blood, and hadn't originally been there as part of the act. Just as she clasped the door handle, which she found wouldn't turn as it was not an exit, her would—be murderer finally removed the axe from the floor, like Arthur ripping Excalibur from the stone, or Thor lifting his hammer. Before Katy had a chance to turn and see him coming, the axe had been planted firmly in the middle of her wrist.

Pulling away, Katy's eyes widened to the size of saucers and she screamed in horror, seeing her hand resting firmly atop the axe embedded in the wall. Shiny dark red arteries jutted from her raw wrist stump. She wrapped her fingers around the base of it and squeezed to simulate a tourniquet or compress. Her mind barely registered the jolts of pain shooting down her forearm, and her eyes barely registered the axe being pulled from the wall, her severed hand tumbling to the ground with a comic book smacking sound.

By the time her processing units informed her that, indeed, the axe was back in the hands of this monster, it was too late. Behind her, the monstrous bringer of death pulled the axe back, winding up like Babe Ruth getting ready to knock one out of the park.

He swung with all his might, the axe making swishing as it cut through the air. A choking/gasping sound pushed through Katy's throat and abruptly ended as her breath cut short due to the axe being planted in her midback. She dropped to her knees with the axe protruding at a rude angle from her and reached with a palsied hand. For what, she didn't even know. Somebody. Something. Anything. As if some invisible lifeline would form out of nowhere and pull her from this situation. Her head fell back. She could see the ceiling. With a cough/hiccup, she spat blood. The last thing she would see was her killer's fairylike boot descending to bend her neck even further back with a sickening and resounding pop.

5

The events at Ghoul Mansion transpired exactly one week after the events at Blood Moon Farm. The bodies of Dennis Hutchinson and Kaitlyn Jones were discovered by a family of four who didn't wish to be identified. Also discovered by the family was the body of Garry Allen, the employee dressed like a murderous lumberjack.

The family of four rushed out of Ghoul Mansion upon seeing the residue of brutal crimes. They would forever be traumatized by the grisly sight of a young woman lying on the floor, hand missing, the vertebrae in her neck poking through the skin, not to mention the man strapped to a chair with his wrists slit and inner skull exposed, or the performer impaled to the wall through his throat. The family explained to interviewers that they told their young children, a boy and a girl, the bodies were fake. Actors pretending to be dead. When their children asked why they were leaving so soon, the parents told them that room was the last one in the tour. Like Blood Moon Farm, Ghoul Mansion was closed immediately and indefinitely. The entire building underwent a clean sweep. Employees and guests were questioned, but all turned up as clean as a baby's bottom.

As it had been for Jack Sayer and Julia Wrightson, the murders were plastered all over the papers and news, and not just local, either. The crimes had garnered national attention. Authorities in Western Pennsylvania acknowledged that they had a serial killer on their hands.

Police searched desperately for patterns but found none beyond the obvious. Of course, it was another young couple visiting a haunted house, but this time one of the performers was a casualty. Never in the history of the United States had a spree murderer targeted local and seasonal attractions repeatedly. This had to be stopped.

This was some of the information that made the *New York Times* and local media outlets like the *Pittsburgh Tribune Review*. Along with a little about the lives of the victims. Dennis was a graduate of Geneva and worked as a male registered nurse for Sharon Regional Health Systems. His fiancée, Katy, also a graduate of Geneva, worked as a physical therapist in a Golden

Hills nursing home. The couple was engaged to be married in May of 2016. Garry Allen, thirty–six, worked at a flame hardening plant in Zelienople called Pena–Flame Industries where a cousin of Ghoul Mansion owner Matt Reynolds was also employed. Allen volunteered an actor and effects artist for Ghoul Mansion in his spare time as a favor to his co–worker's cousin.

Laurie's week had sped past just as every week of late. She had always believed that weeks seem to go faster when they are broken down, segmented, structured. This was another reason she didn't mind having a lot to do, or perhaps it was just an excuse to convince herself that having her plate full most of the time was not that bad when she stopped to think about it. She attended the candle light vigil, along with Maggie and Rick and Darian and Billy. She even saw Marshall Matthews there and took the initiative to talk to him. As it turned out they hit it off well and Laurie's worst fears were vanquished. For one thing, she didn't have to ask him out, because he asked her.

That was good because it saved her the awkward feelings and proved him the proper gentleman. He and Laurie, along with Maggie, Rick, Darian and Billy, were going on a triple date to the Croatian Club, a private club located in Mount Jackson/Bessemer, a township of Willow Falls. Maggie, Darian, and their boyfriends were members

Laurie wrote for the on–campus newspaper, *The Holcad*. Maggie was the head editor and assigned articles. She assigned Laurie—although it was more Laurie's idea as Maggie never demanded anything of her friend—to do a tribute story to Jack Sayer and Julia Wrightson. Laurie interviewed Jack and Julia's friends and family, which was as uncomfortable as she'd anticipate. Not so much their friends, but their families who had just gotten through denial and were progressing into the early stages of acceptance and the cusp of eternal mourning.

Laurie sympathized. At the end of the day, Jack and Julia were still gone but at the very least their memory remained alive. Laurie dedicated her meticulously crafted article to honoring their lives. She felt more than a little guilty accepting the twenty–dollar payment staff writers for *The Holcad* received per article.

How horrible it must have been for the parents of that beautiful young couple to make the trip to their dormitory and gather their belongings. And what about Jack and Julia's roommates? The whole thing was inconceivably awful.

Fortunately, Westminster students and staff didn't have to relive the recent deaths of two of their own during the school week. Dennis Hutchinson, Katy Jones, and Garry Allen weren't killed until the evening of Friday, October the third. On Thursday, the second, Laurie and the six other students in her Shakespeare class had a very interesting discussion with Dr. Abe.

They had just finished the last of the comedies they were reading for the semester and were getting ready to make the transition to tragedies. The final comedy, *Measure for Measure*, perhaps the darkest and most bizarre of the lot, sparked up some interesting thoughts. It ended with a man being sent to suffer three punishments. First, he was to wed all the women he had impregnated. Second, he was to receive numerous lashes. And lastly, he was to be sent to the gallows to be hanged. The ultimate punishment.

Yet the play was classified a comedy. A dark comedy, but a comedy nevertheless. The class discussion got really juicy when Dr. Abe passed out a sheet outlining the history of the tragic play dating all the way back to Seneca, Nero's tutor. Seneca himself wrote at least ten tragedies—all anonymous—and *Didascalia*.

A key feature of Seneca's plays which, according to Dr. Abe, were written for declamation purposes rather than staging, were characters who turned to stoicism. They retained a pessimistic outlook, believing that any achievements would likely collapse and one's best chance for happiness lay in learning to see the cruel, arbitrary world for what it was. Other defining tenets of Seneca's work are the tragic heroes who, unlike Shakespeare's tragic heroes, do not possess a tragic flaw and evoke little or no pity. They tended to give in to inner desires and impulse, which led to crimes of passion. The plays often feature vengeful ghost characters and depict gruesome, deeds.

That was the pre–Christian era. Of course, they also discussed the Christian era with its sin, pride, ambition, and greed. Satan's fall from heaven followed by Adam and Eve's tumble from grace were among the topics at hand. Then there was Renaissance tragedy, which focused not only the fall from greatness, but the soul's damnation, and included a healthy respect for psychology which deepened character motivation and intensified internal conflict. When Dr. Abe suggested that modern tragedy can be viewed as an inner conflict between reason and passion, the waning class discourse picked up new steam.

Laurie was most intrigued by the pre–Christian era. "Ancient Rome had so many bizarre, bloodthirsty, luxurious emperors," Dr. Abe told the students. He also suggested that these works would have been inspired by equally bizarre, bloodthirsty, and luxurious rulers from Greek mythology, such as Agamemnon. Oddly enough, haunted houses worked their way into the conversation, not so much because of what had happened at Blood Moon Farm, but because Dr. Abe was doing a comparison and contrast between society now and society when he was growing up.

"Back when I was your age, haunted houses consisted of somebody standing in the corner in a sheet who would pop out and say 'boo' when you walked by. And you would kind of jump and go, 'Oh' and have a good laugh, and that was it. Nowadays, you've got people coming at you with chainsaws and what–not. Much more extreme than when I was in your shoes. It was simpler in my youth."

Laurie liked things simpler. Simpler was better. She was a fan of the "less is more" approach in horror films. Never show the devil's face. She thought of the scene in *John Carpenter's Halloween* when the monster is disguised as one of the girl's boyfriends, wearing a sheet and big, goofy glasses with holes cut out for the eyes. Laurie still remembered that heavy, marauding breathing coming from behind the ghost's costume. Even now, it was enough to make her shiver.

As for chainsaws, Laurie had recently seen on the news that some California loony was cutting people with a real chainsaw in a haunted attraction out there. The sicko was apprehended and all of Westminster's student body had held their breath, thinking that Jack and Julia's murderer was going to be brought to justice. But, alas, investigators could not connect the chainsaw nutcase to the Pennsylvania killings.

It was early Saturday, October 4, one day after the murders of Dennis Hutchinson, Katy Jones, and Garry Allen. Like the Saturday before, Laurie did her morning routine. Unlike the Saturday before, she had to work today. Fortunately, however, she didn't have to work late tonight. There would be plenty of time to come home, get ready, and go with Maggie and Darian, Rick, Billy and Marshall to the Croatian Club. Marshall didn't know Maggie and Rick or Billy or Darian, but Laurie did, so he was cool with that. Laurie was happy that no longer, well, maybe not no longer, but at least this time, she wasn't going to have to tag along like a fifth wheel. She prayed that she and Marshall would hit it off.

But that wasn't until later. For now, she looked forward to spending a little time with her younger brother, who was up and out the door for school before Laurie's alarm even went off during the week. James was his name. A bright, cute young boy with big, sparkling blue eyes, unlike Laurie's deep, dark brown. His cheeks were lightly freckled, and he rocked a brown crew cut.

James was already at the breakfast table when Laurie came downstairs. As always, her mother was cooking breakfast with the news on. Laurie didn't think that an impressionable young child should be subjected to that side of the world yet, but her mother insisted he didn't pay attention. Laurie was positive that he did since he frequently asked about reported happenings. For a long time, he had been convinced that the bad man was coming to their house to get him.

"Hey, James," Laurie said as she fixed herself a glass of something to drink. "We still going to Sperdute's tomorrow?"

Sperdute's was a farm located in Mount Jackson/Bessemer township where the Croatian Club was also located. Every fall, Laurie, James, and their parents would visit to pick pumpkins for Halloween. The fun didn't end with multicolored pumpkins and squash of varying shapes and sizes, though. There was also a small gift shop. The front porch would be lined with cornstalks and hay bales. Inside, would be jars of homemade jam, freshly grown peppers and vegetables, homemade knickknacks such as jars painted with ghosts and trees and tombstones, among other eclectic items. It was a family tradition.

James's response was a laconic, "Yeah." His eyes were glued to the television and the news of the three most recent murders. Jean Burnette and Patricia Cornwall were covering every grisly detail. Laurie wanted to go for the remote and change channels but found herself wanting to watch too. It was the same old same old. Not so much the same old, but the same as last week's double homicide. A gruesome trio of murders reported by a family of four that wished to remain anonymous.

Anonymous. The word made Laurie think of the film of the same title they were going to watch in Film Criticism. The movie advocated one of many theories as to who actually wrote the works attributed to William Shakespeare. Although Laurie believed the plays and poems were written by the man who born at Stratford upon Avon, she loved a good conspiracy theory every now and them. Hell, everybody in today's society did, or why bother to make a film like *Anonymous*? Was what was going on at these haunted attractions a conspiracy? A double homicide at one followed by a triple homicide at another? Five murders within the span of a week. No witnesses, no evidence.

Her mother turned the TV off. Of course, James protested, but it was all getting to be a little much even for her mother. "Whatever you do," she said, "I don't want you or your brother going to haunted houses, understand?"

"Do you really think that would be on my agenda after what's happened?" Laurie had no intention of going, and she could very well guarantee that James wouldn't consider stepping foot inside a haunted attraction for as long as he lived.

Laurie took a plate from the cupboard. Why would her mother honestly think that she and James would go to such a place? It wasn't as if it was a hobby of theirs anyway. Given the violent acts occurring in such proximity, Laurie didn't think anybody from this area would be visiting a haunted house anytime soon. Hell, she was beginning to think that nobody in the nation would, not with these murders and a nut job attacking people with a chainsaw in California. Laurie also recalled hearing about some guy dying of a heart attack at another haunted house in Pennsylvania and not being found for two days. Passersby mistook him for a prop. Darian had taken a picture of the news story on Facebook and sent it to her.

Society is getting increasingly violent, Laurie thought. *Maybe one day, we'll find ourselves in a nation where people are randomly stoned to death like in that story, "The Lottery."* People enjoyed the macabre. And even the most macabre things could be found in the mundane. That was another thing Dr. Abe had suggested. Kind of going off his haunted house analogy but connected to the tragedies of Seneca and Shakespeare. Gory, vile deeds and actions. People being butchered, chopped to pieces, and baked into meat pies. *Titus Andronicus* was probably the prime example. Certainly, the most blood–letting tale that Shakespeare had penned (unless *Anonymous* was right). Even James had a classmate a couple years ahead of him, R. J. Green, who would tell the kids scary stories about his great–aunt Edna's house, how it was haunted and what–not.

Apparently, tales of demonic activity in that house was a big hit with R.J.'s peers. According to James, he typed them up and brought them to school, passing them out as little booklets to fawning classmates. Laurie didn't know whether James bought into the narrative. R.J. insisted he was only relaying what his family told him and wasn't sure if he believed it himself. But the kid did have a knack for storytelling. After reading one of the boy's more lurid tales, something about a serpent, Laurie had explained to James that R.J. probably drew inspiration from the *Paranormal Activity* film series, and those weren't real. He didn't have to be scared just because it was in print. She sighed. This was the season to embrace the dark side of life, but this year, it seemed like the dark side of life was embracing her.

"Laurie," James murmured as his big sister stacked her plate with pumpkin–spiced pancakes. "Do you think they'll catch it?"

Laurie paused from drizzling syrup over her flapjacks. "Okay, I'm confused. Stop what?"

James twirled a pancake with his fork. "The killer."

Their mother shot a glance at him, and then Laurie.

Dang it, Laurie told herself.

"I knew I should have turned off that station," her mother said.

Laurie laughed. "That's what I keep telling you, Mom."

James stared Laurie down as he took his first bites of pancake. "Well? Do you think they'll catch it?"

Her mother clicked her fork on her plate. "Don't talk with your mouth full." James acknowledged her with a nod and turned his attention back to his sister.

"First of all," Laurie said. "Don't you think we should refer to 'it' as 'him'?"

James shrugged. "I guess."

Laurie rubbed his shoulder. "And to answer your other question, yes, they will catch him. What would make you think otherwise?"

"Well, it's just…to be able to go into a haunted house like that, and get away with everything, it must be pretty smart."

Laurie couldn't deny that her brother had a point. It took some special talent to pull off what this maniacal murderer done. Even a ten–year–old could see that. And James wasn't just any ten–year–old. He was smart. Smarter than he should be. Sometimes Laurie thought he was too smart for his own good.

James swallowed before continuing in his cute little way that made Laurie want to grab and squeeze him. "Didn't you hear what the reporters said? There's no evidence at either of crime scene. No DNA, no footprints, not even a fingerprint. How could a normal guy not leave evidence? He has to be some kind of ghost or ghoul or goblin."

"Okay, that's enough," her mother said. "Get ready for school."

James laughed. "It's Saturday, Mom."

That made Laurie laugh too. *Okay, that's enough.* What would James do if she wasn't here? Who would give him genuine answers and try and help and actually care? It wasn't that her mother didn't care, but she was so self–centered that any problem Laurie or James presented always ended up working its way back around to whatever problems she was having in her own life.

"A Halloween ghost, huh?" Laurie said playfully. "Very creative, little buddy." She could see that he was getting into a better humor, far less pensive than when the conversation began. "How about a rapscallion?" she said. "What if he's one of those?"

James chuckled heartily. "Or an ugly old troll or ogre?"

While the two of them were bonding quite well over such dark subject matter, their mother remained far from amused. You could read it all over her face. Laurie thought of the word 'bane,' derived from the old English word 'bana,' meaning horrible affliction or curse. A bringer of death and disease and plague. A poisoner and destroyer.

And that reminded her of a stanza from *King Lear*. The foul fiend Flibbertigibbet, described as someone who begins at curfew and walks until the first cock. *He gives the web and pin, squints the eye, makes the hare–lip, and mildews the white wheat. Ultimately, he harms the poor creatures of earth.* That sounded very much like a bane to Laurie. Maybe that's what they were dealing with. No, it couldn't be. Laurie tried to shake the silly thought off. This was no time for flippant fantasy.

"Listen, James," she said seriously. "You're old enough to know that none of the things you and I've talked about here actually exist, right?" James nodded. "You're going to see that when they catch this guy. As soon as they catch him, you'll see he's as human as you and me. Understand?"

"Uh–huh," James said absently. Laurie smiled and ran her fingers through his hair. *He's a good kid. He'll get through this.*

As they finished breakfast she went over her plans for the day. She would get some writing done before heading out to guard the lives of the swimmers at school. Then, tonight at the Croatian Club. She couldn't wait. *Whatever happens*, she told herself, *it will turn out all right. No matter what.*

6

Sitting on her chair watching kids frolic and splash in the chlorine water was an easy job; and being that Laurie was an avid swimmer, it did suit her well. Still, this wasn't how she preferred to spend Saturday afternoon. *Oh well.* Her shift ended at six; then she would be off to her house to get ready for her date. Marshall seemed like a nice guy just as Laurie had imagined he would be.

He was quiet and a little introverted, but so was Laurie. He was twenty years old. Going on twenty–one. His birthday was October 31, oddly enough. He was a junior business major from Willow Falls. Apparently, he graduated from high school the same year as Laurie, but not from Willow Falls High. This explained why Laurie didn't remember him. His parents had paid extra tuition for him to attend Willoughby High. After his parents split up when he was in the third grade, his new address was listed with his father in the neighboring township of Willoughby. This worked out nicely since he was a member of the Willoughby High wrestling team. Willow Falls High had no wrestling team.

Marshall was about average height. Five–foot–ten. Healthy and in shape, about 160 pounds. Laurie pictured a washboard stomach beneath that shirt. Hopefully she would get to see it sooner or later. His arms were lean and toned, and exceptionally well defined. What really turned Laurie on, though, was his long, brown bangs terminating at trim eyebrows above his radiant blue eyes.

Laurie thought about things like that, things that all girls her age thought about, though she would never admit it to her parents. Darian and Maggie, sure. But Mom and Dad? That was off limits. These thoughts ran through Laurie's mind, drowning out the laughter and screaming and splashing. *Screaming?* Snapping out of her daydream, Laurie quickly gauged the Olympic-sized pool. The sudden rush of adrenaline heightened her senses until her visual acuity might have been equivalent to a hawk's.

False alarm. Nobody was in trouble. The screams must have been her imagination. Or maybe it was playful. Someone splashed in the face or dunked. A nice big gulp of chlorine was enough to make anyone shout.

Dark thoughts seeped through Laurie's head. What if there was a shark in the water. A great white, black eyes rolling, gums exposed as it sank its fangs into soft, young flesh. Water turning red. If not a shark, a goblin? Laurie pictured a miniature mischief–maker in a hooded outfit, bells jingling on its pointed shoes as it shuffled across the water. A reptilian tale thrashed, sickeningly long fingers, hands with prominent veins and rough skin that resembled a road map. Prognathous jaw lined with razor–sharp fangs, a long, white beard like Santa Clause, Kris Kringle, Papa Noel.

Laurie shivered in her one–piece, imagining the little demon taking huge bites from the necks and backs of the parents, slashing their children's faces. The killer. The "haunted house killer," as the newspapers so generically coined him. Coined it. No. Laurie wasn't going to think that. What was it she'd told James? *When they catch this guy, you're going to see that he's just as human as you and me.*

As Laurie's shift came to an end, she could only think of one headline: "HAUNTED HOUSE KILLER STILL ON THE LOOSE."

She was sitting in front of the mirror in her room combing her hair when she heard the car horn. Maggie. It was finally time. Laurie walked down the stairs. Her father was sitting in his chair reading the paper while her mother perched on the couch watching *Family Feud*. James was upstairs playing video games like *Mortal Kombat* and *Call of Duty* and reading Marvel and DC comics.

"Bye. Love you guys," she said as she stepped outside. "I'll be home after a while."

"Don't be late," their mother said.

Laurie closed the door softly. Maggie had volunteered to drive tonight. There wouldn't be room for all six of them in her car, but it could fit four comfortably. Maggie and Billy and Laurie and Marshall. Maggie had already picked up Billy.

"So where does this guy live?" Maggie asked.

"Right over on Herman Drive," Laurie said, "616." The truth of the matter was that Laurie had been more than a little reluctant to say yes to Marshall's request for a date, just as he had seemed reluctant to ask her. It wasn't because there wasn't a mutual attraction and genuine connection there. There was. Laurie just hated this part of it. The part that would determine whether there would be a second date. She especially hated when her friends got involved. They only wanted to help, but still... It was Darian and Maggie's idea to triple date. Laurie felt uneasy introducing the man she was trying to make the new man in her life, whom she hardly knew herself, to her friends and their boyfriends.

It wasn't that she didn't trust them. She did with all her heart. It just seemed to her that having her date along with them, amplified the pressure to hit it off a thousand-fold. She dreaded sitting there beside him and him beside her, neither saying anything to the other.

It was all too plausible that the night would go like that. They were both the quiet type. And how were going to get some one–on–one time surrounded by four people?

Maggie pulled up to his house, a two–story Victorian complete with English Tudor. Laurie decided to make the best of the situation. It really wasn't that bad. Not realistically all that bad. *Things are always worse in your mind than they are in reality.*

"Maybe I should knock on the door," Laurie said. Normally, the guy picked up the girl, knocked on her door or rang her doorbell, walked her to his car, opened the door for her–that whole routine. Laurie wasn't prissy like that. She didn't feel comfortable being catered to. Besides, it wasn't Marshall's fault it had gone like this. If it was just been him and her, Laurie imagined she would be receiving the treatment whether she liked it or not.

"Not necessary, babe," Maggie said. "He's ready to roll. What a punctual guy." Laurie looked and saw that, in fact, Marshall was on the porch, presumably had been for a while. Just how long, Laurie couldn't be sure.

She thought as Marshall reached for the car door that her nerves were getting the best of her, causing her to think too much. She needed to turn it off if she expected to connect with this guy. He opened the back driver's side door with an audible click and sat in the back seat. His hair was fixed, and he was redolent of Abercrombie & Fitch woods.

"Hello," Maggie greeted dutifully.

"Hi," Marshall responded almost below his breath.

Billy turned and extended his hand. "Billy Johnson."

Marshall smiled and met Billy's handshake with a firm one of his own. "Marshall Matthews." Laurie was surprised. She had pictured him as the type that would offer a dead–fish handshake.

Billy returned the smile. "Nice to meet you, Marshall."

Marshall turned his attention to Laurie. A soft, shy smile broke across his face, so soft and shy that she was amazed he'd had the gall to ask her out in the first place. "Hi."

Laurie reciprocated the soft, shy smile, as well as the hello. Neither of them said anything for what seemed like an eternity, but in reality, was only a matter of seconds.

"How are you tonight?" he asked.

Laurie really smiled big this time. "I'm doing fine, how are you?"

Marshall nodded. "Great. Never better. You look really nice."

Laurie felt blood rushing to her cheeks and hoped it wasn't too noticeable. She didn't want to look like a rosy–cheeked clown.

"Thank you," she said. "You look really nice yourself." She didn't know what more to say. Hopefully her reciprocal compliment would suffice for the time being.

Maggie and Billy exchanged glances.

Laurie had been to the Croatian Club before. While she wasn't a member herself, Rick and Billy were, and members were allowed to sign in two people, which worked out perfectly for this evening since she, her two friends, and her date weren't members. Two members, four guests.

By the time they arrived, it was already full dark. What Laurie remembered most about this place was the downstairs floor, which was where they'd be eating tonight. The other thing was their marvelous fish dinners that her family would order during Lent. You could have your choice of fish or chicken or both, grilled or fried, with a side of coleslaw, fries and macaroni and cheese. You could even get a fish sandwich with cheese, coleslaw, and fries on it. Pittsburgh style.

Rick met them at the door. They walked in and went down the steps. Darian and Rick led the way, followed by Maggie and Billy and Laurie and Marshall. Laurie felt that warm, fuzzy feeling when they entered the basement accentuated with Halloween décor she'd never seen down here before. She had never been here at this time of year.

Rick approached the sign–in lady, who was also the bartender. "Hi," he said. "I'd like to sign in two people."

She smiled as she wiped a mug with a cloth. "Sure. Your name?"

Rick cleared his throat. "Rick Baker, and I'm going to sign her in." He pointed to his girlfriend. "Darian Nicole, and…" He looked at Laurie. Should I sign in you or Marshall? Do you care?"

She shook her head. "No, you can sign him in. I don't mind." Rick probably figured he'd sign Marshall in since he was the most recent guest.

"Marshall Matthews, too," Rick said. The bartender jotted the name on her notepad. Rick and Darian took their seats.

"Name's Billy Johnson," Billy said, "and I'm signing in Maggie Haggerty and Laurie Williams." Their names were written down on the same pad and they were good to go.

Laurie admired her surroundings as they walked to their seats. A tiny hall bisected two platforms. The right–hand side supported leather booths. On the left–hand side were tables. Old–fashioned Tiffany lamps hung above each table and carpeting padded the walls.

Of course, there were also tall tables and high chairs on the floor in front of the bar and seats at the bar counter as well. A banner hung above the entrance: **Undead Ahead**. Soft gold lighting gave the entire room a cozy feel, which Laurie enjoyed immensely.

Rick and Darian had decided on a big round table. There were just enough seats, which made Laurie think of the knights of the table round. A medieval door beside the table added to this feeling, round at the top, a gargoyle head holding the knocker in its mouth. Behind the table in the corner stood a grand piano covered in silky white cobwebs replete with puppy–sized spiders. A banner read: **No Bone Zone**.

A waitress asked the trio of young couple if they wanted something to drink as they looked over the menus. Rick asked what they had on draft, to which the waitress replied, "Yuengling, Angry Orchard, Sam Adams, and Coors."

Rick decided on a Yuengling tall draft, Darian ordered an Angry Orchard. Billy asked if they had Samuel Adams October–Fest to which the waitress replied that, unfortunately, they didn't. Billy settled on a tall draft of Angry Orchard Green Apple and Maggie got a Raspberry–flavored Smirnoff. Then it came to Laurie and Marshall.

"I'll just have water for now," Laurie said. Laurie was more than a little hesitant to follow her friends' lead. For one thing, she didn't really drink. And secondly, she wanted to seem subdued on her first date with Marshall. After one or two drinks, she'd be feeling a little loose as they like to say. What was the other term? Tipsy? She looked at Marshall. "What are you going to have?"

Marshall shrugged. "I was considering a draft, but only if you want one too." He smiled. "I'm not trying to put pressure on you. It honestly doesn't matter to me. I just meant that if you're going to have water, I'm not going to be over here guzzling brews."

After the ensuing, "Come on," and "Just get something," and "Just have one or two," from her four friends, Laurie settled on a hard iced tea, which was met with a round of "heys," and "ho's," and mock applause. Marshall ordered a tall draft of Coors. Luckily, the waitress, who looked to be only about eighteen herself, didn't ask for ID, because at least three of the six were underage. She smiled as she finished scribbling on her pad. "Okay, I'll be right back."

They looked over menus as the bartender prepared their drinks. By the time the waitress returned, they were ready to place their orders.

"Is this going to be separate or all on one?"

"It's going to be me and her," Rick said, pointing to himself and Darian.

"Then me and her." Billy gestured toward himself and Maggie.

The waitress turned her attention to Laurie and Marshall, "And you two?"

Laurie held her breath. She hadn't planned this out. But Marshall wasn't looking at her for advice. "Yeah, us two," he said poking himself in the chest and shooting his finger in Laurie's direction.

"Okay then, what would you like?"

While the others ordered, Laurie leaned over and tapped Marshall's shoulder. "What did you decide on?"

Marshall rubbed his nose as he did one last look-over of the menu. "I was thinking about getting ten hot ranch wings. If I get an order of hot pepper cheese balls, would you want to split them with me?"

"Sure." Hot pepper cheese balls sounded irresistible. She liked spicy.

"Okay," Marshall said to the waitress. "I'm going to get ten hot ranch wings, and she's going to have—" He looked over at Laurie.

"Ten parmesan," Laurie said.

"And can we have an order of hot cheese balls?" Marshall asked.

"Sure." The waitress flashed pearly white teeth. "Small or large?"

Marshall thought about it for a second. "How many come in each?"

"Ten in a small, twenty in a large."

Marshall looked to Laurie. "How many do you want?" Before she had a chance to respond, he hit her with another question. "Think you could tackle a large?" They exchanged smiles. Grinning, Marshall looked back to the waitress and told her they were going with a large.

As they waited for their food, Rick asked the group, "So what do you guys think of the murders?"

Laurie's stomach sank. "Do we really have to talk about that?"

Marshall nodded. "Yeah, that's kind of upsetting dinner conversation, don't you think?" He laughed.

"I just wanted to get your opinions on the subject. I mean, I didn't know those students, Jack and Julia, personally. Did any of you guys know them?"

None of them did. Marshall, being a business major, did have a couple of classes with Jack. Still, it hit close to home for Laurie. Two people so close to here, not figuratively but literally, had just come face–to–face with their mortality. It might have been any of the six of them.

Rick straightened his butter knife. "What I'm saying is this seems to be becoming a pandemic. A double homicide, then a triple homicide at two different haunted houses inside of a week? And what about that sicko in California? This stuff's spreading like the plague."

Billy butted in. "Yeah, and don't forget about the guy that died of a heart attack at that haunted house in PA. His body stayed there for two weeks before they realized it wasn't a prop."

As much as Laurie didn't want to talk about the subject, she had to ask. "Wait. Two weeks? I thought it was only two days." Billy shook his head. "No, it was two whole weeks. Can you imagine the toxic, rotten smell that must have been festering in that house? It's just amazing they didn't realize something was wrong."

Rick leaned forward. "Do you think there's a connection between the murders at Blood Moon Farm and Ghoul Mansion and that one you're talking about?"

Billy shook his head. "No, that guy died of a heart attack, he wasn't murdered. And he was an actor, so where he was when he died was where he was stationed to be. He wasn't posed there or anything. Now, as far as the one in California goes, I'm not so sure."

"I am," Darian said. "They couldn't connect the case in California with the murders here in PA. Police said no connection. Besides, he was mentally ill, and you can see the result. He got caught before he seriously hurt anyone. Whoever killed Jack and Julia, and those other three people at Ghoul Mansion may be psychotic, but not mentally ill."

Rick laughed. "You're splitting hairs, babe."

Darian gave him a playful slap on the wrist. "I'm serious. Think about it. It would have to take a considerable intellect to commit such atrocious crimes and not leave a shred of evidence, witnesses, or anything. How did he even get into the house if he wasn't one of the performers?"

Maggie nodded. "He could be somebody that paid for a ticket. He just hid there and waited. Why he targeted Jack and Julia, I don't know."

"I don't think it was personal," Billy said. "I think it was random. Think about it. One week later, he kills three people from Sharon."

"Yeah, but there is a common denominator," Maggie said. "He's targeting couples. Young couples."

A chill went through Laurie. She glanced at Marshall. He was watching her, barely listening to the conversation. That was relaxing somehow.

"Maybe," Billy said. "But when you stop to think about it, that's mostly who goes to those attractions, right? And don't forget that one of the actors was murdered at Ghoul Mansion. If he was somebody who paid for a ticket and went inside and hid, wouldn't the people who were already in there, like the performers and what–not, have seen him and told him to leave?"

"What do you think, Marshall?" Maggie asked Marshall.

"There's one theory you've neglected," he said with a glance toward her. The others watched him. Even Laurie found her interest piquing.

"Yeah, what's that?" Rick said.

"Well," Marshall said slowly, "I agree with you on the intellect part. His crimes not only have a common theme of violence, but intellect as well.

But don't you think it's plausible that there's more than one killer? He has an accomplice. And what makes you so sure it's a male? Maybe we have a female killer, or killers. Or a male and female killer."

"A killer couple," Billy said with a hint admiration. Then he laughed. "I think you've seen the *Scream* movies too many times."

They all shared a good laugh at that one. As they settled down, Billy looked to Laurie. "Hey, Laurie hasn't weighed in yet. Let's hear from her."

Laurie didn't want to tell them what she thought. It wasn't that she believed what she thought so much as simply thought it. It just popped into her mind. Popped in and lingered there. She was thinking what James had been thinking. What if the killer was a supernatural entity? What if he or she was a demon or succubus? Or even the devil? Funny how you could let a ten–year–old get inside your head like that.

Naturally, Laurie accepted the fact that those notions were entirely improbable. No, not even improbable, impossible. Oh hell, maybe she should just go ahead and say it, make a joke out of it. But could she really joke about something that she hadn't entirely disregarded? In typical Laurie fashion, she finally settled on, "I'm not really sure what to think. I mean, I agree with you guys. I think they're all interesting theories, but, honestly, I'm at a loss. I'm pretty sure you guys covered all the basis. There really aren't any more possible options. It must be one of those explanations. I don't know."

"Nothing like a group of college students trying to solve a string of grisly murders over drinks and wings," Rick joked. They all dabbled in the art of good humor as they sipped their drinks until they saw the waitress coming with their food.

"I have to run to the bathroom," Marshall said. "Plus, I'm out of beer. I think I'm going to get one more. Anybody need a refill?" He smiled at Laurie. "You want another one?"

Laurie twirled her finger around the mouth of the empty tea bottle. "Sure. Why not." Marshall reached over to grab her bottle.

Laurie stopped him. "That's okay, I can get it. I need to stand up for a moment."

She and Marshall walked to the bar. Marshall placed his empty tall draft on the counter, and Laurie set her empty bottle next to it. The bartender cracked another as Marshall headed off to the restroom.

The bartender handed her the freshly opened hard iced tea and went to work preparing Marshall's draft. In her peripheral vision, Laurie saw someone sitting at the bar looking at her. She ignored it for a moment, but the person kept watching her. So, Laurie turned to lock eyes with her admirer.

It was a middle–aged woman. Somewhat heavyset with straw–like salt–and–pepper hair. Her face was pleasantly plump with full, round cheeks. Her upper and lower lips curled in as her mouth made chewing motions even though she didn't have any food. Her eyes were dark and sparkling and seemed to stare right through Laurie. Laurie acknowledged the stare with an uneasy smile, looked away and then back again as she thought she heard the woman mumble.

A broad toothless grin had spread across the woman's face. She said something else but had such a severe case of mush mouth that all Laurie couldn't make it out. The woman stopped after a sentence of two.

"I'm sorry?" Laurie said. She was beginning to think this was one of those times where she was just going to have to nod and go, "Yeah, uh–huh."

The woman spoke again. Laurie didn't even notice her and Marshall's drinks sitting the bar in front of her. She was too busy leaning forward to make out what this strange woman was trying to convey.

Despite the raucous conversation going on in the basement, she finally made out a few words. "It's coming, you know."

Laurie drew back. "Excuse me, but did you say, 'It's coming?'"

The woman stared. Laurie repeated her concern, this time with a nervous laugh. "I don't understand."

The woman smiled and nodded. "It's coming. He's coming. This is the year. The year when you're all going to pay for your sins."

"That's uh, that's interesting," Laurie stammered. She reached for her and Marshall's drinks, but nearly jumped out of her shoes as a hand descended upon her shoulder. "Oh!" she yelped before snapping around to see Marshall.

"Hey." He grabbed their drinks. "You all set to go back?"

Laurie's eyes widened. "More than you know." She looked over her shoulder as they walked back to the table. The prophesizing woman was half–turned on her stool watching them. Laurie shivered.

"You didn't have to wait for me," Marshall said. "I'd have brought your drink to you."

"Yeah, well, it was probably a good idea that someone stayed there. I wouldn't have trusted leaving our drinks with *her*."

Marshall seemed confused. "With who?"

"I'll tell you when we get back to the table." Laurie cast a last look at the woman. She had turned to the counter and was paying no mind to them whatsoever.

When they did get back, Laurie tried to point inconspicuously at the strange woman. "That lady sitting at the bar," she whispered loudly. "She must be really drunk. She said some weird things. I wasn't sure what to make of it." The others gawked. Laurie snapped jokingly, "Don't stare."

"What did she say?" Marshall asked.

Laurie shook her head. "I'm not sure. Something like 'It's' coming,' and then she changed that to 'He's coming,' and 'You're all going to pay for your sins this year.'" Everybody was mildly amused by this except for Laurie and Marshall.

Darian sighed. "This is why I hate this holiday. It's so stupid and unnecessary. I think so anyway. I mean, I'm not sure of the history of it or why we celebrate it, but it just seems like a bunch of wacko traditions and an excuse for crazy people to dress up and act stupid. I say we just skip Halloween and go directly into Christmas."

That last comment made Laurie think of one of her favorite films, *The Nightmare before Christmas*. There did seem to be a blending of the two holidays, not just in Willow Falls, but in society in general. Hell, in the downtown strip, street lamps were decorated with cornstalks on the bottom and Christmas lights on top. No wonder Tim Burton wrote that poem.

The juxtaposition of ghouls and goblins with Santa and his reindeer was certainly an interesting idea to get the creative juices flowing. Laurie thought of the streetlamps, and the ethereal light they cast when dusk settled in. It was an unearthly shade of orange. Halloween orange. Eerie at all times of the year, but especially on fall and winter nights when dead leaves would rustle through that light or the snow would dance in flurries.

Laurie had always thought Christmas Eve was the scariest night of the year, even more than Halloween. For some reason or other, she didn't think it was safe to go outside on Christmas Eve. While she didn't tell James that, she did try to prevent him from stepping foot outdoors on that night. Their parents, too, seemed to share Laurie's hesitancy though they never came out and said it.

With the recent events, Laurie was beginning to recalculate her fear. She sipped from her tea and focused on the group's discussion. The topic had changed from the creepy heavyset woman in the "Undead Ahead" zone.

"Do you think we could go somewhere else?" she said. She laid her napkin across her parmesan-smeared plate.

After some discussion, the group decided Laurie was right. They all had two drinks, and, for the drivers, that was more than enough, but no one wanted to call it a night. They decided on a movie at the dollar theater, Cinema Eight, just over in Boardman, a ten–minute drive.

As they got up, Laurie grabbed her jacket and looked over to the bar counter. The woman was no longer there. She could only gaze at the vacant stool for a moment before Marshall got her attention.

"Hey, you ready?" he asked. He didn't seem to notice that the woman was gone.

Laurie sighed. "Yeah, I was just daydreaming."

Marshall smiled as he donned his jacket. The two of them walked out last, just as they had come in. Laurie didn't bother to look back again. What was the point? Had that woman said those creepy things at all? Maybe one hard tea was her limit. All she wanted to do now was see a movie even though the group had settled on a scary one. What the heck, it was the right time of the year. As they exited into the chilled night, Laurie thought that wherever that woman was now, she probably had a big sloppy smile on her face.

Deputy Flynn pulled up to the abandoned farm house in Willoughby, a township of Willow Falls in Lawrence County. He was on patrol tonight, and didn't mind working the late shift, even on a Saturday night. It came with the territory of being a deputy. The farm wasn't far from his home in Canterbury anyway.

He couldn't get the images from the home video out of his head. Such a loving father and son, both missing. Seventeen years ago, Halloween night. He didn't have to argue hard to get Sheriff Gram to allow him to come and check this house out. In fact, the sheriff thought it was a good idea considering what was shown in the film. Even though they weren't state police, and this was out of their jurisdiction, it *was* their case, and would be negligent not to follow the evidence.

He pulled down the long driveway and was more than a little freaked out as the headlights revealed a foreboding, blue, two–story farmhouse standing out from the shadows and silhouettes of the forest. He parked the cruiser in front of the house. An eerie green glow from the dashboard illuminated his face as he gazed upon the boarded–up house.

He turned the key in the ignition and shoved the car door open with a grating clunk. The woods came alive with the sounds of crickets, owls, and the howling wind. Dead autumnal leaves rustled across the forest floor. Feeling exposed, Deputy Flynn stepped into the chilly night.

He ascended a set of creaking porch steps and tried the door handle. Locked. More than that, it was boarded up, as were the windows. Paint that had once been a vibrant blue was faded and chipped, peeling in places like a tarantula shedding its exoskeleton.

There was no other option. He had to break in. Using his baton and fingers, he worked at the boards partially blocking the doorway. Why the hell did the township of Willoughby board the place up in the first place? Normally, boarding up windows would suffice to keep animals out. Regardless, he managed to pry off the two–by–fours and rusted nails and muscle his way inside.

It was just as he'd expected. Well, several things anyway. The interior was dark. Very, very dark. And cold. But what was really disturbing, in a disgusting sense rather than a scary sense, was the overwhelming musty smell that drenched the air. It was almost as potent as formaldehyde.

Despite the stygian darkness, Deputy Flynn thought he could see dust particles dancing in the empty hallway. He flipped his flashlight on. Straight ahead a staircase rose to a landing and bent back upon itself. Spindles cast stark shadows against the scabbed and shredded wallpaper. He decided to save the upstairs for later.

A door to his right led to a dining room. There was a table and chairs, a chandelier, and a china cabinet filled with antique eggs and dishes among other things. Other than that, there was nothing to see.

Down the hall a second door opened onto a study stacked with dusty old books and yellowed newspaper articles. Several animal head trophies stood out from one wall. Their dead eyes gleamed in his flashlight. He shivered and backed into the hall. He didn't know exactly what he was looking for, but it wasn't that.

He repeated this process through the family room, kitchen, and living room, turning up nothing of real interest. He would have to go upstairs.

As he approached the stairway, a crack sounded. The floor vibrated dimly through his soles and he heard a distant spit of plaster onto a floor. He froze, hand touching his holster. Nothing. Just an old house settling into its foundation. *Like some living, breathing entity in pain?*

Man up, he thought. He shook off the willies and headed up the steps, which creaked like arthritic bones. He stopped at a closed door but stopped as he was about to open it. A plastic license plate was taped to the top doorframe.

Danger Joshua's Room

Upon entering what he presumed to be Joshua's room, whoever Joshua was, he was disappointed to discover no obvious clues here either. The three remaining bedrooms proved just as unhelpful. But he wasn't ready to give up hope just yet. There was still a narrow door directly across the hall from a sagging bathroom he had deemed too dangerous to search. Flynn assumed the door led to an attic.

He turned the crystal knob and found that he was right. Unfinished steps led up into darkness. He tried the light switch on the wall, but all it did was click. Angling the flashlight, he proceeded to work his way up. He reached a landing, rounded the corner, and walked up three or four more creaking steps.

As he wasn't expecting to find anything interesting, he was both amazed and horrified by what he saw. Sitting on a sofa against a back wall to Deputy Flynn's left, were four horribly decomposed bodies. Their clothing was tattered and caked with dried blood, and they appeared to be male. Four young men.

At first he couldn't be sure whether they were props or real. On closer inspection, there was no denying their reality. A toxic stench wafted from bloated, discolored, shriveled, decaying, and maggot festering flesh and bone. Deputy Flynn had to press his forearm over his mouth to repress the bitter bile pushing up his throat.

The attic itself was one big room with a doorway leading into a niche filled with plastic bins stuffed with comic and coloring books. A filing cabinet supported a paper mache skull that looked to have been made in an art class. He considered calling for backup, but this wasn't exactly an active crime scene and his fellow officers would not appreciate having to come out here on a Saturday night. He decided to investigate further, maybe get a little light in here and take some pictures.

Much of the attic floor was littered with candles. In the harsh glare of his flashlight it approximated a miniature, leafless forest. Beyond the candles a small window overlooked the shadows and silhouettes of the actual forest behind the house. In the corner a coffin sat in shadow. His beam illuminated solid oak or mahogany, smooth and freshly stained. A shudder clenched his shoulders. He shook it off.

Inside the coffin was another corpse, bigger than the others. The coffin itself was at least seven feet long, so Deputy Flynn estimated the body had to measure a good six–and–a–half feet. A man, probably in his fifties by the color his hair.

"Oh my god," Flynn whispered. He recognized this man. It was the farmer. The farmer who had disappeared nearly twenty years prior. Moran was his name. Johnathon Moran. Flynn had researched the archives. He'd had to dig a little deep, but he found that he wanted. John Moran was sixty–one years old. His son, Joshua, had been eight, about to turn nine when they went missing October 31, 1998.

It wasn't just the Morans that went missing. There was a group of college boys too. Four, if Flynn remembered correctly. A quick glance at the couch brought memories of newsprint flooding into his mind. The young men ranged from nineteen to twenty–one. Their names were Shawn Dixon, Randolph Stevens, Earl John Rye, and Donald Rightwing.

Flynn couldn't recall if the disappearances had been linked, but it sure as hell seemed like a pretty strong correlation considering now. He remembered reading that friends of the boys had informed authorities had left a frat party and were walking back to the dorm. That was the same Halloween night that John and Josh Moran disappeared.

The body of Johnathon Moran wasn't in the same condition as the boys. In fact, he appeared to be in near–pristine shape. A neat tux and combed hair. Tucked into the coffin padding was a series of photos of him and his son and drawings that Flynn assumed the boy had made for his father. Cute, but in this context, creepy. Sketched by a shaky hand with crayon and colored pencil on sheets of yellow drawing paper, the drawings depicted monsters, dragons, and dinosaurs. One caught Flynn's eye, a rendition of a leprechaun with needle fangs, a pointed hat and shoes, and a long, silky beard in a field of melon vines beneath a sickle half–moon.

How could this body be in such good shape after twenty–five years? Further inspection revealed webs of thin tubes trailing from the farmer's sleeves. They led to a machine in a cabinet beneath the coffin that seemed to be pumping deep blue fluid.

Other tubes were inconspicuously taped to his temples. *Why blue?* Flynn thought. No one had blue blood. The only reason the veins were blue was because they reflected blue light. The blood itself was red, whether it was in your body or out. This had to be embalming fluid.

He pressed his shoulder mic and called for backup, but the only answer was several bursts of static that only vaguely imitated a voice, and not the voice of anyone he knew. "Damned secondhand junk," he said, flicking the mic off. He would have to use the car radio.

A sound startled him. Drawing his gun, he turned to find himself face–to–face with the same mask-like visage that five young people had seen in their dying moments over the past week.

"Freeze!" Flynn screamed. "Don't even think about moving!" The gun wobbled in his hand. He tightened his grip.

The figure simply stood there staring with that teasing, petulant grin. Flynn flicked the safety off. "I'm serious."

Before he could do more, the assailant latched onto Flynn's wrist with a viselike grip. Bone popped. Flynn cried out. The gun twisted, and his hand with it, until the barrel pointed directly between his eyes. The pain flared and steadied, like sitting close to a bonfire for too long. He couldn't stop staring at his hand. A wrist wasn't supposed to bend like that, was it? He willed his arm to move and was rewarded by a spasmodic jerk that threw his assailant momentarily off balance. Flynn twisted his shoulders and torso, tried to step through the hold. An ear–splitting explosion blew through the attic as the gun fired, hitting the corpse of the young man closest to the sofa's end. Flesh and bone splashed from of the back of his softened skull.

With a violent yank, the attacker pulled Flynn's arm out of its socket. The stomach–turning pop was nearly as loud as the gun shot. The weapon fell from his numbed fingers. He screamed in agony. His arm hung limp and useless, a wet noodle.

A strange calmness came over him. Shock, most likely. He got the impression that his attacker could have done a lot more damage had he intended. A fractured wrist and dislocated shoulder were bad, but this man's grip was so strong he surely could have ripped his hand off or tore his arm clean from the socket.

The attacker's free hand flashed. Flynn felt the impact, but only saw stars as his head snapped sideways. He dropped to his knees. Brilliant colors flashed and faded. He felt the killer's hand clamp onto the back of his neck. Flynn stiffened. Images came to him of corpses in full rigor mortis, a line of gurneys stretching down an endless white tunnel. His knees scraped as he was dragged to the embalming machine.

"No," he begged. "No please." Blood dribbled from his mouth.

He dug his fingers into the floor. Bullets of pain shot through him as the wood splintered and ripped his nails from their soft finger beds. Blood streaked the floor.

The killer threw him down. His face smacked the base of the machine. The sound of it pushed at his senses like fingers probing his ears. He spat teeth and willed his vision to clear.

The killer grabbed a handful of hair. Flynn's head pulled back so violently, his neck cracked. The killer grabbed an IV line and jammed its needle-end into Flynn's tear duct. The machine came alive, whirring and flashing. Flynn shouted as midnight–blue fluid sped up the tube toward his eye. Hand flailing from his broken wrist, Flynn tried to rip the needle out. The killer grabbed his wrist. *What am I going to do?* Flynn thought with surprising lucidity. He couldn't resort to biting, as he didn't have any front teeth, and his gun was halfway across the room.

He grappled the killer's wrist with his remaining hand and squeezed with all his might, hoping, praying, it would loosen that iron grip. It didn't work. Nothing worked. He pulled his head back as far as he could. Pain shot through him, but he wouldn't stop, contorting his back in ways that it was never meant to bend.

Finally, he got his knees beneath him and craned himself partway up between the killer's legs. With a grunting howl, he ripped the line from the machine.

The killer released. Flynn fell back. He landed on his shoulders and worked the needle from his eye. *Adrenaline*, he thought. Had to have been. It was the only thing keeping him going. While the killer attended to his machine, Flynn dragged himself across the floor and he reached his shaking hand toward the gun.

It was his only hope. "Ah," he grunted as his finger touched the cold steel gun barrel. He heard footsteps. A large, pointed boot descended onto Flynn's good hand, and bore down. Bones popped. Pain flashed, but it was nothing now. When everything hurts, nothing does. Flynn thrust his bad hand forward. Fingers flopped onto the gray metal revolver. He tried to grip, but it just lay there. So close and yet so far.

The killer grabbed a handful of Flynn's hair and pulled his head up. He pulled cartoonishly massive hunting knife from his belt. Flynn's eyes fixed on the serrated edge, the slightly hooked end of the blade.

It was inevitable now. What was left to try? You can't fight fate. He remembered his father saying that after being laid off in the 90's recession. Flynn's reflection stared back at him from the gleaming metal, as clear as if it were a mirror. *This can't be real.* And yet it had to be. The pain, the blood, the swollen eyes and split lip. The broken nose.

"Boy," he spat. *Tell me you didn't hurt the boy. At least tell me that.* He could deal with four college kids, but an innocent little boy? He had been a little boy once.

The killer didn't answer and didn't strike. The knife continued to taunt.

Answer me, he thought. Silence. The fading thud of his heart.

A violent and uncontrollable fury swept over him. Now his hand did grip, clumsily, but enough to move the gun.

"You crazy m—" But his growling was cut off. With a single upward thrust the blade penetrated his lower jaw, the tip piercing the soft underbelly, his tongue, and the roof of his mouth.

Flynn her gurgling, gagging sounds. Warm copper flooded from his mouth, spattered onto the wooden floor. Flynn prayed the killer was through with him, had done his work, and would leave him to die. Maybe he could to call for help if he could just hold on long enough. He thought of the malfunctioning shoulder mic, the working radio in his car. It seemed an impossible distance, and probably was.

The killer stepped to the side and pulled Flynn's hair. The deputy's back arched to the point of breaking. Pressing the serrated edge against Flynn's scalp, the killer drew the blade back.

"No," Flynn choked through a mouthful of blood. He seemed to float up from his body until he was looking down upon the gruesome scene. *Is there a heaven?* he thought. There was certainly a hell. But then how many times had he reviewed crime scene photos, seen murders acted out on TV? Even now he was thinking like a law officer, weighing evidence, deducing motive, trying to find an objective truth.

The blade sliced clean. A layer of flesh and hair flapped back, exposing the hardened pink bone of the skull beneath. Flynn's final scream echoed through the house, the night, the surrounding woods, perhaps more nightmarish than any sound ever emitted by mortal vocal cords. Thankfully for all but Flynn it went unheard by human ears. The clear hooting of an owl was the only response.

7

The drive to Sperdute's was only about fifteen minutes, but it seemed longer. Perhaps because it was so out in the country, and entirely out of Willow Falls despite being a township of Willow Falls and part of the same county. Perhaps it was because Laurie and James cherished the ride so much. Either way, it always seemed longer on the way there than on the way back.

It was Sunday, October 5, and the Williams family had decided to come a little early this year. Normally they waited until late October to get their pumpkins, but they had learned a hard lesson last year when they showed up two days before Halloween and not a single pumpkin remained in the fields.

Laurie and James sat in the back seat with their windows down. Normally Laurie didn't like to have the window down as it would ruin her hair, but the fresh Sunday air was just too refreshing today, especially since she hadn't gotten a chance to shower this morning. She would have to take a quick one before work. For now, she meant to savor this trip and family time.

Last night had gone well. She and Marshall had some real chemistry, and there would be a second date, a one–on–one that Laurie was actually looking forward to.

James nudged her with his elbow. "Hey, Laurie, what movie did you guys see?" Laurie had to think about it. The title wasn't coming to her.

"A scary one that would give you nightmares for the next three years," she joked. She remembered the title and told him, but of course that wasn't enough. He wanted details.

She laughed. "I can't tell you that." James's eyes narrowed in a cute way that made Laurie want to pinch his cheeks.

"Why not?" he asked.

"Because you have to sleep at night," their father said.

Their mother nodded from the passenger seat. "You don't need to be watching those kinds of films, James. They're not for kids."

James gave Laurie a look that said, *do you agree with them, Laurie? Please tell me you don't. I'm old enough, I really am. You can tell me. I won't have nightmares, I promise. Please tell me.*

But Laurie wasn't about to be taken in. "They're right, sport," she whispered. "Don't worry. It was a stupid movie, anyway."

James gazed out the window as they passed wide open fields and heavily wooded hillocks. The sweet revitalizing scent of the open country in October was abruptly replaced by a rotten stench of manure. Laurie nudged her brother. Several cows stood in a pasture, a couple of bulls, some solid black females, others with more traditional white and black spotting.

Their father pointed to the back of the herd at a white cow with brown spots. "There's a chocolate milk cow, James."

Laurie smiled as her little brother lifted himself as far as the seatbelt allowed and peered intently through her window. James believed that cows with brown spots were the source of chocolate milk. His parents and big sister didn't have the heart to tell him otherwise, but protective measures had been taken. Their parents had convinced him not to mention the chocolate milk cows at school. That way it could be his secret.

"Are those where steak comes from?" he asked.

Laurie nodded. "Yeah, buddy. Makes you not want to eat steak, huh?"

James shook his head as he admired the chocolate milk cow. Laurie laughed a little inside. Seeing these poor, innocent animals did made her want to turn vegan, at least until the next Wendy's sign. She didn't even want to think about veal.

Their father turned onto a backwoods road. They passed a house with a llama in the yard. James recognized it at once. It all made Laurie want to sigh with relief. There was simply nothing like the country. The great outdoors. She wanted more than anything to build a house in this area when she got older. It would have to be after she got a job teaching high school English and got on her feet, financially. A big house, not a mansion. In a mansion there was always the fear that somebody would break in and lurk in one of the million dark, dusty places and corridors that you couldn't be in all at once. A nice, big house, complete with fireplace and bay window that she could look out of as she wrote the next great American novel.

Of course, she would have to be cautious of the wildlife, bears in particular. In Pennsylvania, black bears were the only ones you would run into. They were the timidest of the bear species and were likely to run from human contact, but you always had to worry about getting between a mother and its cub. Plus, if they were seeing llamas now, what other exotic species might have sneaked into the picture since Laurie learned about PA wildlife in grade school?

There were also other things to fear. Darkness, for one. The all–encompassing darkness of the wilderness. Laurie remembered something Darian said a few years back, that somebody who looks in your window can see you because of the light in your living room, while you can't see them because of the darkness outside. Scary, indeed. Perhaps scarier than wild animals. Serial killers.

They passed through fields of corn, vast oceans of starch. Sunflowers grew along the border. They were really getting out there in the sticks or the boondocks now, but not too far. There were other houses out this way besides the farm. Beautiful houses. Some huge Victorian mansions even. But they spaced a good distance apart to the point you could consider them neighbors, but not really.

"We're here," her mother said. Laurie turned her attention forward. The sight of Sperdute's coming into view always made Laurie a little fluttery inside. It was up ahead on the left–hand side. The first structure was a small shop with an old–fashioned country porch. Each pole supporting the overhanging roof had big thick bunches of corn stalks tied around it. Bales of hay were dispersed judiciously along the floor.

Her father pulled into a gravel driveway. Directly across from the shop long wooden crates contained all manner of pumpkins and squash.

"You ready to pick a pumpkin?" Laurie asked. She meant the question to be rhetorical, but James was staring so intently at the gift shop that she wasn't sure if he wanted to pick a pumpkin or go in there first. Traditionally, they would pick pumpkins first and then check out the gift shop.

James turned away from the window. "Yeah," he said, nodding rapidly.

They exited the car as a family and headed over to inspect the pumpkin patch at the base of a low hill. Old Man Spud's house stood atop the rise. It was a warm and cozy log cabin. Laurie had never been inside, but she pictured a crackling fireplace and bearskin rug.

Old Man Spud had come to this country as a young boy on a boat with his father. They were Italian Americans, and very, very conservative. He hated all things democrat, not to mention "niggers" and "faggots." If Laurie ever dated an African American man, she would never in a million years bring him here. The old farmer would probably call him an eggplant or coon right to his face.

There was a variety of pumpkins to choose from., all different shapes, sizes and colors. Orange ones, green ones, bumpy ones, smooth ones. Green ones with orange stripes, white ones, white ones with orange stripes.

James tugged on Laurie's blouse and pointed. "Look at that one. It's gray. Wow. I've never seen a gray pumpkin before." To tell the truth, neither had Laurie.

"Did you know," James said, "that when Stan Lee first invented the Incredible Hulk, he wasn't green?"

Laurie did know that. "You forget that I was just as big of a comic book geek growing up as you are."

James laughed playfully. "Hey now, that's not nice," he said, in his spoiled–brat–whose–feelings–had–been–hurt tone.

Laurie threw him a bone. "Why did Stan Lee change the Incredible Hulk from gray to green? I forget." They approached the gray pumpkin.

James giggled and gave the rind a playful slap. "He wanted the Hulk to be gray because no superhero before had been that color. And when he was first created, Dr. Banner would only change into the hulk at night, and because he is a monster, and gray is a scary color, Stan Lee made him gray."

Laurie nodded. She recalled interviews, how the combination of Dr. Jekyll and Mr. Hyde with Frankenstein had served as inspiration during the Hulk's creative birth.

"The original colorist had trouble making the right shade of gray," James said. "Sometimes it would turn out a different shade of gray or even green, so Stan Lee just decided to make him green."

Laurie hadn't heard that part. She patted his shoulder. It was always fascinating to glimpse the wealth of knowledge stored in her brother's ten–year–old mind.

"Doesn't that look like the head of an alien?" he asked as they continued to walk around to the medium–sized pumpkins. Before Laurie got a chance to answer, he answered himself. "Yeah, it does. An alien. A gray alien. We could get that and just paint two black, almond–shaped eyes on it and a little mouth, and it would look just like an alien."

Laurie thought of a line from Keats, one of her favorite romantic poets. "She stood in tears amidst the alien corn." Of course, he didn't literally mean alien as in the slimy, Lovecraft inspired creatures from those Sigourney Weaver films or *Predator*, but it was always cool to be inspired by words even if they meant something totally different.

What if these pumpkins *were* aliens? Boy that would be a neat idea for a short story. Campy perhaps, but neat. What if all the pumpkins and squash and cornstalks and sunflowers as well as all the other crops were extraterrestrials from parallel dimensions?

When James was younger he liked to imagine he was Godzilla and fight cornstalks, pretending they were giant praying mantises. He'd lift them over his head and throw them, twist them and break them in half over his knee. Oh, it just made Laurie want to sigh. The joys and pleasures of an active imagination. It was truly too bad that most people lost that once they became adults.

"Hey, Laurie," James said.

"Yeah."

"How come we have to die so young?"

Laurie was a little confused. "Where is this coming from?"

James looked at his shoes. "I was just wondering why everybody died so young."

"I'm not sure what you mean, bud. Not everybody dies young. Most people live into their in their mid–to late seventies." She smiled and touched his shoulder. "Some live to be a hundred or more. Not everybody dies young." Of course, there were exceptions to the rule. You couldn't ignore homicide victims or suicide victims; people killed by a wild animal attack, drug or alcohol overdose, or medical issues like brain aneurisms, leukemia, and so on.

James selected a pumpkin. "That's not what I mean. What I'm saying is some animals like the giant Galapagos tortoise live to be a hundred and fifty. And look at the dinosaurs. They were around for a hundred and eighty–five million years. We haven't been around that long. And how about the earth? It's been here for like four–and–a–half billion years. Our lives are like the blink. It just doesn't seem fair."

Laurie knelt to inspect a pumpkin that was flat on one side. It was evident that James had given this a lot of thought. But he gave everything a lot of thought. He couldn't help it. He was a thinker.

She met his gaze. "I see what you're saying, but just because we haven't been around for as long as dinosaurs doesn't mean we're won't be eventually. Most animals don't live nearly as long as we do."

James laughed. "What about chimps and gorillas and orangutans?"

Laurie shook her head. "They live pretty long, but I don't think they make it as long as we do, my man."

Their conversation was cut short as their mother interrupted, asking if they'd picked out a couple of pumpkins. They selected two medium–sized plain–old–orange specimens and carried them toward the shop to pay. A sign outside the door showed that small ones were only two dollars. Mediums cost three, while large pumpkins went for five.

They walked inside the little store which reminded Laurie of the classical general shop in an old Western film. Visiting the shop had always been Laurie's favorite part of the their Sperdute's expedition.

Immediately to the left was a glass counter. They placed their pumpkins on it and went to look around as their father paid. Laurie went one way and James another. Laurie liked to check out the jars of homemade jam which ranged from blackberry to boysenberry to elderberry to strawberry, blueberry, and everything between. Elderberry was Laurie's favorite, and according to the woman who worked the counter last year, it was also the favorite of most people who passed through. Laurie just loved it on toast or a muffin or bagel with extra crunchy, reduced–fat peanut butter.

She grabbed a jar and looked to her mother. "You care if we get a jar of this?" Her mother shook her head no.

Her father and James were on the other side of the store sifting through fresh red, green, yellow, and orange peppers. Some of the peppers were round, others elongated like witches' noses. Her father tossed handfuls into a shopping basket while James examined jars of sweet, hot, and mild pepper rings. Laurie had to give it to her father. The man knew how to cook peppers. Any recipe you could think of—pigs in a blanket, stuffed pepper soup, even fried peppers on wheat or white bread. All were irresistible.

Laurie tucked the can of elderberry jam in her arm and continued around the shop. There was an opening toward the back that looked out on the barn. It wasn't much to see, but the wall past the opening featured a scythe, a pitchfork and an array of laminated newspaper clippings, yellowed with age. The center of the store held bales of hay with miniature scarecrows attached to posts for decoration.

Beneath the newspaper clippings was a display of decorated mason jars. Most were painted black with gray tombstones and spooky classical ghosts poking their heads out from scraggy trees with faces of their own. Some had lids, while the others contained orange wax candles and had checkered cloth wrapped around the brim. Laurie wondered if any of them had ever held moonshine. That had been a big industry in these parts during Prohibition.

Laurie's tour came full circle. She met her brother and father at the glass counter. They each got what they wanted. Laurie and James had pumpkins. Laurie had a jar of elderberry jam, and James a jar of mild banana peppers. Her father bought a basket of regular peppers, mostly the elongated kind and seemed to have one of each color. They were going to be enjoying fried pepper sandwiches this evening.

James helped himself to a handful of candy corn from a dish.

"You can have a sucker too if you want," said the nice woman behind the counter. It wasn't the same one as last year, but she had similar features.

James sifted through the array of suckers. Grape, lemon, root beer, and butterscotch. At last, James decided on a butterscotch.

"Find everything okay?" the woman asked.

"Sure did." Their father paid. They gathered their belongings and were out the door. Their mother was already sitting in the car.

Laurie glanced over her shoulder. Old Man Spud stood by his porch with his black Lab at his side. Laurie couldn't help but recall one of her favorite horror films. That dog looked like something straight out of *The Omen*. She acknowledged the old man with a nod and a wave. He dutifully waved back. *Got to love the old–time Italians,* Laurie thought as she got into the car. He might be a creepy old bigot, but he had manners.

She closed the door, sealing off another annual trip to the farm. She was starting to get hungry. She'd go home and have a golden crisp apple with peanut butter for a snack before work. That sounded like a healthy enough treat. And satisfying too. Her father had put their pumpkins in the trunk and they would carve them and light them up in the next week or so.

"You guys got everything, right?" their mother asked. Laurie, James, and their father replied in unison that they did. So that was that. And they were on their way.

Until next year, Laurie thought, and she was certain James was thinking the same thing. But a tendril of dread crept through her musing. *What if there isn't a next year?* The way things were going, it seemed entirely possible.

8

Inquiry was a class geared toward reading, writing, and thinking. But some things seemed so preposterous they should be illegal to think about, or at least talk about. That's what Jamie Woodward thought anyway. Jamie was a student in the LLP department, taking Inquiry with one of Laurie Williams's favorite professors, Dr. Perkins. Her class was a small one, consisting of six students including herself.

The LLP program was designed for non–traditional students. Most were older than the typical student enrolled on campus. At twenty–four, Jamie was the second youngest person in the class. The oldest was a forty–three–year–old male history major. What was nice about being in the LLP department was that tuition cost six thousand a semester rather than forty–five thousand. No room, no board, none of the excess baggage of being a traditional eighteen–year–old freshman out of high school. The only downside was you couldn't participate in extracurricular activities. Well, the athletic ones anyhow. If you wanted to, you would have to pay extra. But Jamie wasn't interested in that, just finishing her degree.

It was Monday, October 6, and she was at Lake Britain, a small lake tucked away in a pocket of woods behind the field house. Her objective was to procure another entry for the ever–expanding journal she had to turn in at the end of the semester. This was a descriptive entry detailing the reflection of trees and telephone poles on the water. Being a half–decent writer, she didn't mind this assignment. She had arrived at Lake Britain just as the sun rose. Autumn rays sparkled off the crystal blue surface. There was that early–morning nip in the air, and all was still a bit hazy as dawn mist rose from the rippling water. Jamie had trekked through dew–ridden grass, soaking her shoes, and approached the edge of the water, where she now sat Indian–style with her notebook on her thigh.

She began to scribble thoughts and did a double and then a triple take at the reflections of the trees and telephone poles. This assignment had the potential to showcase everyone's writing ability and perceptions. But that was the problem, too. Jamie worried this would become less about creativity than logical thought. Not that there was anything wrong with thinking, but Dr. Perkins kind of alluded to what the class lecture would be. He wanted them to discuss how mature students perceived the world. He would probably to ask if the reflections were still there if the observer closed their eyes or looked away. Jamie understood how liberal arts students tended to think. The majority would probably say no. It was just like the classic question: "If a tree falls in the woods and no one hears it, does it make a sound?" So many people said no, and it always made Jamie laugh. That was like saying that if you blasted a radio and then left the room, it would stop making noise.

Jamie remembered a friend who had taken the Inquiry class with Dr. Perkins telling her that one of the students that year had claimed that humans needed to perceive things, physically or otherwise, for them to exist. Not only did he say the reflections in the lake would go away and the tree wouldn't make a sound, but that if humans were to suddenly go extinct, the earth would vanish. Fade into thin air.

This was beyond absurd. By that logic, if someone were to close their eyes or go blind, the world outside him would no longer exist. "You can't talk sense to a fool," Jamie's grandmother had said. Jamie found that to be quite true.

Dr. Perkins liked to give the class "brain teasers." The last one went a little something like this. "A teacher told her students she wished yesterday was tomorrow. That way today would be Friday. What day did the teacher tell her students this?"

Upon hearing the question, Jamie had sensed it would require a lot of thought. It did but it didn't. The answer was actually quite simple.

Two students answered Thursday. Another said Saturday. Jamie figured it out before the rest of them. Sunday. You couldn't think in terms of yesterday being the literal day before whatever day it was. You had to do a bit of backtracking and then work forward. If yesterday was tomorrow, then today would be Friday. Well, comes after Friday? Saturday. So, if Saturday is tomorrow, today is Friday, but Saturday isn't tomorrow. You had to think back to the beginning of the riddle: if yesterday was tomorrow. So, the day before today was Saturday, because if it were tomorrow, today would be Friday, but it wasn't tomorrow; it was yesterday, so, by process of elimination, the day the teacher told her students had to be Sunday. You had to jump back a few paces and then forward like a game of chess. You may sacrifice a pawn or a jester along the way, but, ultimately, it would serve the greater purpose. Jamie laughed. Why a teacher would be talking to her students on a Sunday was an entirely different riddle.

As she sat there scribbling, she was suddenly distracted by the sound of two crows cawing. A sense of dread came over her. She looked up and saw birds fluttering out of the treetops across the lake. They were huge and *so* jet–black. Their wingspans appeared to stretch ten or even twenty feet. Of course, Jamie knew this was an illusion. The documentaries she'd seen on TV, along with tales she'd heard about thunderbirds, were playing tricks on her. Thunderbirds were mythical beings from Native American lore, gods in the form of massive birds. The flapping of their wings generated thunder and lightning and they sometimes carried off children in their wretched talons.

As the couplet flew overhead, Jamie saw that they were two perfectly normal–sized crows, flapping and squawking. But the feeling of uneasiness didn't end. It had been there all along in fact, and not because of the ridiculous notion of giant god birds. No, this feeling had been there before the birds. She had just refused to acknowledge it until now.

From the woods across the lake, she felt a presence. Adding to the unnerving feeling, was a fleeting movement of shadow upon shadow. Was somebody watching her? Some *thing*? She squinted and barely made out a blobby, amorphous figure partially blocked by undergrowth. She sensed eyes, cold, implacable eyes fixated on her. She tried to ignore it and focus on her writing, but there was also something in the lake.

Whatever it was, it was floating, a vaguely humanoid shape floating face down. She dropped her notebook and pen and stood. The bobbing thing worked its toward shore. As it drew close, she determined that in was in fact a person, a male, and he didn't appear to be in good shape.

"Oh my god," Jamie said. "Are you okay?" She prayed to the good Lord above that this was somebody playing a prank, but as time continued to draw out like a blade, it was beginning to look otherwise.

The body was dressed in a policeman's uniform. Jamie splashed into the fifty–degree water. As she stood a little less than waist deep in the freezing, lake, she saw that, yes, this was a police officer—or had been. She began to whimper as she realized the man was missing his scalp. The entire top of his head, flesh, hair, the whole nine yards, had been cleaved off, exposing white bone.

She flipped the body over and shrieked as life–drained eyes gazed through her to the vast eternity that was the sky. Jamie's friends sometimes teased her about her eyes looking like this when she was exceptionally drunk. Her friends called them "doughnut eyes."

Lake Britain shortly became a crime scene after Jamie rushed back to her cell phone and reported the incident to the authorities. Police were able to identify the man as Deputy Michael Flynn, who had gone missing two nights before. There was no sign of the man's cruiser, but according to Sheriff Gram of Canterbury County, Flynn had gone to inspect the old Moran farm Saturday evening after he and Flynn watched old reels of home video footage depicting John Moran and his son, Josh. Local police were going to dispatch a unit over to the Moran farm to see if they could find anything after fishing Flynn's corpse out of the water.

Westminster had taken not just one, but two hits—the murders of two of their own students, and the body of an officer from a neighboring township found in their lake. Faculty and students caught wind of the situation quickly and gathered in flocks outside the yellow police tape as authorities conducted interviews. Red and blue lights flashed through the early morning.

This hustle and bustle and commotion didn't become the small campus. It didn't seem to fit or belong. Not one bit. As this out–of–place commotion transpired, students, staff, along with the entirety of the police force, remained blissfully unaware of the eyes watching them from across the lake. Only Jamie felt them. She told the authorities that she thought she'd seen someone in the woods. The police told her that they would do a sweep once things calmed down a bit.

The same set of eyes that had been watching Jamie now had something much larger to feast on. With one gloved hand, the observer pushed the branches down to get a better view. He admired them just as they admired his handiwork on the foolish cop who was too stupid to leave him alone. Heavy, animal breathing penetrated his mask, but he was far out of earshot of the authorities and spectators.

With impeccable timing, he released the branch, which popped up and concealed him just as Jamie Woodward turned in his direction. She found the shaking of the branch to be curious, but it was the least of her worries right now. The spectator of spectators played that role for a while longer before receding back into the woods.

9

The incident involving Jamie Woodard discovering the mutilated body of Deputy Michael Flynn in Lake Britain occurred on Monday, October 6. That was just three days prior. Today, on Thursday, October 9, Laurie had plans to go out and eat dinner with Marshall at six o'clock at Twenty–Six Bar and Grill, which was a sports bar on the East Side on East Washington Street in Willow Falls. As much as Laurie had been looking forward to this night, she just couldn't shake the horrible thought of the events that had occurred just this Monday.

After talking to Marshall about it, she discovered that he shared the same sentiments. Regardless, there was nothing they could do about it now, apart from trying to move forward and try to carry out a normal routine. Dean Anderson had implemented a curfew for all students who lived on campus. Naturally, they already had a time when they were expected to return to their dorms, but the dean had bumped it up just a tad bit earlier. Students who had evening classes with long walks back to their dorms, from Old Main over to Hillside for instance, were cautioned to not go alone. As Dean Anderson noted in his most recent e–mail, "We live in dangerous times, students. I advise all of the student body as well as faculty to be on their toes, alert and extra cautious."

With the discovery of Deputy Flynn's body, some of the pieces of the puzzle were beginning to come together for people like Laurie, who had been interested in the case from the get¬–go. After all, it wasn't like some government cover–up or conspiracy for God's sake, like Roswell or Area 51. It wasn't as if the police were intentionally trying to cover their tracks or had anything to hide. Flynn had gone to the Moran Farm, where John, the man who owned it, and his son, Josh, had gone missing some seventeen years earlier.

The reason he had gone there, was because two rolls of film that were home video footage of John and Josh were found stuffed in Jack Sayer's eye sockets at Blood Moon Farm. Long story short, Flynn went to the farm, and two days later, they found him scalped and floating face down in

Lake Britain. But what was most telling, was that Jack and Julia were killed at a haunted house, and according to some of the old newspaper clippings and archives Laurie had read, Johnathon Moran set his farmhouse up as a haunted house around Halloween time. Also, Jack and Julia went to Westminster College in Willoughby, where John's farm is located.

Perhaps more importantly, or perhaps not, was the fact that John and little Josh disappeared on Halloween night 1998. Were they murdered? Laurie couldn't help but wonder. Was it the same murderer who had been responsible for the disappearances of John and Josh that was responsible for the disappearances of the four boys whose names Laurie couldn't quite put her finger on? Shawn was one of them. Yes, Shawn. Shawn, Randolph, Earl, and Donald. The bigger question would be if the killer who had taken these six individuals seventeen years ago—if they had been taken by a killer—was the same one who had targeted Jack and Julia at Blood Moon Farm, and the three other victims at Ghoul Mansion.

It was starting to look like Willoughby had a serial killer / mass murderer on its hands. Thank God, Laurie thought to herself, that he didn't seem to be targeting citizens in Willoughby, Willow Falls, or any of the other townships at their homes. Not that she wished him to claim the lives of those partaking in annual Halloween festivities, but two random events at two separate haunted houses in neighboring counties wasn't enough for the good denizens of Lawrence County to worry about locking their doors during the day–time. That is until the body of Michael Flynn had been found toothless and scalped in Lake Britain. The students at Westminster College seemed to be in more danger than the families in Willow Falls and Willoughby.

It was all more than a little much to think about. At last, Laurie figured that it was probably best not to try and dissect the mind of a maniacal madman. That was something that nobody could relate to or make sense of except for a highly trained and qualified psychiatrist.

As close to home as the action was getting, Laurie just wanted to stay alert and cautious. Sure, she was scared, but she couldn't stop living her life. She just kept telling herself that she had to have faith, and that soon, very soon, this bastard would fall into the hands of police custody. In the meantime, she would try to enjoy the rest of her evening. She was going to spend it with Marshall at the bar in which he apparently was a regular every Thursday night since he was eighteen.

Marshall was knocking on her door at quarter to six, just as he'd said he would. Not a minute late and not a minute earlier. Laurie had been ready well in advance. He didn't have to knock long before she was out the door and into the car, even before he even had a chance to hold the door for her.

Twenty–Six Bar and Grill was named that because the owner was number twenty–six when he played football. And it wasn't just his number, but his brother's, his dad's, and both of his uncles. They all played in high school and in college. In fact, two of their jerseys had been framed and hung on the wall. Laurie knew that because she'd been there before. She just wasn't sure exactly whose jerseys those were. But it didn't matter. They were all the same anyway, right? They had the best wings in town, with an array of flavors ranging from wet ranch, dry ranch, hot ranch, wet Cajun, hot and sweet honey brown, five AM's, and Ryan's. Thursdays were wing nights, when wings went forty cents apiece. And they had dollar beers, as well. Miller High Life Light. Not that Laurie cared much about that, but she supposed if you were a beer drinker and you didn't mind light beer, you couldn't beat it. It wasn't called the "Champaign of Beers" for no reason.

They pulled into the parking lot. Laurie was admiring the flaming sky, a mixture of powder blue and gray, hot pink and orange at the horizon. The air had a bite to it, which was not surprising considering the time of year and time of day, and Laurie just couldn't wait to get inside the nice warm bar.

"Little chilly out tonight, huh?" Marshall asked after seeing Laurie crossing her arms tightly.

"Sure is," Laurie answered.

"That's okay," Marshall responded. "A nice stiff drink will make you feel all warm and snuggly inside."

Although it hadn't been that long, Laurie had grown to become accustomed with Marshall's humor. For one thing, he knew drinking wasn't her cup of tea, so to speak. He had seen how conservative she had been on the last date, not to mention the fact that she told him she didn't like to drink. Secondly, no self–respecting twenty, soon to be twenty–one–year–old, would ever dream of using the phrase "nice, stiff drink," and that's exactly what Laurie told him as a joke. Marshall knew she had a point.

He led the way as they walked up the sidewalk. Laurie admired the rose–colored stones covering the tarp out front. Deep–green plants jutted out of them like Carrie White's bloody hand at the end of the film. It had been a while since Laurie read the novel, so she couldn't recall if that was in the ending of that or not. The plants were such a vibrant green that Laurie thought of it as a color that hadn't been classified yet. Life green, she thought, was a pretty fitting moniker. But getting back to the rose–colored rocks, Laurie couldn't help but think of the recently discovered large theropod dinosaur, *Apatosaurus*, a contender for largest carnivorous dinosaur of all time, rivaling *Tyrannosaurus Rex*. Its bones were discovered not just in packs, but in a quarry the color of the stones in front of Twenty–Six. Is name literally translated to "Earth lizard of the rose–colored rocks."

Above the door, inscribed into the gray, concrete section of the building in big bold letters, was "Twenty–Six." On both sides of the entrance door and running across the top and just below the name of the establishment, the building was painted maroon with gold trim. Maroon and gold were the colors of the East Side Rams, a former football team here in Willow Falls

What Laurie remembered most about this place was the photo of an old man on the wall. He was obviously a football coach. That was evident based on his East Side Rams hat and whistle. The last time Laurie had been here, she'd asked who that man was. As it turned out, he was the owner, Denny Flora's grandfather, who was responsible for starting Pop Warner football in Willow Falls.

They walked inside, and there was that tell–tale creaking of the door that Laurie recalled so well. It seemed so loud that Laurie felt as if all eyes were on whoever it was that walked into the bar. It was always so dark in there; Laurie remembered that as well. Not just dark, but smoky. Smoky and dark. Or maybe it was so dark that it just seemed smoky, because you weren't allowed to smoke in here until after ten.

That much Laurie did remember. That along with the fact that the last time she had been in here, the walls were a rustic orange. Now they were a soft, pleasing shade of periwinkle. There was a table tucked away in the corner immediately to their left. The corner of the bar was directly ahead of them, and adjacent to the opposing corner at the other end of the bar were comfy, leather chairs that were like stools and had backs. Lining the wall behind the bar chairs were several small tables with stools. The men's bathroom was directly behind the corner of the bar furthest from the door, while the women's restroom was on the left–hand side down a small hallway that ran parallel to the men's and led into the basement. If one were to turn right from the men's restroom, one would go into the back section of the bar, where the bartenders walked in and out of, and where the bar wrapped fully around.

If one were to make a left before the men's bathroom, one would run into the jukebox. To the left hand–side of the jukebox, if one were facing it, was a door that lead out onto the side patio. The side patio was especially nice to sit on during summer nights. But even on fall nights, it was very pleasing, and literally a breath of fresh air. There was yet another corner tucked behind the men's room and to the right–hand side of the patio door.

"Where do you want to sit?" Marshall asked. Laurie scanned the small bar. There weren't really many options to choose from, but she decided on the bar for the time being.

"We could just sit at the bar for now," she answered. They took their seats in the center of the bar. "If you want to, we can go outside on the patio after a while," Laurie told him as they were sitting down. "It's a nice night for it."

Marshall agreed with her. "Yeah, maybe we'll go out after we eat if that's cool with you."

It certainly was with her. The bartender, whose name was Greg–o, came over to Marshall and Laurie and asked them what they'd like to drink. Actually, he asked Laurie what she'd like to drink, and placed Marshall's Miller High Life Light in front of him, which he dutifully grabbed and pulled in toward himself before taking a nice, hearty swig. Although Laurie didn't like to drink, she figured this was a bar and one or two wouldn't hurt, so she ordered an admiral and diet coke with a lime.

"Going big tonight?" Marshall asked as he took another gulp of the foaming, amber liquid.

Laurie was amused. "I wouldn't call it going big so much as having a few." She chuckled. "I guess if you consider mixed drinks going big regardless of how many you're having, then yes, I am going big. I just hope I don't regret it in the morning."

As Greg–o was mixing Laurie's drink, Marshall said, "You won't. Trust me. That stuff goes down like water. It's so sweet. It doesn't even taste like alcohol. You'll think you're drinking a regular diet coke."

Greg–o placed Laurie's drink in front of her. Going off Marshall's last comment, she remarked, "Yeah, but it's the stuff that goes down like water that comes back to bite you in the ass."

Marshall had to agree with her. "That's the truth. Just have one or two, that's all I'm doing. Someone's got to drive my car home. Probably wouldn't look too good if I had to have my mom come and pick us up."

"Your friend here need a menu?" Greg–o asked Marshall.

Laurie figured the reason he didn't ask Marshall if he needed one was because, being a regular in this place, he probably knew the menu off by heart.

"Yeah, I think we're going to be getting ready to place an order," Marshall told him.

Greg–o was a big guy. Big and bearded, with a full, curly head of hair. He played in a band; Laurie could tell by the look of it that he was a musician. Marshall had even told her that the cook, whose name was Jay, short for Jason, played in a band. Both he and Greg–o would play whenever Twenty–Six had "Jam Nights" the first Friday of every month. Greg–o placed a menu in front of Laurie, which was simply a horizontal sheet of paper. Laurie thought to herself that Greg–o's pale and freckled fingers seemed to blend with the whiteness of the paper.

Laurie took a moment to look over the menu, asking Marshall what certain flavors of wing's tasted like and which ones he'd recommend. It took a couple minutes, but they decided. Marshall ordered ten wet ranch with a large side of Cajun fries, while Laurie settled with ten hot honey brown. The rule was you had to order at least ten. You weren't allowed to split five and five. Even if you ordered a dozen, you couldn't split six and six. You had to order at least twenty if you wanted to split between two different flavors. Even at that, it only cost the customer eight bucks on wing night.

Marshall had to explain this to Laurie, who had just noticed that there was a waitress working behind the bar as well as Jeff. "What's her name?" Laurie asked gesturing in the direction of the short, dark–haired girl dressed in black who Laurie was beginning to think was gothic or emo.

"That's Sally," Marshall told her. "She's the other bartender. But she's not actually tending the bar tonight per se. The way they do it is they'll have two people working at a time. One will be doing the bar, like Greg–o, and the other, Sally, will be doing tables. But that doesn't mean that she can't get you a drink if you ask."

Laurie was sure that she already knew this. After all, it wasn't her first time there. Fortunately, there wasn't many people there tonight, so their food came fast. Jeff placed Marshall's wings and Cajun–seasoned fries in front of him, the wings oozing white like melting candle wax. Laurie got her sweet honey brown, an enticing mixture of red and brown sauce, thick and hearty.

Marshall thanked Greg–o before tearing into a wing. Laurie was picking through hers, trying to pick out a nice leg, all the while trying not the get sticky sauce all over her fingers. Oh well, that's what they gave them the wet naps for. Laurie wasn't a big wing eater—wasn't a big eater, period— but five or six wings went a long way with her. She would always start by eating all the legs, then finish off with the wings—that is, if she could finish. At last she settled on one. Her mother often teased her, telling her that she ate like a chipmunk, taking such small bites. She didn't bite wings, however. In typical woman fashion, she picked them apart with the tips of her fingers. Marshall placed his basket of Cajun fries with ranch dipping sauce in between them.

"Help yourself," he told her. "I don't think I'm going to be able to finish them all. I think my eyes were a little bit bigger than my stomach."

Laurie had to admit that they did look a little tempting and told Marshall that she may have a few in a little.

They finished their food, or most of it anyway, then sat there and conversed, enjoying each other's company.

"So, what do you think about the murders?" Laurie asked. She didn't want to blurt it out like that, but found that the way their conversation was going, she was having difficulty easing it into the topic. She didn't want to talk about such grim happenings, as she wanted to try her best to enjoy this night out, a nice little break from school and work, but it was festering in the back of her mind. Was it that she had to hear someone else's opinion to set her mind at ease? Perhaps. But there was always the possibility that it wouldn't be a good opinion.

"I'm not sure what to think," was Marshall's initial response. Laurie just nodded her head and waited for him to continue. She could tell that he was still pondering. "I think that something is rotten in the state of Denmark." The faintest smile formed on Laurie's face. Marshall repeated, "I don't know what to make of it. I mean, I know enough details about the case to know that this all must be connected in some way. It just can't be a coincidence. From what I've heard and read, the police found two rolls of film stuffed in Jack Sayer's eye sockets. This film turned out to be home video footage of a farmer and his son from Willoughby who went missing on Halloween night seventeen years ago. One of the cops investigating the case goes to the abandoned farm and two days later, they find him dead in Lake Britain."

Marshall was more or less giving Laurie a synopsis of the case. She was more than familiar with all the gory and mysterious details. "Yeah, I know all that," she informed him. "What I meant was, do you think the killer, whoever he is, is still around here?"

Marshall paused for a moment, taking some time to think over the question. It wasn't that it was a difficult question, but it was. "Well, what makes you think he would still be around here? Is there anything to suggest that he was here in the first place?"

Laurie was a bit puzzled. Of course, there was evidence to suggest that he was in the area. Marshall recognized his blunder and was quick to correct it. "That's not what I meant. There was the farmer and his son who went missing, the home video footage of them, and the cop who got murdered in the farmhouse. I didn't forget about that."

Laurie corrected him this time. "No, but you did forget about the four Westminster college students who went missing that same night."

Seeming surprised for a moment, Marshall finally came to his senses. "Oh yeah, I did forget about that. That was what, the same night the farmer and his son went missing, right?"

Laurie shook her head yes. "Yeah, six people all go missing the same night seventeen years ago. Two of them lived in that farmhouse, and the friends of the other four claimed that they were walking home in that direction and would have passed the farmhouse along the way. And the farmhouse was set up as a haunted attraction on that night. Two and a half decades later, there's five homicides at two different haunted attractions, and a murdered deputy who was investigating the crimes."

This was all getting a little repetitive to Laurie, but she couldn't help it. Sure, it disturbed her, especially considering how close to home all the commotion was hitting, but she couldn't deny that as much as she was disturbed by it, she was equally fascinated by it—not fascinated in a morbid sense, but she found it interesting. And even her interest wasn't born out of the macabre killings, as much as it was trying to put the pieces of the puzzle together and crack the code. Ultimately, she wanted this bastard to be apprehended. She surmised that the interest was akin to a history major having an interest in the Holocaust. It wasn't because they were fascinated by the torturing, experimenting, and killing of millions of Jews so much as the history of it all. Whether anybody wanted to admit it or not, there was a tale to be told here. A much larger story even than the one that everybody, even the detectives in charge of the case, were aware of.

Almost as if he'd read her mind, Marshall stated, "There is a bigger picture here. Like I said, I'm just not sure what it is. But what I am sure about, is that this person can't be that smart. He's bound to mess up sooner or later. There's no such thing as a foolproof crime or criminal. At least I don't think so. He's going to slip up. And when he does, the police are going to nab him." Marshall paused to take a sip of his second beer before continuing. His last four words were like the exclamation point on the topic and addressed concerns of Laurie's own. "Or her. Or them."

Laurie couldn't help but notice the role reversal at work here. Wasn't it just the other day that she was telling James this? That whoever it was that was doing this would soon make a fatal blunder, and his reign of terror would come to an end just as quickly as it began. Then she got to thinking. Was she just telling James that, or did she need to hear it for herself? Maybe that's why, subconsciously, she may have asked Marshall his opinion on the subject matter. Nevertheless, she didn't want to talk about it any longer, and she was glad to see that Marshall shared the same sentiments.

She quickly changed the topic, having satisfied what she set out to find, and throwing the whole issue on the back burner. "So, who did you use to come here with?"

Marshall seemed happy to be transitioning into a different subject. "My buddy Jeremy Ryan. You know who he is? He's a couple years older than us, but he graduated from Willow Falls High."

Laurie had to think for a moment. Jeremy Ryan. That did sound hauntingly familiar. "Yeah, I think I remember him," she responded. "Big, tall kid, right? About six foot four?"

Marshall nodded. "Yeah, that's Jeremy. I didn't really know him so much in high school. I met him when I worked for the city that one summer."

Now Laurie was starting to remember. "Oh yeah, didn't you work as a security guard with him?"

"Yeah, I did one year, but that's not during the summer. That's in the fall and winter. Right after Halloween when they start putting up the Christmas displays."

Laurie was interested now and had completely forgotten about the previous topic. "Oh yeah, how does that work now?"

Marshall cleared his throat before taking another chug of beer. "Well," he began. "You know how Cascade Park does their annual 'Cascade of Lights' event?"

Laurie answered that she did. She loved going to that event annually. Taking James through, and tuning into 94.5 Three WS, the Christmas station, as they drove through the park.

Marshall continued to explain. "They've had issues with people stealing the cords for the displays. They strip them and sell the copper. They can't take the displays themselves. For one thing, they're too big and heavy and it just wouldn't be practical. Plus, they're anchored to the ground. So, starting November 1, they'll start putting up lights on the dance hall and new restrooms and what—not, and some ground displays. Once they attach the cords, they need people to do security. And the way they do it is, they have eyes in the park at all times. They work seven to three, so they'll have someone come in and work the afternoon shift, three to eleven, and someone to work the nightshift, eleven to seven."

"Do the shifts alternate or stay the same?"

"No, they alternate," Marshall told her. "Like the year I did it, it was me, Jeremy, and this lady, Fay, who works for public works. She's a full—timer, but doesn't have a CDL, so she was kind of forced into doing it. She only works afternoons, and the way we did it was, me and Jeremy would divvy up the afternoons she was off and the nights. But the thing was, she was only off on Mondays and Tuesdays. She worked Wednesday through Sunday afternoons. So, between the two of us, there was only two days of afternoon shift that we could choose from. I usually worked them both because Jeremy liked the night shift. Brian, who's in charge out there, posted a schedule for each month. It usually runs from November up through the end of January until they get all of the displays down."

Laurie was very interested in this. Up until that point, she hadn't been aware that all this went on at cascade. "So, what do you have to do?"

"Nothing." Marshall's response was funny and surprised her so.

Laurie wasn't fully convinced. "You don't have any responsibilities whatsoever?"

Now it was Marshall's turn to laugh. "Of course you do. You have to keep an eye on the displays, make sure that nobody's tampering with them. All you do is drive around the park once an hour. Other than that, you could do homework, study, surf the Internet, watch TV, read or sleep. You have a key to the front gate, that way if you wanted to go anywhere, you could. Hell, you could go get dinner if you were working the afternoon shift or breakfast if you were working the late shift. You could even go home really. Just so long as you came back."

"What's Jeremy doing now? He had a kid, right?"

"Yeah, a daughter. He just got married back in August. Last I heard he was working out Sylvan Height golf course until his layoff date in November. Then I think he's going to be doing security again. I know he and his wife just got an apartment right next to the high school. I'm pretty sure he plans on going to the police academy at some point." Marshall got to thinking. "Hey, Cascade Park is having Octoberfest. We should go."

Laurie told him that this weekend was no good for her, but next weekend would work. She asked him what they were having there, to which he replied German food and beer. He even told her to invite Darian, Maggie, Rick, and Billy along. It sounded like fun to her.

Marshall asked Greg–o for their tab. He paid and left a tip, and he and Laurie were out the door. "What do you want to do now?"

Laurie wasn't sure. She told him that it didn't matter to her. "Well, you want to come over for a little bit?" Marshall asked.

"Sure," Laurie answered.

As they stepped out of the darkness, Laurie expected to walk into even more darkness, but it wasn't the case. Sure, it was dark out, but she and Marshall were bathed in the eerie, orange glow of the streetlamps.

"God, I hate those things," Laurie remarked.

Almost instinctively, Marshall commented, "What, the streetlamps?"

Laurie wasn't surprised. It seemed that everybody in this town was freaked out by those things. It just seemed to be an otherworldly shade of orange. Halloween orange, Laurie thought to herself. "Yeah," Laurie answered. "They're just so unsettling. But I'm sure it's that way in every small town." Despite her last statement, Laurie wasn't sure that it was that way in every small town. Nevertheless, she was looking forward to spending the rest of the evening at Marshall's house. It was going to be the first time she would be there. Admittedly, she was a tad bit nervous to meet his parents, but that fear subsided when Marshall told her that his parents weren't home, and that they would have the whole house to themselves.

Almost instantly, Laurie's anxiety about meeting Marshall's parents was replaced with a new anxiety. Being that they would have the house to themselves, would Marshall want to make it to home plate? She didn't think he would. Not just yet. He didn't seem like the pushy type. Laurie wasn't sure if she was ready for that anyway. Sure, maybe things would get a little frisky, but Laurie could handle that. She was ready for it. She kind of wanted to. But if he didn't pursue it, she wasn't going to push it. She told herself, whatever happens would happen, and, regardless of whatever did, it would turn out all right. They walked hand in hand to his car.

10

Allison Check had been a 911 dispatch operator for ten years. She was an overweight woman, mid–forties, with bulging eyes. Growing up, she was often teased and picked on. Being heavyset was the primary dartboard that drew her cruel peers' aim, but her somewhat bulbous eyes didn't help. *Frog eyes. Fish eyes.* Funny how people so stupid could be so smart when it came to ridiculing others. But that was in the past. It still seemed to pop into her head from time to time, especially when she was tired or anxious. This job required an attentive ear and entailed a good deal of responsibility. Those traits seemed hard to hang on to on nights like tonight when her eyelids weighed a ton apiece and she just wanted to rest her head.

There always seemed to be more distress calls this time of year when the whackos come out of hiding to cause mischief. That was one of many reasons she hated Halloween. It just seemed like an excuse for weirdos to act even weirder than usual. A Get Out of Jail Free card. As she thought these thoughts she twirled her pudgy finger, which culminated in a long acrylic fingernail, through her mug of foaming latte and made snap, crackle, pop sounds chewing on a stick of Trident. The mug read: *I ♥ My Cocker Spaniel.* Which was mostly true, except when he chewed up her slippers. The large pink heart reminded her of Valentine's Day, a holiday that she loved, probably her second favorite after Christmas, due to the colors. The warm reds and pinks and purples and whites. Not to mention the chocolates, cordial cherries, coconuts, caramels, and almonds.

The phone rang. Slurping lukewarm foam from her fingertip, she moved her gaze to the blinking red light. *Such nice thoughts, which will soon be displaced by a potentially severe crisis.* She brought the receiver to her ear and removed her chewing gum.

"Nine–one–one what is your emergency?" A mechanical humming sounds for a second or two before she heard a voice.

"I'm tired of people thinking that they can turn this holiday into a mockery of everything it stands for." The voice sounded artificial, hitting tones both too high and too low for a human range.

At first Allison was at a loss for a response. Should she hang up? She couldn't hang up. Her supervisor would flay her alive. Her eyes narrowed. "Sir is this an emergency?"

"It is. Your full attention is required. I need somebody to hear me." The more she heard the voice, the more inhuman it sounded. It had to be one of those devices meant to disguise the speaker's voice. This person probably wasn't experiencing an emergency, but likely *was* the emergency.

Don't be so judgmental, Allison. Maybe he's had a tracheotomy. "Sir, you need to tell me specifically what the emergency is. You are aware that it's illegal to prank call this number. It's a very serious offense. So, if this is some kind of joke—"

"This is not a prank. This is as serious as it gets."

Allison didn't know what to say. She only waited and listened. It went against her better judgment to tie up this line for some whack job Halloween prank, but there was something in his cadence that demanded she hear him out.

"People have forgotten the true meaning of this holiday. There's more to this time of year than donning fancily wrought attire and gluttonously garnering all the sweets as your stomach can handle."

Allison rolled her eyes. Perhaps this wasn't serious after all. Some self-righteous prick throwing a hissy fit about the commercialism of Halloween.

"Sir, this doesn't sound like an emergency. This isn't a complaint line."

"I am your killer."

Allison's blood ran cold. "Sir, what exactly are you referring to? Because if you think this is funny—"

"I am your haunted house killer. I took it upon myself to take the lives of five individuals at the Blood Moon Farm and Ghoul Mansion establishments, respectively."

Allison's stomach dropped. She felt as if she'd taken a shot from a sledgehammer to the abdomen.

"Of course," the voice continued, "I wouldn't want to neglect the ill–fated police officer who thought the best course of action was to go nosing around in my business."

Allison's sleepiness was completely gone now. She had to keep this psycho on the line, so the call could be traced. This person wanted to talk, had things to say, so she was going to let him talk. Still, if this person really was the killer he probably wouldn't overlook the fact that a phone call could be traced. She had the sneaking suspicion that regardless of how long they conversed, the call wasn't going to be traced.

"People have forgotten what this season truly entails," the voice said. "The significance of it all, as opposed to the superficiality that has contaminated it like the plague. Let me ask you something. What do you think the significance of Hallowmas is?"

"Uh…"

"You don't have to answer that. I'll answer it for you. It angers me beyond words how much of a mockery the eve of November has become. Its power has been forgotten, life force drained. I plan to rectify that. Permit me to inquire something else of you. Do you know anything about natural selection?"

"I know a little," Allison said slowly.

"A little is all you need to know," the voice said. "Because the rest you will learn as we go. I shall teach you. Not just you, but everybody. You see, while I personally may not be famous, I am still famous because my actions are famous. And do you want to know why they're famous?"

Allison wanted to tell him that it was more like infamous, but she felt it best not to interject.

"They're famous because of the brilliance. You may label me insane, but would an insane person really be able to pull this off? I think not. But the true reason they've garnered such renown, is because I've shown society the true meaning of this holiday the way nature intended it." He stopped.

"I think if you've set out to make a point, you've made it," Allison said to fill the silence.

"That's a hasty assumption. Maybe I have opened eyes, but the message hasn't fully sunk in. You see, I've come to learn that the only thing people truly respect is fear. Fear wakes the sleeping. The great awakening is upon us. I am an agent of this awakening. I restore balance to the natural order. There will be more bodies tonight. Stop me if you can. But keep in mind the injustice your forces would be carrying out by attempting to do so."

"I need more," Allison said. "I don't fully understand what you're saying." *Keep him talking.*

"Thank you for your time." An audible click sounded. The phone went quiet.

Allison hung up with a trembling hand. She pressed *Police* on the quick dial pad. Flashbacks came to her of those prank calls she'd received when she was younger. "Fish eyes!" "Frog eyes!" How innocent they seemed now.

11

The Fortress of Fear was a tempting proposition for any haunted house fan. Located in Garrison, Ohio, it was a three–part attraction. First was the titular Fortress of Fear, a seventeenth–century–themed castle where visitors navigated long narrow halls and dusty corridors long abandoned by the living. At least that was how the promoter advertised it. The second attraction was a sensory pandemic entitled Fearanoia. This was a factory–themed warehouse where contaminated workers resided. Contaminated workers who wanted to make the visitors their next coworkers. A skull bearing the biohazard symbol marked the factory on the site map.

This year brought a new addition. The Zombie Abomination. The website said that fans of first–person shooters would really get a kick out of this attraction. It was described as an intense and interactive shooting challenge where visitors became part of the zombie SWAT team. *Grab your weapons, man your stations, and let the hunt begin.*

Dan Full-Forth and his wife, Liza, a tall, thin woman with cherry–colored hair, had already gone through the Fortress of Fear and Fearanoia. Now for the *pièce de résistance*. Zombie Abomination. This was the main reason they came this year—the main reason Dan came anyway. A die–hard gamer, playing games like *Call of Duty Ghost* for hours on end, who also enjoyed horror–themed games such as *Bioshock*, *Aliens*, and *The Evil Within*, an attraction like Zombie Abomination was right up his alley.

He had kind of dragged Liza along, but she didn't mind because she was aware how passionate he was for first–person shooters. She had stayed up late with him many a night after the kids were in bed, mindlessly staring at the screen until her eyes burned, clicking away at the controller buttons until it felt as if she had developed carpal tunnel. Of course, she was no good at those games. Dan killed her easily when she played against him, but that was a rarity. Typically, they played online as a team. Oftentimes, his Facebook posts would highlight how fortunate he was to have a wife who would get *out of bed at three in the morning to game with him.*

They trekked through a path between towering cornstalks. Dan led the way, joking to Liza that she was too flighty to find her way out of this maze. With her leading they'd probably get lost in there forever and freeze when winter rolled around. Liza, ever the good sport, found this quite amusing. She didn't focus so much on the maze aspect of the attraction as she did the cornstalks, which made her think of crop circles, the mutilation of livestock, and alien invasion. More like *Signs* than *The Shining.*

Liza kept an outstretched arm, hoping that the tips of her fingers would touch Dan's back. He was moving a little fast for her.

"Dan, slow down, you're going to get me lost in here. Jesus." She laughed.

"Quicken the pace, woman. At this rate we'll starve to death and wind up in here forever."

Liza shook her head. "You know, smart–ass, if we starve to death, we can't wind up in here forever."

"We certainly can," Dan said over his shoulder. "Think about it for a second. It'll sink in."

Zombie Abomination. Of course. Liza recalled a tale from her Greek mythology class in college. "Theseus and the Minotaur" was a very famous story that prominently featured a maze. Funny how her mind worked. She must be spending too much time playing video games with Dan. When a cornstalk maze makes you think about aliens and a giant, part man part bull monstrosity, you must have an overactive imagination.

She focused. There really were things lurking in the corn, ready to pop out at them. Not insectoids or parasitoids or a man bull, but zombies. Rotten, lurching, undead corpses that wanted to eat their brains. How was that for imagination?

The first zombie emerged. It was more traditional than the ones that inside Fearanoia. Those zombies were dressed in scrubs and doctor's coats with stethoscopes around their necks and scalpels and various other murderous medical instruments in their rubber–gloved hands. The idea of scientists and surgeons transformed into hordes of undead was rather brilliant in Liza's opinion. Dan would probably agree. A brain surgeon becoming infected with a sickness, transforming into a blood–thirsty ghoul who wants to eat brains—that was pretty cool. The zombies in the cornfield weren't like that. These were more akin to the rotten, decaying, maggot–infested specters that lurched about in those classic, B movies shot in Western Pennsylvania.

Dan aimed his gun and scored a direct hit, causing the actor's suit to light up. He pretended to be hurt and receded, moaning, into the corn. Liza fluttered with excitement. "Good job, babe."

"That's what you have me for, right, babe?" Laughing and leaning forward, he planted a kiss on her lips.

Everything seemed to happen so rapidly after that. Sudden stops, pivots, bursts of speed, and of course, zombies bursting forth with outstretched arms. Dan didn't miss once.

He was getting a little ahead of her, but she wasn't having much trouble keeping up until her foot landed in a divot that sent her tumbling onto her face. Although she took quite a spill, she wasn't that banged up. No cuts, bruises, or blood, which was surprising because she felt as if she'd bit her lip when she hit the ground. Her chest and stomach took the brunt of the fall. It was a little hard to breathe for a few seconds, but nothing serious.

Dan was no longer there. Panic fleeted through her. Not that this was anything serious, she just didn't want to get separated. Slowly she got to her feet and began walking. Dan couldn't have gotten that far.

She rounded a bend and found herself facing a dilemma. There was more than one path from which to choose. Four, in fact. No sign of her husband.

"Dan," she called out. "Where are you?" He didn't answer. "Dang it," she growled. He was probably so absorbed in his zombie shoot that he wouldn't hear her if she was standing right next to him. Her best bet would be to call his phone, but she what were the odds of him hearing his phone if he didn't hear her voice? Oh well. It was worth a try. She rummaged through her purse. The fall had shuffled things pretty good.

Dan reached for the phone in his pocket. His wife was no longer behind him. She'd probably try to dial him. He figured he'd beat her to the punch and take a little starch out of her *how could you not notice I wasn't with you?* argument. He began backtracking as he pressed numbers. He didn't have to sift through his contacts since he knew her number by heart. It was a shame that most people probably had to consult their contacts for even their closest relative's number.

He was too busy looking down to see the gloved hand that shot out, clamped his mouth, and pulled him into the field. The phone fell from his hand and began ringing the theme from *The Walking Dead*. Liza.

Dan was thrown hard to the ground. The back of his head smacked the hardpack, sending stars across his field of vision. He blinked and blinked again. Looming over him was a figure clad in a medieval–looking Halloween costume. Gloves, boots, a belt, a cutoff with a cross on the chest, tights, a bearskin cloak, and the most surreal mask Dan had seen. It glowed vibrantly, a grinning face superimposed by a frowning face.

Dan spat a fragment of corn stalk from his mouth. "You can't do that," he said. He was aware of the haunted attraction code of conduct. Performers couldn't lay a finger on you so long as you didn't touch them. This performer, if he was a performer, which Dan doubted as he seemed sorely out of place, had crossed a serious threshold. Through gritted teeth,

He raised his gun and fired. "You're dead, you mother" A boot crashed into his jaw, knocking him flat. The shooting stars returned, even more vibrant and radiant. He rolled clumsily onto his chest.

The assailant straddled him and thrust an arm under his chin. His throat stretched. His head pulled back. Dan tried all he could, pounding and clawing and digging his fingers into his attacker's arm, but nothing worked. Something crashed into his temple, setting off an intense ringing in his ears. The next impact fractured bones.

Dan thought of playing dead, but he couldn't stop his wheezing breath or the rhythmic groans that seemed to originate in his chest. He had to get out of here. Escape. Somehow, someway.

As the attacker hovered over him, Dan's shaking hands slowly eked him forward. Blood gushed from his nose and mouth and forehead. His eyes stung and teared.

He managed to get a few feet ahead before risking a glance back. He was not being pursued but watched. The attacker simply stood there. *Why isn't he following?*

Dan reached a little further, his pulls gained a little strength. If he could make it to the path, someone would notice him. Someone would help.

Methodical steps sounded. Cornstalks cracked. Dan moaned and pushed himself even harder. The steps quickened too. *Damn.* A boot pressed into the middle of his back, pinning him.

Dan tried to push up, but he was too weak. His assailant easily pushed him flat. Dan's chin planted in the mud, his teeth gnashed. He didn't see the revolver aimed at the back of his skull. The barrel was encased in a silencer, but it stilled popped off quietly as the trigger was pulled again and again.

Twenty–four hours after the execution–style murder of Dan Full–Forth, visitors at Kennywood Park's Phantom Fright Nights were going about their business as if nothing had happened. It wasn't that they didn't know about it. Most did, but that incident happened 90 miles northwest of Kennywood. All the way over in Garrison, Ohio. It seemed light–years away. Besides, Kennywood was an amusement park, not a haunted attraction. Sure, they had Phantom Fright Nights in October, which overlaid haunted attraction themes to the Pittsburgh amusement park famous for its towering wooden coasters, but it wasn't a typical haunted house. Scary sure. Perhaps too intense for very young children. In fact, it wasn't recommended for children under thirteen. But at the end of the day, it was a public place. Very open and crowded with people.

There was only one entrance and security was strict. Security guards with metal detectors manned the gates. There was no way in or out if you wanted to commit a murder. When it came to not being able to commit the perfect crime, Kennywood seemed foolproof.

Noah's Ark wasn't a particularly huge ride, nor was it thrilling. But it was fun. And safe, many people would call it. A safe enjoyable ride for people who didn't like roller coasters. It was closed in and confined and didn't go terribly high. Just high enough, actually. It was, as its name implied, an ark, and it rocked forward and backward like a pendulum.

During the summer exotic animals looked out of its windows—zebras, lions, crocodiles, buffalos, giraffes, hippos, rhinos, and elephants. During Phantom Fright Nights these creatures were replaced by all manner of grisly horror figures and faces. Of all the spectacles of terror, which included Bio-Fear, Voodoo Bayou, Mortem Manor, and Villa of the Vampires, the Noah's Ark ride remained a favorite.

Tonight was a special night, the thirteenth day of the thirteenth year of the Phantom Fright Nights event. Promoters used this to hype the entire weekend, even selling tickets half off.

Tyrell Brown half–admired and half–challenged the ark as strobe lights lit it up like a rainbow. The sight was beautiful. Even a guy like him couldn't deny that. That was why he admired it, but he challenged it for a different reason. Mentally, he dared it to scare him. A big guy like him shouldn't get scared of a kiddie ride.

"Man, you expect a big guy like me to be scared of some Bible school ride?" he said to his girlfriend, Shannon.

Shannon snickered. "Baby just shut up and enjoy the ride. After this, we'll go do that ride you wanted to do. The Terminator or whatever it's called."

"It's actually The Exterminator."

Shannon rolled her eyes playfully. "Whatever."

The Exterminator was an indoor coaster, pitch–dark and impossible to see except for moments when it would light up, usually when the cars spun or made a loop. The theme of the ride appealed to Tyrell, a quarantined facility infested with giant vermin. The cars were designed to simulate the box carts that miners rode in the olden days. Cow–sized rats like in Stephen King's short story "The Graveyard Shift" inhabited the ride, along with a deranged, pickaxe–wielding lunatic straight from *My Bloody Valentine*.

The young African American couple finally "boarded the ark," as Tyrell put it. Inside, it was dark, very dark. Tyrell began to complain about how cluttered it felt. Shannon shushed him, and the ark began to rock.

Darkness coupled with the swaying motion wasn't a good combo for Tyrell. He held onto Shannon as the ark began to pick up speed. Horror faces and figures appeared sparingly from the darkness, eliciting nervous laughter and timid screams. Tyrell found that he was actually impressed by the ride. As much as he hated to admit it, he was more than a little scared, but it was a fun fear. The kind that makes you feel alive.

One particularly creepy face impressed him the most. The eerie, grinning mouth and upward slanted eyes glowed whitish yellow. The face, like others on the ship popped in and out of the darkness. There must be two of them, though. Twins, but not quite. Something about that expression. Was that a frown or a smile? One would appear and a moment later the other. There must be two actors

A very cool effect, he thought. But it went away for a while. Tyrell kept an eye out for those faces, even as his mind harkened back to his Bible school days. Being Catholic, he recalled readings his class discussed and did activities on. He had attended on Wednesdays after school and Sundays in the fall and winter and recalled gazing out of a small classroom widow at the blazing, late–in–the–year sky.

He remembered how beautifully the church was decorated during the Christmas season, and Easter too, the pink, purple, and white candles of Lent. He also remembered the fear some of his conservative Catholic teachers had installed in him; the fear of going to hell. One of his teachers had said that when you die, your soul stands at the pearly gates, and God either says "come in," or "good–bye." Even at a young age, he realized how loving and forgiving God was in the New Testament and how wrathful he was in the Old Testament. Noah's Ark, of course, was in the

Old Testament, when God, fed up with the sins of the world, wiped out humanity with a catastrophic flood. Maybe that was why he was scared now. He had stepped back to a time when God was pissed off. Were these hellish figures agents of this wicked God?

His ruminating was interrupted as the grinning, glowing mask appeared from the darkness again. It seemed even closer than last time. He nudged Shannon, but she was unresponsive.

The mask flickered on and off. Each time, the expression changed. Tyrell frowned. How was this possible? Were the two actors leap–frogging each other? He continued to nudge Shannon but couldn't seem to get her attention.

Grinning and frowning, the faces zeroed in on Tyrell. He realized that Shannon was leaning against him. In fact, he felt as if he were supporting her entire frame. Her head slumped against the top of his shoulder. *Why is she resting her head on my shoulder?* It did seem strange. He shrugged, trying to get her to lift her head, but it just flopped down. Something wet and warm was running down his chest underneath his shirt. He felt it with his hands, and although he couldn't see it, he could tell it was sticky.

Blood. It had to be blood. Shannon was bleeding. Tyrell began to panic. She must have hit her head or butted heads with someone. He grasped her around the waist. She seemed to be unconscious.

The boat lit up. Tyrell caught a glimpse of something protruding from the opposite side of Shannon's head. Then the light was gone. Blindly, he reached, and his fingers wrapped around the wooden hilt of a steak knife. Tyrell's touched the cold blade in Shannon's ear canal.

Tyrell quickly side–stepped. Shannon's body collapsed. Tyrell began hyperventilating as he felt a presence standing beside him. Snapping his head around, he all but screamed when he saw the face.

It was in fact one face. The same face making both expressions. He couldn't move his eyes from the chameleonic visage as it morphed from one expression to its opposite with each turn of the head or different refraction of what little light there was.

Tyrell couldn't be sure if he was thinking about screaming or actually starting to scream. He would never know. His high–pitched and helpless sound abruptly cut off as a butcher knife rammed into his mouth. The cold steel made scraping, squeaking sounds as it slid through gaps between his incisors cleaved his tongue and drove into the back of his throat.

Several miles away and not long after riders aboard Noah's Ark discovered the ill–fated Tyrell and Shannon, a museum was indulging in festivities of its own. The Carnegie Museum of Natural History was hosting its annual "All Things Creepy," event, where children could explore the exhibits and collect candy. It was educational and a valuable learning experience. Aside from *real* mummies and bugs, there were enough skeletons to satiate any dinosaur lover.

Many science centers affiliated with Carnegie were hosing similar events. Even the aviary and library were having trick–or–treating. But the Carnegie Museum of Natural History had a lot more to offer for both adults and children.

At least that was what Sam and Samantha Tibald thought. Their kids, Sammy Jr, age eleven; and Tracy, age seven, were dinosaur fanatics. By default, the Tibalds' answer to where they were taking their kids trick–or–treating was handed to them, unlike so many things in life. And it wasn't just dinosaurs. Sammy Jr. had a keen interest in history. Pharaohs, mummies, temples, pyramids, ancient Egypt, the whole nine yards.

One of the scariest exhibits let viewers get up close and personal, albeit in a safe environment, to the deadliest spider in the world, the Brazilian wandering spider. In the promotional photo, the creature, which resided in banana trees, was reared up on its back legs with its forelegs pawing at the onlooker like a begging puppy. Slick black fangs glistened, and Sammy imagined he could see its mandibles twitching even though it was a still image. Looking into those clustered black eyes that radiated a sense of instinct, survival, and hunger, made Sammy Jr. think of just how alien such creatures were. Why did God have to create things that were so scary? So ugly?

Regardless, they were here now. While Sammy would have been excited to go trick–or–treating anywhere, it was a thousand times better at the museum. The museum offered a glimpse into the rich history of our majestic planet. For Sammy, it was a glimpse into the future too. He was going to be an archeologists or paleontologist. It was rare for even high school kids to know what they wanted to do with their lives, but even at eleven Sammy harbored a passion that burned with the intensity of a million suns. Nothing would stand in the way of his goals.

Sammy and Tracy led the way, wending their way through the crowds, which seemed larger than usual this year. Sam and Samantha always let the kids go first. It was only logical. If kids walked behind you, how could you keep an eye on them? Somebody could swoop in from the side and snag them away before the parents even knew they were gone.

The museum was big, but not as large as the Natural History Museum in New York City, where it would take a few good days to see everything and truly appreciate it. The first thing they went through was the mammal hall, beginning with African mammals and Asian mammals. Birds came next, then the amphibians and reptiles hall. They strolled through biodiversity and environmental halls, the hall of North American forests, the hall of oceanic life. Human origins and cultural halls featured Asian and African peoples, and then there were the earth and planetary science halls, where visitors could observe meteorites. Sammy found this almost as interesting as dinosaur bones.

The hall of human biology and evolution presented an in–depth investigation into the theory of evolution. Displays illustrated the path of human evolution and explored origins of human creativity. Life–sized dioramas revealed human predecessors such as *Australopithecus afarensis*, *Homo ergaster*, Neanderthal, and *Cro–Magnon*. It also featured ice age art found in the Dordogne region of southwest France, including limestone carvings of horses. Quiet conversations echoed through the halls, punctuated occasionally by a baby's cry or girls squealing at one display or another. Girls really shouldn't be allowed in here. They couldn't handle science. He glanced at Tracy, moving her lips as she read from a plaque describing what might be evidence of an ancient sacrificial rite. Well, maybe some of them could.

What can be more interesting than human evolution? Sammy thought. It tackled the big questions like: Who are we? Why are we here? Where did we come from? Most people operated under the misconception that we evolved from apes or monkeys. He even remembered one person saying it was hard to believe that we were once a baboon. This was amusing to him and he was always quick to correct people. Human evolution didn't mean we used to be crap–tossing arboreal savages, but that we shared a common ancestor with said crap–tossing arboreal savages. He excused himself between an elderly couple, probably grandparents to the clot of babbling kids blocking this display and moved on.

There were two dinosaur halls. They toured the hall of ornithischian dinosaurs first, which consisted of the beaked, herbivorous dinosaurs, like the duck–billed dinosaur, *Edmontosaurus*. The second hall feature saurischian exhibits, lizard hipped dinosaurs such as the mighty king of them all and Sammy's favorite, *Tyrannosaurus Rex*. It also featured some close runners–up, one of which was a meat eater with the most wicked–looking fangs of the bunch, *Ceratosaurus*, and the gigantic meat eater that predated *T–rex*, *Allosaurus*.

After it was said and done, Sammy and Samantha each held a bag and a bucket overflowing with succulent treats. That was another thing about the museum. On the streets, all these other kids would be competitors for a limited resource. Here, there was always plenty to go around.

"You guys all set?" Sam asked. As reluctant as they were to say leave, the kids had seen everything they wanted to and got everything they wanted as well.

As they were making for the exit, something caught Sammy's eye. It looked like an asteroid or meteor, but not a full one. It had been cut in half across the hemisphere. Either that or the bottom half was embedded through the floor.

"Look, Dad," he said. "It's a new exhibit." Firmly nestled in one of the caverns of the mock–rock, was a pair of elevator doors, whose metal was as clear as a mirror. It served its purpose and drew the family of four to it. Rather, it drew the young ones, who dragged their parents with them. A crowd was gathering, and Sammy wanted to make sure they got a place in line.

A plaque read: "A Journey into Earth's Past."

"I know what this is," Sammy said. He was excited as he always was when given the chance to enlighten others.

"Yeah, what is it?" Sam said.

"It's this small room, and there's a TV screen, and it makes you feel like it's moving, but it's actually not."

"So, what's the point?"

"The point is, it makes you feel like it's going down into the earth, and on screen they show which layer you're in, and what creatures lived during that time." Why did it take adults so long to grasp the concept of *cool?*

His dad shot a glance at his mom. She gave a subtle shake of the head. She didn't like riding elevators, claiming they made her stomach and brains fall into her toes. Her lack of enthusiasm wasn't surprising to Sammy. What he didn't expect was that Tracy wasn't interested in getting on the ride either after she found out it was an elevator. Sammy tried to explain it wasn't a literal elevator and they weren't actually descending to the earth's core, but she still wanted no part of it, especially after he shared the revelation that it was dark inside the not-elevator. Plus, it was about rocks.

"Okay then, champ," his dad said. "Looks like it's just you and me."

"Your loss," Sammy said to his sister, but she still wouldn't bite. An elevator dinged. The doors opened, and a surprisingly large crowd exited. All the people getting off seemed content. They must know a tad bit more than they did when they started. Like Dad always said, the more you know, the better off you are.

The car wasn't initially dark, but it was jammed to capacity. More than that, it was hot. Sammy's nose wrinkled. It smelled like bad breath and salty sweat. He looked up at his dad to see that an intense grimace had contorted his usually calm features. He shot Sammy a look of distaste, and the two of them shared a laugh without even having to tell one another why. Fortunately, the smell grew faint quickly.

The lights dimmed before darkening entirely, very much like a movie theater. This got Sammy to thinking. He couldn't wait to go see the new *Jurassic World* movie. The tight room went quiet, apart from a few murmurs, a cough, and somebody clearing his throat.

At last an image came on. It was the point of view of a man holding a cartoonish drill and dutifully drilling into the ground. A voice came over the intercom. "Today we are going to be taking a journey into earth's past," he said in the pleasing, mechanical male voice so typical of all recordings.

As they "entered" the different layers of the earth, Sammy's father got the distinct impression that this did capture some of the cinematic magic of being in a movie theater even though it was an exhibit at the museum. Despite its charm, he found his mind wandering. It wasn't long before he had completely drowned out whatever sounds there may have been in the confined space. He lost track of body parts jostling his, his son's hand grasping and releasing his at intervals. Unfortunately, he was too busy pondering how someone who was claustrophobic would have a terrible time with this exhibit to see the glowering face that hovered over his son.

Sammy gasped as a gloved hand wrapped his forehead and pulled his head back. A harsh steel blade slid across the boy's throat, leaving a paper-thin slice. Streamlets of deep red blood flowed from the wound, which gaped as the boy's head was pulled back further.

Sam's scream scared everyone. Not only did it pierce their ears, but it drowned out the voiceover and drew everyone's attention to him. He took one look at his bleeding son and went into crisis mode. He grabbed the knife hand. Sammy's head sprang forward, he coughed several times, and his eyes reeled up toward his father. Sam began to overpower the assailant. They went to the floor, people cramming into each other to get out of the way.

Out of breath from the several seconds of giving it his all with the knife—wielding stranger, Sam looked up at his son still standing beside him.

"What's wrong Dad?" he said. The lights came on, not in response to the commotion but because they had reached the end of the exhibit.

Speechless onlookers tumbled from the elevator like liquid pouring from a carton. Sammy peeled away the latex neck piece he had been wearing, which was dripping with corn syrup stained red with food dye.

Sam could taste his heart in his mouth, the texture of the ventricles and aortas, the warm, coppery flavor of blood. He looked down to see that he had tackled a husky boy. Sam peeled the hideous mask from his face to reveal a teen only a year or two older than his son. Tears glistened in his wide eyes.

Sam wiped cold sweat from his forehead with his sleeve and slid off the attacker. The boys exchanged glances that suggested they knew they were in deep shit. *What were we thinking?*

Sam stormed out of the exhibit, nearly yanking his son's arm out of its socket. He snapped back around. "Just what the hell do you think you were doing in there?"

Samantha was waiting for them. "Honey, what's the…"

"Not now," Sam said. He turned back to Sammy. "Do you think that was funny?"

"Dad, I can explain."

"Well, you sure as hell better make it good."

"I'm sorry. It wasn't supposed to scare you, it was a joke."

"A joke? Are you kidding me?" He glared at the teen who made little Sammy seem frail. "And what about you, what's your story?"

The boy stared at his shoes. "I…I was told to do it."

"Told? By who?" He scanned the lobby for suspects. The crowd had dispersed. They'd probably relegated this to the tasteless Halloween prank it appeared to be.

The boy looked up. "A man…he gave me the neck piece and fake knife. He told me to pick a family and get the child to go along with the joke, to scare the parent."

Sam's fists clenched. "Are you kidding me? You mean to tell me that some random guy just pulled you off to the side and asked you to get someone else's kid to act like they were being murdered just to scare the parent? Do you know how ridiculous that sounds?"

There was an audible gulping sound as the boy swallowed. "I know it sounds crazy, sir, but it's the truth."

Sam scratched above his eyebrows. "And how did he get you to go along with this ruse, Sammy? You're smarter than this."

Sammy showed an awkward grin. "Candy, Dad. A whole bag of candy." The boy nodded at a second bag bulging from Sammy's fist. Sam snatched the bag away.

"He told me to tell your son I work for the museum," the teen said. "Sir."

Sam yanked the first bag of candy from Sammy's grip.

"Hey, what are you—"

"I wouldn't push it," Sam growled.

"He was a very nice man," the teen said. "He works here."

"Pretends to, more likely." Sam looked around the lobby again. No one was paying particular interest to them. "What does this man look like?"

"He's a security guard by the tyrannosaur exhibit. He was telling me all about how the T–rex that's on display here is the holotype specimen or something like that. I don't know, I've never heard the word. I think it means the first one discovered. By Barnum Brown back in—"

"Let's just stay on topic for the moment. You said he was working by the T–rex exhibit?"

The teen nodded.

"All right let's get to the bottom of this." Still holding the boys' candy, started toward the dinosaur halls.

"Honey, don't you think we should speak to—"

"No, I'm going to this guy one on one and get some answers. This bastard's going to lose his job if I have anything to do with it." Sam was nearly speed–walking when he heard the teen's next sentence.

"He's probably not going to be there. He said he was heading back to his desk by the entrance."

Sam turned on a dime and the entire clan sped for the entrance/exit. An unusually large crowd had gathered. Sounds of overlapping conversations reverberated from the walls. Many had their camera phones out.

He extended his arm behind him to keep Sammy and Tracy back. His wife grabbed both children and pulled them close. But that couldn't stop the wailing and gasps of shock from entering their sensitive ears. Even the teen boy cringed.

One of the dead security guards wore nothing on but a pair of Fruit of the Looms and black crew socks. He had been suspended from the ceiling with lengths of steel chain crusted with rust. One chain had twisted his head nearly all the way around, leaving an ugly purple welt. A swollen tongue protruded from his mouth. The other guard, whose nametag read Dale and who was still dressed in his full attire, sat in his wheeled chair beside his hanging partner. But he wasn't better off. He was missing his head.

But nobody had to look hard to find it. It was placed between his thighs. Long strands of flesh splayed from his severed neck. His eyes were comically wide. A leather strap bound his face and a blue foam was stuffed in his mouth. Police pushed the crowd back. Sam looked down at the candy bags. There was just no way either of these boys was getting this candy.

12

Exactly one week after the horrific trio of events in Garrison Ohio and Pittsburgh, fall was really in full effect. The leaves had been growing more intense day by day leading up to this beautiful Saturday at Cascade Park with her boyfriend and friends. There was a nip in the air. Winter was right around the corner.

Laurie normally looked forward to Christmas. There were so many traditions that she just adored, like eating wings at Our Gang's over in Sharon. Probably the best wings on the planet. After they would eat dinner, which usually consisted of their world–renowned wings and fries, usually with fried veggies for an appetizer and maybe a burger, the Williams family would head over to Kraynak's and Santa's Christmas lane. Then Cascade Park would have their annual Cascade of Lights, a choreographed display that ran through New Year's Eve. James especially enjoyed that.

Given the circumstances, Laurie wasn't nearly as excited as usual. She couldn't wait for Halloween to be over, of course, but Christmas seemed so far away. News of the triple murders this past Saturday had pushed her and her friends over the edge. They'd had enough of this chaos. Darian was right that this holiday was just an excuse for freaks to come out. People used to worship demons, even the devil on that night. Could that have something to do with these murders? Were they sacrifices?

No, whatever this was, went deeper than that. Ritualistic sacrifice seemed too cliché for a killer of this intelligence and originality. Still, if somebody wanted to argue that this holiday at its core was about devil worship, they wouldn't be technically wrong. She hoped this madness would come to an end once Halloween was over. She prayed it would be anyway. At least there wouldn't be any more haunted house attractions after the clock struck midnight on the first or second of November.

This killer wasn't targeting the suburbs or butchering men, women, and children in their peaceful houses. At least not yet. He or she targeted haunted attractions. Laurie wasn't an expert on serial killers, but this one seemed to have a different *modus operandi* than others she had been exposed to—Dahmer, Bundy, Gacy. This was a whole different beast.

Octoberfest was a very nice event at the park. It wasn't quite as well attended this year, for obvious reasons, but it was still a good time. Laurie and her friends would never dream of setting foot in a haunted house, but that wasn't what October–fest was about. It didn't center on Halloween or All Hallows' Eve or any of that "crap," as Darian put it, but was more about the fall season in general. Vendors sold German food and beer, arts and crafts, and there were even a couple of autograph signings. The man who played Eddie on *The Munsters* had set up a table next to John Kolb, former Pittsburgh Steeler defensive lineman and four–time Superbowl champion. Laurie knew John personally. She had taken his health science course at the community college.

There was also Darrell Denko another famous football player. Darrell played for the New York Giants and was a resident of Willow Falls. Children's author Randy Ryan, also a local of Willow Falls and author of such titles as *My First Baseball Game, My Trip to the Museum,* and *Hunter's Christmas Memories* was there as well, signing copies of his books.

The murder count was now ten if you just counted the haunted houses, and not the farmer, his son, the four college boys, and Deputy Flynn. Detectives had not formally connected those murder to the others yet. Laurie believe they were. The heart that was pumping blood through the veins of this ongoing tragedy was beating from the Willow Falls area.

The three couples had gone through their dutiful meet and greet before entering the park. They'd kept in touch through texts during the week but really hadn't talked much.

"Boy, I'm really going to savor this," Rick said. "After this crazy–ass week, I could really use some lax time. And it always helps when there's German food and beer involved."

"Yeah," Billy said. "Good call coming here, Marshall."

Marshall, humble as ever, told him it was no problem. He had worked here before and knew that events like this were usually a lot of fun.

"Well, I don't know about the German food and beer part," Darian said. "But from what I see, it looks to be pretty nice."

"What's wrong with German food and beer?" Rick asked with a chuckle.

"Nothing, I suppose, if you're into that stuff."

Thoughts of kielbasa and sauerkraut tumbled through Laurie's mind. She hadn't realized how hungry she was.

"Now that we're here," Billy said, "where should we go first?"

Nobody really cared so long as they got a chance to see everything. Vendors and entertainment were set up around the outside of the midway. Unlike the Italian Festival, there wasn't live entertainment. At that event, they usually had Frank Sinatra imitators in tuxedos performing on the old train station platform.

The couples decided to stroll around the midway, check out the different vendors, then tour the rest of the park and come back for food. Seeing the park in the fall was as exciting as anything else in Octoberfest. Cascade Park was beautiful during the summer, but nothing could compare to the scenic foliage of the fall.

"We could go down this way," Marshall suggested after they had nibbled and drank enough to sate their appetites. He pointed past the french fry stand and carousel. "That takes us past the playground. I figured we could head down that way, then take a stroll down the lakebed, and come back up through the grove and around the pool."

Nobody objected, so they started walking. All of them were dressed appropriately given the chilly fall weather, which made the walk brisk and refreshing. It was nice there wasn't a ton of people crowding the park either. A few parents lounged on benches as their children slid down the playground slides, but that was about all they noticed as they walked past the bocce courts.

"We sure picked a perfect day for this," Rick said.

"True dat," Darian said. "It's been so long since I've been here, but as I walk around, it comes flooding back. Sometimes we forget the true power of our past." Something caught her attention. "Hey, Marshall, what's that building up there?" She pointed to a small structure atop a steep hill.

Marshall laughed. "Oh that. It's called the Rappid Tappets. I think they spell rapid with two p's in the name. It's mainly an old storage building, hardly ever used. There's a pool table and a leather sofa and some old plaques dedicated to past employees, along with ceiling tile and pipes and a bunch of other crap like softball trophies and stuff."

Darian nodded. "I can't believe I don't remember it. It's like I've never seen it before in my life."

"I'm right there with you," Maggie said. "I have no recollection whatsoever of that building."

Marshall smiled. "That's actually not as uncommon as you think. A lot of people don't notice it. Even people who work here. But I can assure you, it's always been there."

They rounded a bend and started along the straightaway past the old cobblestone restrooms on their left, blissfully unaware they were being followed. Not in a literal sense, but a pair of eyes followed their progress to the old bridge.

The figure stood comfortably concealed behind the Rappid Tappets, a gloved hand wrapped around the side of the building. His body was only a quarter exposed, with the bulk of the obstruction between him and his prey. Should any of the young couples turn their heads, all he had to do was take a quick step back and he would be completely invisible. But he didn't have to worry about that. No one turned. No one looked. No one knew. This was just the way he liked it. As he grew increasingly excited, his breathing grew heavier and rasping.

They crossed the first bridge and then the second and headed down the long road of the lakebed. Laurie noticed that the road was lined with streetlamps and could just imagine how creepy this narrow stretch must look at nighttime. That long, dark path seeming to go on forever into pitch darkness, with only dim Halloween–orange illumination until the black swallowed you completely.

"Hey, I know you guys probably don't want to talk about this," Billy said, "but I was wondering. You guys heard about the most recent murders, right?"

Darian, Maggie, and Laurie moaned. Even Marshall was on board for that one. But Billy had caught Rick's attention.

"Yeah, I think everybody has," he said. "There was, what, three of them, right? Three groups. Phantom Fright Nights, Fortress of Fear, and uh…what was the other one?" He clicked his fingers several times.

"Carnegie Museum," Billy answered. "All Things Scary."

"And the one guy," Rich said, "they found him strung up like a scarecrow, right?"

"Sort of," Billy said. "Actually, I read it was more like a crucifixion. Nailed to a cross by his hands and feet. A wooden spear jutted out from his ribs. A burlap sack was tied around his head."

How awful, Laurie thought. Her stomach curled into a tight ball.

"It was his wife that found him, wasn't it?" Rick said.

Billy believed it was. Either that or the officials. Either way, Billy told the group, the man had been with his wife, they got separated, and he was attacked and killed.

"So, he actually died by being crucified?" Maggie said. A morbid fascination underlined the disgust in her tone.

Billy shook his head. "No. According to the autopsy, he was shot six or seven times in the back and the head, execution style."

"My god." Darian's hand covered her mouth. "That is harsh."

"Then of course you had the young black couple were stabbed to death on the Noah's Ark ride," Billy said. "But what happened at the museum that was even more unusual. I guess this teenager was told by a security guard to fake killing another kid in front of the kid's parents. For candy." He shook his head. "Kids. Well, the teenager found another kid to go along with it and long story short, kid's dad finds out, takes his son and the other boy to the security station, and what do they find? Two dead guards. One was missing his uniform. And here's where it gets really twisted. The candy that the supposed security guard gave to boy was tainted. Laced with arsenic, razor blades in it, all kinds of shit."

"And on that note," Darian said, "I'm glad the haunted houses around here have been closed."

"Yeah," Maggie said. "It's too bad that one nutcase has to ruin the fun for everyone, but that's usually how it works. Besides, who would feel safe going there with a maniac on the loose?"

"Yeah, but just how nuts do you think he is?" Rick said. "I mean, obviously the guy's got issues, but in order for somebody to pull off what this guy's pulled off, there's no way that he's completely insane. I mean he must possess some degree of intelligence. A high degree, I would say."

Those unintentionally kind words did not go unnoticed. The three young couples were being paralleled from the side. Their follower walked softly despite a plethora of fallen leaves and twigs. The hill was heavily wooded, so he didn't have to worry about them seeing him, especially considering he was nearly on the walking trail. Not only did he watch, but he now listened, savoring the sweet words. Like anyone, he appreciated receiving recognition for his work. That was the point of embarking on this endeavor in the first place (one of them anyway), to get people to see what was right in front of them. They still hadn't heard exactly what he was trying to tell them, but that was okay. They would in time. A little more work was required.

"Hey, Marshall. What are these posts for?" Maggie pointed to a couplet of wooden posts at the base of the hill ahead to their right.

"Those are markers. Exits from the walking trails. There's two down here and two more up top by the girl's section of the complex. Jeremy and I have to weed–whack all four of them. You wouldn't believe how out of control the weeds and plants get around here, especially up top."

"How are the walking trails here?" Maggie said. "I've thought about coming here and doing a mile or two, but never get around to it."

"You're better off walking through the park," Marshall said. "It's much nicer. The trails are very narrow. You have to worry about poison ivy, poison oak, and poison sumac. Plus, the walking trails themselves are uneven and rocky. It's not like Pearson Park. And that's not even the worst part."

Maggie squinted. "Well, what *is* the worst part?"

"Bears."

Everybody began to talk at once. Laurie was the one who finally spoke louder than the others. "You guys get bears around here?"

Marshall cleared his throat. "From time to time. It's not common, but we do get them. Jeremy and I used to take the Gator back on the trails, and we actually saw one."

"Are you kidding?" Laurie said. "How close did you get?"

"What kind of bear was it?" Darian asked.

"It was a black bear. They're the only ones native to Pennsylvania. And to answer your question, Laurie, we got very close to it. Actually, he got close to us. We were on this trail right up here beside us. We'd just crossed the bridge on the trail, and we weren't in the Gator because it wouldn't fit. From where we were sitting, we could see the grove. Anyway, we sat there for a while, when all of a sudden, we hear a huff. We look down the trail a ways, and about fifty feet from us is a freaking bear. He was huge for a black bear too. I'd say between five and six hundred pounds. Its gut nearly dragged on the ground."

"Maybe *he* was pregnant," Darian said with a grin.

"Could be, I didn't get close enough to check."

"So, what did you guys do?" Laurie said.

"We sure as hell didn't stick around. We couldn't go forward, so we ran back across the bridge. There was no room to turn the carryall around, so we just put it in reverse and backed our way out of there. Jeremy was driving. I kept my eye on the bear."

They came to a locked gate. A burn pile stood to one side, piles upon piles of twigs and sticks and branches overlooking a decline leading into the heavily wooded area behind Cascade Boulevard. Laurie turned to start back.

"Right here where we are now—" Marshall gestured to the burn pits— is where the second incident occurred."

"Oh, crap," Billy said. "We better pick up the pace."

Marshall smiled. "Actually, it was just a one–time thing. And we weren't even sure it was a bear. Nobody actually saw it, but there was strong circumstantial evidence."

Laurie wrapped her arm around Marshall's for comfort.

"Nobody actually saw a bear?" Rick said.

Marshall shook his head. "We didn't, but Jeremy and I saw another one that same summer, from a more comfortable distance I'm glad to report, so we know they do come around. But what happened here was, we had a hopper that we were throwing our trash in for a while. It was nearly full, so we came down to dump, and some animal had scattered trash all over the place."

"Raccoons?" Billy said.

"I was about to get to that. The trash I'm talking about was in bags, some of them filled with rocks and weeds, others weighted down with water. They weighed a hundred pounds easily. And they weren't on top either. So, I would say that negates any possibility raccoon. Of course, there's the possibility of it being people, but what would they look for in a bunch of black garbage bags that would be worth the effort of digging them out?"

Now that Marshall had everybody on edge, thinking that at any moment a bear was going to come crashing out of the wood, the group was more than a little anxious to get out of the lakebed. Before long, they had crossed the bridge again and were heading into the grove. On the left–hand side of the bridge was a tree that was sort of tucked back in a corner.

"You see this tree right here?" Marshall said. "Last year on Christmas Eve, Jeremy was working security on the afternoon shift. I guess when he was doing a round, he lost control of the truck and crashed into that tree. Fortunately, he didn't get hurt, but they had to send the truck to public works to be scrapped and replaced."

As they walked through the grove Laurie relished the sound of a running creek. Heading up the hill, they passed shelter seven and eight, which was eerily tucked away in a corner near the top of the hill. Passing the old swimming pool and locker rooms on their right, they made their way up a one–way–street bisected by a moss–covered boulder, past the overlook, to the straight road that would take them to the shop. The road offered a beautiful view of the gorge.

"Hey, Marshall," Maggie said. "That chimney down there. Didn't a famous writer live there?"

"Yeah. Back in the early fifties and sixties. Hannibal Kane. He was a horror writer. Many literary critics hailed him as the next Lovecraft or Poe. Today he's widely considered the Stephen King before there was a Stephen King."

"Wow," Maggie said. "Have you read his work?"

"Sure have," he said. "Overall, he has a very good body of work. He wrote about twenty novels and three collections of short stories. His most famous works are *Jack Knife Jump*, *Blueberry Vines*, *The Strep Throat Ripper*, and *The Gorge*."

Laurie was familiar with most of Kane's work as well, especially the four Marshall mentioned. *The Gorge*, Laurie recalled, was the name of the section of the park where Kane lived and still was to this day. She had read that book growing up but honestly didn't recall it. The one she did recall was *The Strep Throat Ripper*.

They finally reached the maintenance garage. "So, when you guys do security," Laurie asked, "is this where you stay between rounds?"

"Sure," Marshall said.

"Is it heated?"

"No, but that's okay. Typically we're driving around every hour or two. Sometimes we'll pick an area and sit there for twenty minutes or a half hour, just to let people know that we're here in case they don't notice the truck parked by the door. But it's not bad because there's heat in the truck. Radio too."

"Doesn't it get creepy out here by yourself?" Darian said.

"It must be eerie during the winter," Billy added.

"It's very eerie," Marshall said. "Picture this. You guys know what this park is like during the summer, right? Blue skies, green grass, trees thick with life, the park full of people laughing and talking and walking their dogs and jogging. Even now you see how it is. Now picture this. It's pitch–black, there's not a soul in sight, snow's falling, wind's howling, and there's Christmas music faintly playing throughout the entire park."

"What do you do if you actually see somebody?" Maggie asked.

"Call the police."

"Don't they give you weapons or anything?" Billy asked.

Marshall laughed. "There's a baseball bat in the garage and all kinds of other tools. Sledgehammer, pitchfork, axe, spade shovels, flat–head shovels, you name it. Really, we don't have anything to worry about. We're in the garage most of the night, and both doors are always locked. When we're not there, we're in the truck. What's the worst that could happen? If someone comes at you, drive away or run them over." He laughed. "The only thing that really creeps me out is that little window in the main door by the desk. I find myself checking it quite often. Every time I look, I expect to see Michael Myers staring in."

They continued talking as they crossed the bridge. On the right–hand side was the underpass. Laurie thought she saw a glimmer out of the corner of her eye. She did a quick glance, but it was nothing. It was dark under there, but not dark enough to conceal anything reasonably sized. Maybe it was an animal. She squinted to get a clearer view. Nothing. Still she couldn't shake the feeling that something was there. Something was living under there and wanted her to join it.

She shook the ridiculous feeling and caught up with Marshall. They were coming up on the midway. Now it was time to sample that German food and rich German beer. Not too much, of course, at least for Laurie.

Their stalker didn't stop at the lakebed but crossed into the grove and observed them from behind the old restrooms, before climbing up the hill to further observe them from behind shelters seven and eight. He was forced out of his element just a little as he trailed them to the overlook. This was where he'd decided he'd followed them long enough.

He set his sights set on new prey, a woman sitting at one of the benches, eating lunch with her girlfriend. He observed them for a while, waiting to make his move. Before long, the friend got up and went to the restroom. He waited until she was safely gone, then moved in with the grace of a deer in open field or a great white shark cutting through the water. Before she could react, he was on top of her.

A muffled grunt sounded as he wrapped an arm around her waist and pulled her to her feet, the other hand clamped across her mouth. He felt the scream building in her throat, her lungs struggling to expel, but that was going to get her nowhere.

The ill–fated woman kicked and thrashed to no avail. Her assailant's arms were lean but muscular. He jerked her out of sight, dragged her to the end of the fence and stepped around and through the opening. The woman was hysterical, but defenseless.

A rocky outcropping overlooked the steep descent into the gorge. Step by step, inch by inch, he forced her closer to the edge of the outcropping. She planted her feet and pebbles scattered, their clicks and clacks echoing as they tumbled down into the dense foliage.

In a last–ditch effort, she bit down as hard as she could on her attacker's finger. Blood filled her mouth with a coppery taste. Her attacker growled. His voice was inhuman, unearthly, and animalistic.

He contemplated snapping her neck or crushing her windpipe or maybe tearing her throat clean out, but that would be too easy. He wanted to savor this as long as possible. Those six had whetted his appetite for something big and showy.

He toyed with her for a while, choking her then letting her breathe, squeezing her until he heard ribs crack, the stroking her hair. Pain and hope intertwined, a delicious mix.

When he decided he'd had enough fun with this one, he shoved her forward. Her arms wind milled as she tried to gain her balance, but that was not an option. Almost as an afterthought, she screamed and screamed very loudly, then fell and tumbled and bounced down the rocky ledge. The annoyingly high–pitched screaming cut off as she disappeared into the tree–tops and was replaced with crunching and crashing sounds as her body fell through branches and rolled downhill. This lasted for a while, growing further and further away, before all sounds ceased.

He leaned out to try to catch sight of his kill before disappearing into the brush. Voices sounded from several directions, but not the one in which he headed. He was satiated. For now.

13

Rick, Darian, Billy, Maggie, Marshall and Laurie were among the people who went to investigate the screams. They were shocked to find that there was nothing there. No blood, no people, no evidence of an attack. The overlook was just as it always was, quietly overlooking the gorge. A woman said that her friend was missing, but they could find no trail to follow.

"Could it be a bear?" Laurie whispered.

"I don't think so," Marshall said. He pointed to a scrap of cloth caught on the edge of the fence guarding the overlook cliff. The ground looked to be disturbed there too.

The woman's friend began crying hysterically, and everybody knew why. What they couldn't figure out was, why had her friend gone on the other side of the fence? You didn't have to be FBI or CIA agents to suspect the woman had screamed as she fell.

After they called the authorities, the group of six stuck around to see what would become of this incident. Laurie wanted to believe that, God forbid, if this woman did fall to her death, it was an accident. The knot in her gut told her otherwise. Even if the body was recovered, would there be a way to determine whether it was suicide or homicide? If it was murder, maybe they would find skin under her fingernails or a trace of her attacker's DNA. Her friend seemed too genuinely distraught to be a suspect. Boyfriend? Husband?

Something… else?

The authorities arrived and turned the quaint overlook into a typical crime scene cordoned off with yellow police tape and overrun with men in blue suits. The woman's friend identified herself as Jamie Weathers, and her friend was Susan Coulter.

A thorough search of the gorge resulted in Susan's mangled body. At that point the police sent everybody except the girlfriend home. The group of six didn't have a problem with that anyhow. They'd seen enough for one day.

On their ride home, Marshall and Laurie didn't talk. What was there to say? They were both there; both knew what had happened. There was no need to discuss it. As much as Laurie didn't want to admit it, her subconscious was telling her that the events that had garnered nationwide attention were hitting closer and closer to home. She shuddered. Had the killer been in the park that whole time? What if he following them? Was that what she'd glimpsed in the underpass? What she had felt?

14

The weekend came and went. Monday and Tuesday were a blur as well. For Laurie, getting through those two days was key because once you reached Wednesday, it was hump day and you were three steps closer to the weekend.

On Wednesday, October 22, Laurie, Maggie, Darian, and Marshall sat together in Patterson Hall for another class of Math Perspectives. It was interesting, Laurie found it hard to concentrate on much of anything. After class, Dr. Lennox told the students the math department was having a seminar the following evening in the Hoyt Science Center basement. The seminar was going to be an interesting one, concerning robots and robotics in general. As a plus, the hosts were serving Oreo cookies and chocolate milk.

Laurie figured they would have a decent turnout, especially math and science majors, but she wasn't going to be able to make it, nor was Maggie, Darian, or Marshall. She and Maggie were going to have to dedicate a little time to one of their side jobs. The department that published *Scrawl*, the on-campus literary magazine, didn't have the budget to do a fall edition. Instead, thanks to Maggie's suggestion, they were publishing what she termed "Mini Scrawl," to be featured in the student newspaper. Laurie and Maggie would be reviewing submissions.

Class let out, and Laurie told Darian and Maggie she would catch up with them later. She waited for Marshall to gather his belongings. Laurie was heading to Intermediate Spanish with Dr. Barnaby in the field house. Marshall's next class was Statistics in the Hoyt Science and Resource Center, just across the bridge from the field house. He accompanied her from Dr. Lennox's class every Monday, Wednesday, and Friday. Laurie looked forward to their little on-campus walks on those days.

It was nice; Laurie and Marshall got to see each other all five days during the week. On Tuesdays and Thursdays, Marshall had Bio in the Hoyt Science and Resource Center and Writing in Old Main. Laurie would commonly cross paths with him on her way from the McKelvey Campus

Center, named after notable Westminster alumni and business mogul Andrew McKelvey, to Patterson Hall. Laurie thought that one day, Marshall would be as successful as Andrew. He certainly had the brains for it.

They held hands as they walked down the steep hill outside Patterson Hall. At first, Laurie hadn't felt comfortable holding hands in public, and Marshall wasn't a big fan either. He didn't like to hold hands in public, one of a few traits he claimed to have inherited since his father had said the exact same thing to his mother when they were first dating. But Laurie and Marshall had been together for a month now, and given the potent chemistry between them, they felt more comfortable interlocking fingers for others to see.

They entered the steepest part of the hill. Marshall extended his free arm for balance. "So, busy night ahead of you, huh?"

Laurie sighed. "Yeah, I'm all caught up school–work–wise. After this class, I'm going home to work on stuff for *The Holcad*. Got some editing I have to do, and there's submissions for *Mini Scrawl* to read. I feel really bad having to reject some of them. Believe it or not, most are pretty good. Really good, actually. It's just that we can only publish a few. Even if we had the budget to do a fall edition magazine, we couldn't take everything."

Marshall shrugged. "Hey, it's the publishing industry. Rejections are much more common than acceptance. Think of it this way: you have the power to decide what gets published and what doesn't." Marshall laughed. "Look at you go, Ms. Publisher."

Laurie smiled broadly and shoulder–bumped Marshall before telling him to shut up. They planted a kiss before parting. His fingers lingered in hers as he pulled away. *Text me*, he mouthed.

Laurie acknowledged the sexual tension brewing between them. She was growing more and more ready with each passing day. Still, she was nervous for several reasons, inexperience being one. She had only been with one other man. *To hell with that*, she thought. Even if she had never been with a man, she was old enough and mature enough to decide what she would and would not do.

Marshall had to fight off the throbbing in his manhood as he walked away. Laurie's velvety skin and sweet, sweet scent was just overwhelming sometimes. She was warming up to him. He wasn't about to rush it or be pushy, despite his almost daily urges to pounce on her like a lion, rip her clothes off, and go to town in front of the whole campus, faculty and students alike. *Wait*, he thought. All he could do was wait. When the time was right, it would happen. *Good things come to those who wait.* At least that's what he hoped.

Neither noticed the shadowy figure trailing them. Shadowy because he was dressed in dark attire and usually stayed within the confines of the shade trees along the hillside. Nobody seemed to notice him. If they did, he was just some strange man dressed in dark clothing, nothing too unusual. Of course, they never caught a good glimpse of his face. Was it because he was just that good, or was it something else? Were young minds too preoccupied with other things—texting, tweeting, Facebook, talking, to friends—to take notice? In any case it was Halloween season, and they were bound to encounter strange sights and people emerging from their dark holes.

The select few who did notice weren't so certain. By the time one or two people thought they saw him and tried to reassure themselves he was there, he was gone.

15

"Is this the road?" Patricia Cornwall asked as the van bounced down the rocky dirt path that was nearly too narrow for it. She gripped the steering wheel so tightly her knuckles turned white. Her young cameraman, Derek, who was new at the station, did a double take to make sure, then nodded to reaffirm that it was in fact the road. He was a twenty–three–year–old man, recently graduated from the University of Pittsburgh. He had majored in digital and media arts and minored in film and was enrolled in courses at the Art Institute Pittsburgh Filmmakers on Melwood Avenue.

An aspiring filmmaker, he figured that his first job as a cameraman for a local news station, would be at least a start. Hell, who was he kidding? As tough an industry as film was, this job was more than a start, it was a darn good supplement to his resume. He had always been fond of documentaries, even the docudramas and scrapbook documentaries that frequently aired on the local station, WQED. Newscasting was not far removed.

Patricia was a little like a parasite, though. She knew darn well that making documentaries was a goal of his, so what did she do? Coerced him into coming to the crazy–ass haunted farmhouse of John and Josh Moran. This freaked him out more than a little, especially given the recent circumstances of the deputy who was found floating in a lake, toothless and scalped.

Being the blood–sucker she was (Derek couldn't think of a better analogy, which was probably why he was a film major as opposed to an English major) she talked him into coming to the farmhouse on this *particular* night. He had asked her why. Did she want to play detective? Maybe find a clue, crack the code. Solve the mystery. If that was the case, it wasn't going to be worth it. The police had already searched the house from top to bottom and didn't find a shred of anything. She told him this was his opportunity, his chance to catch a break. She was no small fish in a big pond, but the biggest fish in this market.

"Think of it this way, Derek. It's like making a horror documentary. You know, like those found–footage movies you love. *The Blair Witch Project.* Think of it that way."

"I'm really not interested in being a part of a real–life *Blair Witch Project*," he'd said. "You saw how that turned out for that crew, real or not."

"Well, there you go. You just answered your own worries. That wasn't real so what do you have to worry about?"

"Have you forgotten what happened to that cop that came to this farm?"

"We don't even really know that he made it to the farm. That's partly why we need to have a look around."

Derek sighed. "Who's to say we'll make it to the farm?"

Patricia shrugged. "I can see why you'd be nervous but think of it this way. If we catch this killer on film or find some overlooked evidence that lands this sick creep behind bars, it will launch our careers."

Derek rolled his eyes. At the end of the day, her career was all she cared about. He would become an asterisk, if that. If they got themselves killed, she would mis out on, what, 20 years of life? 25? He was talking 50 or more.

"Not only will this skyrocket us into stardom, Derek, but think of the wealth. Remember that guy who took the Kennedy photo? He made a lifetime's living off that."

Derek blew out a breath. He had lost the argument and he knew it. "How can you be so sure we'll find something?"

"I guarantee it. Now, before you storm out of here, just hear me out."

As it turned out, Patricia had a plan or two up her sleeve. She wasn't about to enter the battlefield without an ace in the hole.

"You know," he said after they had jounced through another violent bump.

"Don't tell me," Patricia said. "You're having second thoughts."

"No, it's not that."

"Don't tell me your conscience is eating you up."

"Of course it is, but that's not it either."

"Good, I was hoping you wouldn't pussy out on me."

Derek shifted in his seat. "I just…I think what we're doing is wrong. Now don't panic, I'm not backing out. I just think that maybe we're kind of shitty people for stooping this low for a marginal amount of fame and wealth. Jesus, we're like cliché morons straight out of the movies."

Patricia waved his comment aside. "Wow, wow, wow. Did you just say, 'marginal amount of fame and wealth'? I don't think you realize the full potential of this endeavor."

Derek sighed quietly. At the end of the day, as good a persuader and manipulator as Patricia was, Derek had agreed to this. He was along for the ride through his own volition. His hand hadn't been forced. Not entirely.

"Boy, you weren't lying," he said, gazing out of the window. "These woods are creepy."

Patricia smiled. "Very. Just don't puss out on me."

Derek cast a sharp glance in her direction, a dirty little grin beginning to form on his face. "You know, that's the second time you've said that. Do you want me to show you just how much of a man I am?" Sure, she was old, but not that old. And she was attractive in a manufactured way.

"I don't think so," she said laconically. "Keep your widdle wee–wee in your pants, daddy–o."

"Who says that?" Derek said. "Just coming along and not getting you fired should earn me something. Word around the office is that you'll sleep with anyone with working genitals."

"Oh, is that 'the word?'"

"Yeah, it is." He'd only actually heard that from one person, a janitor down on the first floor, but it sounded right Women didn't get anywhere in the corporate world without sleeping around.

Patricia gave him a half-smile. "Well the word is wrong, Derek–boy. I don't give a rat's ass about working genitals. What I don't do, is sleep my way *down*." She paused. "Even if you did turn me in, it's too late now."

"Why?"

Patricia sniffed. "You're my accomplice. All I'd have to say is that you knew everything and that at no point did you try to stop me or report it to our superiors. Not to mention that you've helped me plan this, and well, here we are now."

Derek nodded slowly. He had sealed his own fate by handcuffing himself to her. The best he could do now was tag along and hope for the best.

"In the meantime," Patricia said, "you can sit there with blue balls or try to appreciate the chance I'm giving you, which is much more of a gift than pointless, mindless sex."

"Yes, ma'am." He tried to make it sound passive-aggressive, but it came out more passive-passive. In truth it did hurt a little to be rejected by an older woman. Any woman, really. He wasn't a bad looking guy, and his butt was nice and tight according to his college ex.

Patricia drove in silence, except for the constant screeching of the van as it tried to tear itself apart. It was getting dark now. The headlights showed packed dirt pocked with potholes.

"Do you think we're bad people?" Derek said as they approached the farmhouse.

Patricia nearly pressed the brake through the floor, bringing them to a screeching halt and nearly making Derek scrape his head off the dashboard. She resumed driving slowly.

"We're *not* bad people," she said. Her emphasis on 'not' made Derek wonder if she meant that or she was trying to convince herself.

"Let me tell you something, Derek. Throughout history, people have perpetrated hoaxes more elaborate than anything we might dream up. I'm talking on a much grander scale."

"Example?"

Patricia's eyes darted. "Okay. You're familiar with the Patterson Gimlin film, right? That footage shot around in 1967 that supposedly shows a female Bigfoot walking across a dry creek?"

"Sure. But they never actually proved it was a hoax. I mean, people have called in claiming they were in the gorilla suit, but they've never actually proved it was any of them."

"Oh, come on, Derek. Have you seen the video? It's clearly a person in a bad ape costume. It was a man in a poorly constructed, haphazard suit. Special effects professionals have confirmed as much."

"But on that same note, they've had some of the best anatomists in the world examine the footage, and they concluded it was definitely no suit."

"Well, whatever, you get my point. What about the crop circle phenomena? Or the Sturgis photos that supposedly show the head and neck of an extinct aquatic reptile in Loch Ness, Scotland. Some guy came out years later and admitted to taking the photo in his freaking bathtub. We could sit here all day and talk about Bigfoot and the Loch Ness monster and aliens, but that's not what we came here for."

"We weren't talking about those creatures *per se*. We were talking about hoaxes like the one we're about to attempt."

"What we're doing is perfectly harmless," Patricia said. "In the grand scheme of things."

Derek sighed again. The insatiable appetite of Americans. Nothing was ever good enough, and that's what led to trouble. He just hoped this antic didn't get them into serious trouble.

He worried that it would as Patricia parked the van in front of the blocky farmhouse.

A chill shot down Derek's spine, so potent it felt as if it traveled through his legs and came out of his toes. He tried to push it aside.

"Man, looks like nobody's been home for a while. That place is darker than a witch's tit."

Patricia shook her head and narrowed her eyes. "What the hell does that even mean?"

"Nothing. Just trying to lighten the mood a little."

"Now's not the time for jokes. Now's the time to stay focused, hit your spot, get the shot. We've passed the point of no return."

They gathered equipment from the back of the van. Derek didn't take his eyes off the house the entire time. It towered above them with its boarded–up windows. *It's like the head of a monster*, he thought. A monster whose eyes had been stitched together or sown shut. Everything that could make a house creepy, every element that would make any home foreboding, this house had going for it—peeling and faded paint, a creaky weathervane, branches that scraped the shutters.

"You sure you can handle this?" Patricia asked. "You look scared as shit."

"Yeah," he said, not really paying attention. "Can we go through the sequence one more time?"

Patricia walked him through her masterplan yet again. Derek would dress in some goofy Halloween costume and pretend to be the haunted house killer. He would attack her while she was reporting. Supposedly, Derek was filming, but the camera was mounted on a tripod.

During the attack, the camera would be knocked over using a tripwire, and sounds of a struggle would ensue, during which Derek and Patricia fought off the attacker together. It seemed kind of amateur to Derek, but he figured, with good acting, they would be able to sell it.

As much as he wanted to tell her there were people actually dying here, which made what they were doing all the more immoral, as much as he wanted to tell her that the real killer would still be on the loose and, if anything, this would only make the trail all that more cold, he didn't say a word. She gave him a bag containing a costume he had never actually laid eyes on before. He hoped it wasn't cartoony. A goofy–ass costume would ruin the effect.

He got the camera set up and programmed it to turn on and begin filming in under ten minutes. Patricia would be reporting from the front yard while Derek came around from the back.

As he walked around back to get dressed, he glanced up at the house silhouetted against the darkening sky. It resembled some oversized armless horror suffering from a violent itch that needed scratching from the gangly arms of its fellow monsters. He tried not to stare but was running out of options as far as things to look at. It was either that, or the harsh contrast of shadows playing in the darkened woods behind the house.

The sooner this is over with, the better, he thought, again and again. Whatever notoriety they gained from this wouldn't be worth it. Maybe to a person as morally ambivalent as Patricia, but not for Derek.

He set the bag down. "Can't wait to see what I'm dressing as for Halloween," he whispered. He wondered how accurately the costume Patricia selected depicted the real haunted house killer. Did anybody know? Everyone who came in contact with the freaking guy died. Maybe he didn't wear a costume at all.

Derek opened the bag and pulled out the costume. At first glance, it seemed pretty basic. Dark tattered jeans with dirty work boots that would add about three inches. A yellow flannel shirt with thin red stripes and only one sleeve. The left sleeve was missing.

He began changing, but he couldn't figure out the purpose of the missing. He fumbled through the bag and came across a gardener's glove. He slipped it on his right hand and grabbed something hard. He pulled it out and was shocked to see an arm piece like on some robot or cyborg. *I guess that's my left arm.* It covered his shoulder all the way down to his wrist. His bare hand jutting from the mechanical wrist stump looked a little silly, but then he found the glove that was to go on his left hand. This one was actually a claw with long fingertips terminating in equally long talons.

The *coup de grâce* was the mask, a bisected face. The right half was a green–eyed, brown–haired werewolf with exaggeratedly long yellow fangs. The left half was a demented scarecrow head fashioned from a burlap sack with a creepy grin stitched onto its mock face. He slipped the mask over his head.

He noticed something new about the house, one of those old cellar hatches comprised of two wooden doors that flipped open. He hadn't seen one in years. Not in person, anyway.

A scratching sound came from the wood. *There must be an animal inside, trying to get out.* The hatch wasn't locked. There was no chain binding its handle, no padlock. *Has to be a cat*, he thought. He had a soft spot for cats, even feral cats. He approached and heard a mewling sound. The least he could do was let the poor thing out.

He flipped one of the doors and jumped back several feet farther than he thought was possible. It was a cat all right, a large solid black cat with the most striking green eyes Derek had seen.

A high–pitched screech emitted from its mouth and quickly morphed into a chilling hiss. Derek watched as the cat was engulfed by darkness. It was almost as if the cat's fur and the shadow merged into one.

He heard another sound. This one he couldn't explain, couldn't quite put his finger on. He turned and looked directly into the cellar's stygian blackness. Was there something else down there? Another animal maybe? He moved closer. The sound stopped. It simmered down as he neared and stopped completely once his foot touched the door's base.

Something sprang from the darkness. It seized Derek's shoulders and sucked him into the blackness with it. They were swallowed by the absence of light. In Derek's case, it was forever.

As Patricia was readying herself, she noticed a figure coming toward her rather quickly. "Derek, what are you doing? I'm clearly not ready. The camera isn't even on."

It wasn't Derek. Or maybe it was, but it sure as hell wasn't the costume she'd found. "What the hell are you doing? Where did you get that mask? It's not—"

The figure slashed across her face with an exaggeratedly long hunting blade, cutting both corners of her mouth. She screamed and fell back, knocking the camera over. As she struggled to right herself, the mask-wearing figure placed the hunting knife into a leather holder attached to his hip. She ran for the van. He cut her off with one leap. She veered for the forest.

Her attacker gave her a little head start, amused, as she tripped over her own two feet and made for the surrounding wilderness. When she was out of sight, he began walking.

Run, he thought. *When I catch you, I'm going to cut your heart out.* He began to pursue at a breakneck pace as the camera on the ground turned on.

Patricia flew aimlessly through the woods, maneuvering around trees, trying to keep her footing on the uneven terrain. With no moon in the sky, she could barely see her outstretched hands.

She would keep running. There was no chance of her getting tired and stopping. Not *the* Patricia Cornwall. Her adrenal glands were secreting enough juice to keep her going until her heart exploded. She was hell–bent on keeping her footing too. She wasn't about to trip and fall, sprain or break an ankle like they did in the movies. *Hell*, she thought, *even if I do, I'll keep running and running and running.*

A stabbing pain seared through her lower back. She stumbled and violently gasped for air. Her knees scraped the hard ground. She reached around and tried to grab whatever had stuck her. She grasped something made of wood. A handle. Whatever was attached to that handle was buried in her.

Footsteps closed in. *Run*, she thought. She tried to get back to her feet, but whatever it was that was embedded in her lower spine made that impossible. Crippling pain shot through her. The footsteps continued to approach until they were directly on top of her.

The masked man got a firm clasp on the weapon and yanked it free with a loud slurp. At last, Patricia saw what it was: a hatchet or tomahawk.

Please, dear God, let it be quick. Don't let him torture me. Was this what she got for her plotting? Had she brought this punishment upon herself? *You reap what you sow.* The thought was hers, but also came from outside her. *Isn't that how the expression goes?*

As she began to crawl away, a vise–like hand wrapped her ankle and pulled her back. "No," she screamed. "Please, no!"

Her attacker began hacking rapidly, violently, and furiously at her hip. Patricia's screams were high–pitched and terrible as rusted blade grated on bone, and blood splattered as if spewing from the mouth of Mount Saint Helen's. He hacked and hacked and hacked. Very messy work.

Patricia's breath became shallow. Blood oozed from her mouth as the killer finally separated the lower half of her torso from the upper half. *Run.* Even with entrails hanging out, she tried to crawl to safety. The killer threw the weapon into the ground blade first next and seized the top half of Patricia Cornwall by her shoulders. He lifted her to eye level, causing more entrails to spill out.

Miraculously, she still had some life left. "Pussy," she mouthed.

With a violent thrust, the killer impaled her torso on a jagged tree branch. The arm of the tree crunched through her spine and exploded through her heart. Her arms and head hung limp as she dangled there. Blood dripped from her mouth.

The killer admired his handiwork only for a moment before grabbing her ankles and dragging her lower half behind him. He would return for the upper body later. When he got back to the front yard, he found that the camera meant to film the prank was indeed working.

It dutifully filmed the front yard and the front of the house. More specifically, the green uncut grass and the base of the porch. While it filmed these still, creepy frames, the sound of approaching footsteps were heard. The killer's feet found their way into the frame. He fumbled for the camera then brought it to his face for a full shot of his hideous visage, the dark eyes, lack of color and exaggerated facial features, along with the sharpness of his teeth. He clicked the camera off.

16

Patricia Cornwall and her cameraman, Derek Finch, disappeared on the night of Wednesday, October 22, the same day that Laurie and Marshall had unknowingly been trailed on the grounds of their supposedly safe, campus. She didn't hear about the incident until a few days later, and it just so happened that she heard it from Marshall. It was Saturday, October 25, and Laurie was lying there in her nice warm bed. She always dreaded those moments waiting for the alarm to go off.

It wasn't her alarm that snapped her out of her hazy state, but the sound of her phone notifying her of a text message. It was Marshall, and what she read didn't make up for the annoying ding.

Did you hear what happened?

Laurie tensed. It could be good news, but she doubted that very much.

What happened with what?

It was a moment before he got back to her. As she waited, she turned off the alarm on her phone. She was wide awake now.

The phone dinged.

The newswoman Patricia Cornwall and her cameraman went missing.

Let me guess, they were last seen going to the Moran farm?

Marshall's response caught her off guard. Nobody knew where the crew was when they disappeared. There had been no trace of them or their van since Wednesday.

They continued the conversation as Laurie got ready for work. All the general questions were asked, whether it was connected to the murders. On both halves, the answer was not *I don't know*, but an emphatic *yes*.

Did these events bother them? Sure. But, as much as they bothered, and even frightened Laurie and Marshall, they were soon all talked out about them. Nevertheless, Laurie had something to look forward to after work tonight. Movie night with Marshall. It was a breath of fresh air.

She knew that she was about to see James. And if she knew James as well as she thought she did, he would have caught wind of the missing reporter and cameraman. Maybe not though. If he didn't say anything, she wasn't about to bring it up.

He already knew what happened at Cascade Park; there was nothing she could do about that. It was difficult enough to keep tragic events from a young boy, but James was not just your run of the mill boy. He was very observant and had an eye for detail. Even the smallest things didn't slip by him. It wasn't so much that Laurie was afraid of upsetting him, but that she honestly didn't know what say.

Maybe James and his classmates were as tired of the constant flow horrible news as she was. It didn't help that the media kept trying to cram more down their throats. Speculation upon speculation, theory upon theory and only the barest coverage of facts.

Not only was it refreshing to know that she would spend the evening with Marshall, but she got yet another breath of fresh air when she went downstairs. James wasn't there. He was still cuddled in his bed, sound asleep.

17

Work went by fast, certainly faster than she thought it would. Maybe it was because she had been counting down the minutes. For most people, that made the day go slower, but not Laurie. At least, not the way she did it. She didn't so much count down minute by minute as break her day into segments. Only so long until break, and, after break, only so long until lunch, and so on. Before she knew it, she was getting dressed and leaving.

Although she liked her job and couldn't realistically think of one that suited her more properly, except for writing for the student newspaper, it always seemed that the most magical moment of every workday was when she got to go home. She supposed the same held true for everybody. At least for the people working their way through college.

As she walked to her car, it would be inaccurate to say she felt safe. She didn't feel safe, which was why she moved at such a brisk pace. Out here in the parking lot everything seemed vulnerable, especially this time of night when the main illumination was the eerie orangish glow of the streetlamps. Halloween orange, as Laurie came to think of it. As she reached her car and jangled through her keychain to unlock the door (the battery on the automatic door opening button was broken) she couldn't shake the feeling she was being watched. It wasn't so much a presence so as the feeling of being unprotected.

Her surroundings were shrouded in darkness, and here she stood in the middle of this vast open parking lot with the light from a half-dozen streetlamps shining down. It was like being on center stage. Before long she located the proper key and was in her car and out of that parking lot before she even had the chance to bat an eyelash.

The figure watched her from the cover of darkness. He was safely in shadow while this young beautiful girl was entirely exposed in the lamps' glow. He could see her very well whereas she would never see him even if she looked directly at him.

He liked to push his luck, see how close he could get to his target without being seen. It was a challenge. He was the archer or rifleman approaching a fawn, the poacher coming up on a lion. And besides, how much was he really risking? What would this fresh slab of meat do if she did see him? She would scream and fumble for her keys and get in her vehicle and peel away, tires screeching, the scent of burning rubber redolent in the cool night air.

This thought excited him, but he couldn't remain much longer. The girl was leaving, and he had to follow. He wasn't going to strike. Not yet. Taillights winked at him in the distance.

It wasn't a terribly far ride to Marshall's house. Laurie was lost in her thoughts as she drove. The outside world flashed into her peripherals, a mixture of silhouettes, shadows, and orange light. The radio was turned down to the point where it was barely audible.

She hadn't noticed the vehicle behind her, a bulky shadow advancing at a breakneck speed. She adjusted the mirror to get a better view and saw that it was a pickup truck with its headlights off.

The truck only slowed when it was practically on top of her. They were still outside of town, and there was nobody else on the road. Some asshole driver riding her ass. Its headlights must be broken, which might explain why it wasn't passing.

She felt a bump. It wasn't just a gentle tap either, but hard enough to snap her head back slightly and make her drop her cell phone. Looking into the rearview, she saw that the truck backed off. Maybe it was just an accident. The truck's high beams flashed on, blinding her. She shielded her eyes and looked away, and that was when she heard the horn blare.

The truck pulled into the left lane and began speeding at an even faster pace. *This isn't a passing zone,* Laurie thought. Her grip tightened on the wheel, and she glanced from the corner of her eye as the truck pulled beside her. It didn't pass but slowed to match her speed.

What the hell is he doing? Laurie was more than a little worried.

The truck swerved, coming close enough to nearly contact the driver's side door. Laurie braked and swerved right. Was this maniac trying to run her off the road? *What should I do?* She dared not stop.

She tried to speed up, but the lunatic managed to keep up with her. She told herself to remain calm, but that was easier said than done. She didn't want to pull over, but maybe she should. What if he got out of the truck to finish the job?

Although it was dark, Laurie noticed the details of the rundown truck. She couldn't find the exact make and model, but it looked green. Boogeyman green. With splotches and faded areas. The bed of the truck was filled with hay bales. She thought she saw pumpkins in the back as well, but she couldn't be positive as she could barely see through the two–by–four rails lining the bed.

The green pickup swerved again, coming close enough to take her breath away. It didn't hit her though. That was good, wasn't it? She tried to concentrate on the road ahead as the pickup touched doors with her. Maybe this was just some local having a laugh at her expense. But at the expense of what? Her safety? Her life?

She was only five minutes from the township. Sheetz' lights would look like the pearly gates now. There would be people there. Police. If only she hadn't dropped her cellphone. Or better, if she had hands-off phone reception in her car. She would call 911 and have this fascist arrested before he knew what hit him.

Again and again, the green pickup swerved, sometimes touching Laurie's door, other times coming dangerously close. This game of cat and mouse continued for what seemed like forever before, at last, Laurie saw the red and yellow lights of the Sheetz station. *Please*, she prayed. *Please back off once we hit town.*

The lights grew brighter and brighter, closer and closer. Under normal circumstances it would have been funny that she was considering the local Sheetz, an infamous 2:00 a.m. hotspot for hungry and drunken night lifers, a safe haven.

The truck slowed as they drew closer to town. Laurie slowed too and pulled onto New Wilmington Road. She checked her rearview. The truck was stopped at the line where Mercer Road met New Wilmington Road, the invisible line between country and civilization that Laurie had envisioned in her mind.

The high beams shut off, shrouding the maybe-green vehicle in darkness. Laurie drew further and further away. In her side mirror, she thought saw the hulking truck make a U-ey and head back the way it had come, but that could have been her imagination.

Laurie wondered if she should call 911. It wasn't exactly an emergency any longer, but it surely had been one. She imagined herself speaking to the operator. A green truck, maybe, holding hay and pumpkins maybe, maybe a male driver, heading north(?) on New Wilmington Road. What a disaster.

The drive to Marshall's house was a blur. It seemed like she just blinked and there she was parking in front of her boyfriend's house. She sat in her car for a minute, trying to come down from the stress high. She was pretty sure she saw Marshall peek out of the front window but paid no mind. She needed a moment to get herself together and gather her bearings.

After a couple of shaky inhales and exhales, she pulled the key out of the ignition and opened the door. Her arms shook with the effort. Even her legs were wobbly as she walked up the steps to the porch.

Marshall could tell something was wrong by the expression on Laurie's face, not to mention the shakiness in her voice as she tried to formulate a sentence. Her breathing was short and choppy, and tears welled in her eyes. He wrapped his arm around her. "Come inside," he whispered.

He sat her on the couch in front of the TV. "What happened? Are you hurt?"

Laurie shook her head. "This truck…this truck."

"A truck? What about a truck? Did you almost get into a wreck?"

"No. After work. On my way home. Mercer Road. This truck tried to… to run me off the road."

Marshall couldn't believe what he was hearing. "Are you sure? What was he doing? Was he riding your tail?"

Laurie swallowed hard. "At first, he was, but he rear–ended me. A couple times, actually. Then he pulled up next to me and started swerving into my door. I didn't know what to do. I nearly went off the road."

Marshall was shocked. "What happened? How did you get away?"

"Once I reached New Wilmington Road, he stopped."

That made sense to Marshall. It would be easy to pull off something like that on Mercer Road. It was pretty rural and at this time of night, there wasn't much traffic. New Wilmington Road was a different story. There would be heavy traffic, regardless of the time of day.

"Are you okay? Do you need me to call your parents?" Marshall wrapped his arm around his shaken girlfriend. It felt so good to give her comfort.

Laurie sniffled. "I'm okay. I'm not hurt. It was just scary." She looked into Marshall's eyes and a smile spread slowly across her face. "You probably guessed that already." She laughed.

"Maybe we should call the police," Marshall said.

"What good would it do? I didn't see the license plate, and I couldn't make out the make or model of the truck. All I know is it was a beat-up green-ish? pickup."

"That's what we'll tell them, then. That's enough information. That way they'll peel their eyes for a faded green pickup on or near Mercer Road."

"Green-ish," Laurie said. "Maybe gray or charcoal or one of those jobs held together by body-putty. I don't think it'll help. Besides, I'm not sure he was trying to hurt me. Could be some drunk asshole having a laugh."

"Laurie," Marshall said, "that drunk asshole having a laugh could have seriously hurt or even killed you. Plus, he's breaking like a gazillion laws."

"Yeah, I know. I just think it'd be pointless to contact the police. I mean, I've never seen that vehicle before, and I didn't even get a look at the driver's face."

The young couple sat on the couch and discussed the predicament for a while longer. One thing led to another. Laurie pulled in close to Marshall for comfort and did nothing to resist as he pulled her in tighter and tighter. Marshall smelled her sweet perfume. It was the most intoxicating fragrance his nostrils had experienced.

They kissed. He slipped his tongue between Laurie's pliant lips. She did the same. The two sat on the couch, making out with an unprecedented intensity. Marshall nipped Laurie's lower lip, then worked his way down her neck. Her skin was so soft, so smooth, so sweet. Laurie moaned. The sound sent fluttering sensations through Marshall's body.

Laurie's chest heaved. She moaned again and Marshall, somewhat forcibly, worked his way on top of her. His hands slid down her hourglass torso, groping her hips.

Outside, they were being watched. The same figure from behind the wheel of the faded green pickup, watched through the window behind the couch. He had parked his vehicle a few blocks down. He didn't want the girl to happen to look out and see the vehicle that had nearly run her off the road parked across the street. Not that he was afraid of being caught. He just wanted to carry on his work without the concern of being exposed.

He stood a safe distance from the window so that his breath wouldn't fog the glass, but he could still see his hideous reflection in the window, and through that reflection the two young lovers so passionately entwined. The act was alien to him. He hadn't come here with the intention of watching two people copulate; he simply came to watch and watch he did.

Marshall and Laurie continued necking for several minutes before Marshall made the move. Like going in for the kiss at the end of a first date, the time seemed right to cross the next threshold. He worked his hand up from her hips and unsnapped her blouse.

Laurie stopped him dead, grabbing his hand and gently guiding it to less erotic terrain. Marshall felt as though a rock had been dropped directly into his abdomen.

"I'm sorry," he said. "Am I pushing too hard? It's just—"

"Can we go upstairs?"

That sick, dropping feeling suddenly evaporated and was replaced with by the flutters. He smiled and took her hand. "Sure."

Laurie's eyes wandered as she and Marshall partially undressed. Beside his bed was a dresser with three shelves. Above the dresser mirror was a shelf, lined with figurines. Laurie stopped him.

"What's the matter?'

"I'm sorry," Laurie said. "I couldn't help but notice your museum." She gestured toward the shelf. "You never told me you were a collector."

Marshall laughed. He sounded a little embarrassed. "Yeah, it's a hobby of mine. A lot of that stuff is rare, worth a lot of money."

Laurie took a moment to admire her boyfriend's mini museum. It certainly was beautiful. The colors of the diverse figures, along with the sculptures, molding, and points of articulation, certainly would be eye candy for the young and imaginative.

Marshall was quick to draw her attention away from his nostalgia shelf and back to himself. "We're kind of in the middle of something here," he said with a chuckle.

"Oh sorry," Laurie said. She laid on the mattress. "Your collection is so beautiful." She paused. "Just like you."

He grinned and planted a kiss on her lips. "No need to be sorry," he whispered. They continued, but it wasn't long before they moved to the next phase. Marshall pulled his shirt off, before unsnapping Laurie's. She ran her fingers down his back, her artificial nails gently scraping his skin, sending chills down his spine. Marshall fumbled for his belt buckle, and it was only a matter of seconds before he was stripped of his jeans and down to his underwear.

Before Laurie knew it, they were wearing nothing but undergarments. Marshall in his boxers, Laurie in her bra and thong. She reached behind her back.

"Wait, wait, wait," he stammered. "Are you sure you're ready? I mean, I don't want to do this if I forced you or made you feel pressured."

Laurie rolled her eyes and smiled. "Jesus, Marshall would you stop being so sensitive?" She said this, deliberately trying to sound snobby, and her effort to make them both laugh worked.

"I have GCD," Marshall said.

Laurie raised her eyebrows.

Marshall laughed. "Guilty Conscience Disease. It's plagued me from adolescence. Every time I had an opportunity to take a hit off a joint or sip whiskey or… he motioned to her… you know, I just have to take one more second to play the role of the good and loving son or boyfriend before my conscience lets me continue."

"Is it contagious?" Laurie said.

"Let's find out." Marshall unbuttoned her bra and slid it from her shoulders. His breath cut short at the sight of her breasts and erect nipples. They were perfectly shaped and symmetric. He worked his mouth down her neck onto her chest. His teeth clamped gently on her tender nipple.

Laurie moaned, and Marshall took the next step He pulled her thong down her ankles more forceful than he intended. He was fully erect now, and Laurie seemed interested. In seconds, his boxers were on the floor.

"You do have protection, right?" Laurie whispered. He looked up from her belly button, smiled, and waved the condom he had been palming the entire time. Laurie giggled. He loved the way her stomach tightened when she laughed. She was so beautiful, so intelligent, so perfect in every way.

Marshall tore open the package with his teeth and slipped the lubricated rubber onto his manhood, relishing the burning intensity he felt. He entered her, buttock clenched. Laurie gasped and moaned so loudly that her cheeks pinked, presumably with embarrassment. The condom was ultra–smooth and cool as it expanded the nerves inside of her. Marshall thrust his hips slowly at first, before quickening. Laurie arched her back and lifted her hips and tightly clenched buttocks with each thrust.

Marshall bit his lower lip so hard that he thought tasted blood. Desire built and built inside him, until he was on the verge of erupting. His penis was painfully hard. He imagined skin stretched so taut it sparkled, veins on the verge of bursting.

His toes clenched, his buttock flexed, and he was done. A series of violent pulsations shook him as he climaxed. Marshall draped over Laurie, the two of them gasping for air. They had been so worked up and excited that it was surprising to hear just how out of breath they were.

The figure had watched as the young man led the young woman upstairs. Soon they were gone, and he was left staring at his ever so hideous reflection. It was as if he was watching himself fantasize about the two of them together. But, if that were the case, wouldn't he imagine himself with the girl instead? That wasn't what he wanted. Not even what he wanted to think about. Copulation didn't disgust him, but it didn't do much for him either. In fact, he was entirely indifferent to the act. His passion ran in another direction.

Still, he had felt compelled to climb onto a railing and pull himself up to the roof so that he could continue to watch them through the bedroom window. In the process, he discovered something about himself. It did enrage him, more so than he'd thought it might. Seeing the actual act for the first time made his muscles and bones well up with rage. He clenched his fists so tightly they trembled, His fingernails dug into his palms, leaving little sickle–shaped cuts. The pain he felt, what little there was, increased the throbbing that had begun to develop in his crotch.

Such contradictory feelings. Hatred. Anger. Excitement. Arousal too. Maybe, just maybe, he was more capable of experiencing the emotions of members of his race he'd sworn to hate. This upset him, as he had even disassociated himself from the qualities of the beings: he hated, or at least thought he had. He leaned in closer. His breath fogged the glass.

"This may sound cliché," Laurie whispered in Marshall's ear. Her breath tickled him and made the hair on the back of his neck stand up, not to mention causing his sex to twitch. "But that was amazing."

163

Marshall laid his head on Laurie's chest. He wanted to be as close to her as possible. He wanted to cuddle and squeeze and never let go. There was nothing more organic or comforting than their flesh becoming one. If he could squeeze her as hard as he could without hurting her, he would. He laid on top of her, and she laid beneath him and it was perfect.

Outside, the wraith–like figure hopped into the yard. Boiling with rage, excitement, and jealousy, he glared at the bedroom window. He felt confused but also, more than ever, ready to strike. It was only a matter of time.

18

It was Tuesday, October 28, and Laurie was walking with Darian and Maggie from Film Criticism over in the McKelvey Campus Center to Shakespeare in Patterson Hall. Of course, she'd already informed her two closest friends of her intimate evening with Marshall this past Saturday, and they were more than a little happy for her, and more than a little curious. The inevitable questions ensued. Was it good? How big was he? How long did he last? Did he make you cum?

"You guys," Laurie said with a laugh and shake of the head. "I thought we were juniors in college, not juniors in high school." Not all their questions were serious, but at least some spawned from genuine curiosity, and maybe a shred of the adolescent girls still had in them shining through.

"It's only natural to ask these things," Maggie said.

"In the interest of full transparency," Darian added.

Laurie couldn't get mad with her friends or even irritated. This was the best she'd felt about herself in a long time. Marshall made her feel beautiful, and alive, and she would much rather discuss him with her friends than the incident with the pickup.

"It was amazing," she said, starting a round of giggles.

Her friends had suggested she report the truck incident to the police, had, but Laurie's mind was set. Her gut instinct told her it wouldn't do any good. On the other hand, what would it hurt to stop at the Willoughby police station and file a report?

Taking into consideration the madness that was sweeping this town, perhaps she just wanted to discard any event that didn't end in death. That certainly wasn't a coping mechanism she learned from her mother, whose over–the–top worrying about everything and anything sometimes drove her crazy. Laurie tried to worry less than her mother, but she had to be careful and draw the line somewhere.

She believed she had found a comfortable middle ground between worrying too much and too little, but overthinking was another matter. The incident had been over for three days, but she couldn't stop thinking and rethinking it. There was an elephant in the room. At least for her.

What if that driver was the haunted house killer? The Cascade Park killer. The Moran farm / Westminster College killer. Not that he had claimed a victim at Westminster College. Not yet anyway, but Deputy Flynn's body had been discovered in Lake Britain, and he, along with four former Westminster students, had last been seen at the Moran Farm.

Laurie was glad none of her friends had brought up that possibility. Even Marshall, who usually did not neglect even the most–minute aspects of a situation, hadn't entertained that thought.

Who, besides her neurotic self, would think of that? Sure, it was a possibility, but what were the odds? Didn't madness inspire madness? It stood to reason that impressionable locals might commit copycat crimes to get some attention of their own. That seemed more plausible than this maniacal truck-driving serial killer setting his sights on Laurie, some random girl he had probably never laid eyes on. Or had he? She had been feeling watched an awful lot of late. Though that was probably a result of the unstable social climate rather than some heightened awareness of hers.

She almost didn't notice that she had already walked into Patterson Hall, past the Beeghly Theater sign with its mocking and petulant drama faces. This glimpse was enough to make her want to shudder and turn her head. It reminded her of the killer's mask.

They got to class and conversed a little more as they awaited the fashionably late Dr. Abe. Autumn sunshine slanted through the windows, lighting a sea monkey parade of dust particles. Ever since she was a little girl, Laurie could tell the difference between late afternoon sunshine and early day sunshine. She had a knack for that kind of thing—picking up on detail, intricacies, idiosyncrasies, you name it. Just like the way that the sun shone differently on Sundays. It had a warmer, richer glow indicative of the week coming to an end for the purposes of forging a new beginning. Laurie used to hate Sundays growing up. She would develop headaches stressing herself out over having to go to school the next day.

Today the class would discuss the first act of *Hamlet*, the bard's most famous tragedy. Many critics considered it the greatest of his collected works. It had so much to say about what it means to be human, and so much to read into its exploration of life's absurdities.

Essentially, what the play said, or one of things it said, was that we are all on the same journey. The scene that illustrated this best was when Hamlet stumbles upon the two gravediggers dressed as jesters who unearth the skull of Hamlet's former friend and mentor, Yorick.

In life, Yorick was a jester and this occupation, coupled with the gravediggers dressed in the same manner, poked fun at the senselessness of life. It doesn't matter whether we are a king, a prince, an heir, a jester, or the lowliest peasant alive, we are all on the same journey to the grave.

What was it that Hamlet said about a man eating a fish that fed on the worm that fed on the body of the king? Is there a true hierarchy? Does it matter? Death is the great equalizer, whether you are king, fish, or worm.

"Hey, everybody," the girl who sat behind Darian said. Her name was Jessica Hanse, Laurie recalled, and at the beginning of the semester she had called herself a Shakespeare fan, but not enough so to actually read the playwright's works in her leisure. Despite that, she always seemed to be the one who talked the most during class.

"As you guys know," Jessica continued, "this Friday is the thirty–first, and since fall break begins tomorrow and we're off for the rest of the week, I thought it would be fun if the student body partook in some annual holiday festivities. So, a couple of my friends and myself are having a haunted house in the library."

There was an awkward silence. Laurie certainly knew her thoughts on the matter and was pretty sure the rest of the class was thinking the same.

Jessica carried on. "Now I know it may seem in bad taste, I get that, but it's not meant to be disrespectful to the victims, primarily Jack Sayer and Julia Wrightson. We just want to have a little fun since none of the haunted houses around here are open. It will give the students something to do on Halloween instead of going to the frat houses and drinking.

"So, you're all welcome. I don't want to give too many details because I don't want to spoil anything for you if you decide to come. But if you do join us, you're more than welcome. Oh, and before I forget to mention it, it's totally free."

Laurie didn't know what to think. Was it a good idea? Was it a bad idea? How could she know? It couldn't be all that bad, could it? If this was a rash of school shootings, they wouldn't shut down all school functions for everyone else. She did ponder whether the decision to set up a haunted house in McGill Library was distasteful, considering two former Westminster students had been murdered a little over a month ago.

19

October 30, the night before Halloween commonly referred to as Mischief Night or Devil's Night. It was a Thursday, and since none of the three couples had to go to class the next day, they decided to do something fun. Once again, Laurie and Marshall found themselves at Twenty–Six, only this time, they were joined by Darian and Rick and Maggie and Billy.

The place wasn't too packed when they arrived, and there were a bunch of seats open at the bar. By seven the place was in full swing. It wasn't as busy as most Fridays and Saturdays, but the wing night regulars were there.

These were the same twenty or thirty people that showed up every Thursday night. A couple were teachers that Laurie recognized from her days at George Washington Intermediate School. And Willow Falls High School's head baseball coach would usually pop in on. Then there was the crew that worked for the borough of Willow Falls

Looking around and seeing people laughing, drinking, eating, and being social made Laurie feel warm inside. She saw why Marshall liked coming here. Everybody knew everybody, like a little family or community. Sure, it was nice to go new places, but new places and faces always brought a few you couldn't trust. At least here you could feel safe.

By this point, the men in the lives of the three college girls were aware of the haunted house that Jessica Hanse and her crew were setting up in the McGill Library. Initially, they had shared the same concerns the girls expressed, but none of them had plans for the following evening. There was always the option of passing out candy, but they weren't really game for that. "Man, it's like we're a bunch of Grinch types on Halloween instead of Christmas.," Billy joked.

After a little discussion, they decided to check it out. Even a generic haunted house could be interesting, and a little entertaining. It was something to do. Even if they hated it, it was free.

"I have to take my little brother trick–or–treating, but we can go after that," Laurie said.

"What time is trick or treat this year?" Rick asked. Laurie had to think about it for a moment.

"It's from four to six," Laurie said.

"They make these kids start so early anymore," Darian said. "Remember when we were kids? We wouldn't even start until it was pitch–black out. It's a shame that times change like that. So many freaks come out of the woodwork these days. We lose our traditions."

Laurie agreed wholeheartedly, but there was one correction that she would have liked to make. Freaks did come out and mess around this time of year, but it wasn't just an annual problem, it was year–round. Older generations were ridiculed for talking about how much safer it was when they were children, but Laurie felt there was a hint of truth to that. Her father said growing up was peaceful—no drug problems, no crimes, no violence. You didn't have to worry about locking your doors at night. Everybody was friends and neighbors. Nobody bothered anybody else. If two guys got in a fight, it didn't matter who won or who lost; after the fight, it was over. No grudges. Nobody was shot or stabbed.

Was life really like that? A depiction straight out of a Norman Rockwell painting? White picket fences, children playing hopscotch and jumping rope beneath the cool shade of oaks and maples, stay–at–home moms, and apple pies fresh out of the oven cooling on the window sill. Maybe each generation thought theirs was the best, most peaceful, and safest. Her grandmother and her grandmother's mother would have told their kids the same thing. Was there any truth to those notions? There had to be.

Laurie remembered her father saying that he didn't think the earth was going to last much longer. People were the cause of it. Throughout the ages, there had been many predictions about when the world's demise. People quit their jobs, gave up life–savings, to protest and warn others that the rapture was imminent, Judgment Day would soon be here. Sinners and zealots would be swallowed in the lake of fire and a select few sucked up into the sky for eternal life. Of course, none of this came to fruition. But just how far away was it? Eventually, mankind would implode upon itself like a neutron star.

Maybe every generation thought that what little peace and solitude they had outweighed the violence and hatred. Maybe they just savored the peace and love they did experience. Or maybe they didn't think it was all that good growing up, but seeing their children's generation, their childhoods didn't seem all that bad. Laurie sympathized with the generation of her future children—if there was going to be a generation for her future children. With so much mayhem in the world of late, it was hard to be sure.

20

The big day had finally arrived. Not that Laurie considered Halloween to be the big day. It wasn't like Christmas. She never really got all that amped up about Halloween even before this year. She wasn't looking forward to it. But in a twisted sense, she was, because the sooner it got here, the sooner it would be over. She glanced at the clock as she hammered away at the Mitsubishi keyboard, finishing articles for the student newspaper and acceptances for the few submissions lucky enough to be featured in *Mini Scrawl*. More than an hour to go.

She was soon lost in her own little world, as was typical when she or any self–respecting writer was busy at work. A reminder popped up on the screen. Trick–or–Treat started in five minutes. James would knock on her door any moment.

She saved the important documents on her flash drive. Laurie always made sure to save her files in more than one place, just in case a malfunctioned. The last thing she needed was to be working on something for hours and then lose it forever. That would be enough to make anybody want to pull their hair out.

James knocked lightly. "Laurie? Are you ready?"

"Just a moment," she said. She stood and stretched and tried to put the worries of the world behind her. She didn't want her anxieties hinder James's good time.

She went to the door and flicked off the light switch. She already knew what James was going to be, but she hadn't seen him wearing his costume, and she was looking forward to it. She opened the door and there he was.

It was a dark one–piece outfit, sort of like a leotard made of spandex. The taut black material covered James from head to toe. The front of the outfit showed a traditional skeletal system, but the bones were bright green. Boogeyman green that glowed mildly in the dark. The mask showed a smiling skull of similar color.

"Do you like this green?" he said, rocking the costume in full view of his sister. His voice was muffled.

"Do I like the green?" Laurie said, not quite understanding. "Why wouldn't I like green?"

"You don't think it's too green?"

Laurie could see what James meant. Although it was green, almost chartreuse, it was not the hideous neon green found on shirts worn by public works employees, that vibrant yellow–green you could see eight miles away. Still, it was a nice relatable green.

"Green is my favorite color," she said.

"Well, I think it's too green." James said. "Booger green." Laurie couldn't help but laugh as well as feel a tad disgusted.

"Has Mom or Dad seen you, kiddo?" She knelt and straightened his mask.

"I don't want them to see before we go out. I wanted you to see it first. You're closer to my age, and you appreciate the stuff I'm into in a different way." It was a complex notion for a ten–year–old, but not for James.

Laurie smiled. "Well, let's get you some candy." James liked that idea. In that respect he wasn't unlike other ten-year-olds.

Their parents sat on the steps of their front porch. Their father held a plastic jack–o'–lantern filled to the brim with candy. Their mother sat beside him keeping him company, but she had the backup bowl behind her on the off chance that they ran out of candy.

Usually the Williams' block didn't get too busy on Halloween. "We live on a block of misers," Laurie once said when she noticed that nearly every house on the street had their doors closed and their lights off.

James wanted Laurie to go outside first. He hated leading the way, especially when he knew people were expecting him. Their parents didn't turn their heads as they were occupied by a group of trick–or–treating children.

After the kids got their candy and returned to their parents on the sidewalk, Laurie walked down the steps, slipping her way around her parents. James was still on the porch.

"Don't turn around yet," Laurie said. Her mother's face spread into a smile as she half-glanced over her shoulder. Her father simply looked on, but his eyes were smiling. James slipped around his mother and posed, head held high, chest out, hands on his hips.

"Oh my," her mother said. "How cute."

James rolled his eyes beneath his mask. It was typical for mothers, regardless of how scary or badass their child's costume was, to regard it as cute or adorable.

"Good choice" their father said. "Very bold."

Her mother snapped some photos of James and his sister. They said their good–byes–be–carefuls and were on their way.

Laurie looked around as she walked beside her brother. Their street wasn't too busy, which didn't surprise her. "Where to first?" she asked.

"We might as well hit this street first," he said. "It looks like there's a few passing out candy."

"Sure thing." None of the houses were particularly decorated. Those that were had conservative themes to say the least. Sad-looking jack–o–lanterns, wimpy sheet ghosts, spiders on a string.

"Looks like the Cleavers are passing out candy," James said.

Oh, the Cleavers, Laurie thought. *What a joy.* Their names might evoke a typical middle–American suburban family from the 1950's, but these Cleavers were far from archetypical. They were religious conservatives, who believed every word of the Old Testament literally and didn't expend one brain cell interpreting parables or metaphors. Their son, Jason, was the same age as James.

Laurie didn't have a problem with their beliefs, but she did have a problem with the fear and judgment that families like the Cleavers tried to impart on unsuspecting people. This is a sin, that's a sin. You are going to hell. Gay people condemned to eternal damnation, and so forth. James had stopped hanging out with Jason after Jason told him he wasn't very "Christian–like."

"They need to go back to Kentucky where they came from," their mother had said upon hearing that. That vehemence had surprised Laurie, but also made her a little proud.

They turned up the sidewalk. Laurie admired the English Tudor house the Cleavers lived in. It was a pretty house, but creepy. The windows were always dark and the trim dividing their panes looked like asylum bars.

They mounted three squeaking steps. What bugged Laurie most about the Cleavers was that their own skeletons were as numerous as anyone else's. Mr. Cleaver was supposedly guilty of an infidelity with a neighbor and it wasn't uncommon to empty liquor bottles in their recycling.

"Trick or treat."

"Hello James." Mr. Cleaver, whose wife was nowhere to be seen, knew it was him since this green skeleton was accompanied by Laurie. He scratched his trim mustache and adjusted his spectacles. "Miss Williams."

Laurie smiled in a hopefully non-skeezy way. He placed a piece of candy in James's bag, along with a tiny scroll that would contain their usual Halloween Scripture, Titus 1:15: *To the pure, all things are pure, but to those who are corrupted and do not believe, nothing is pure. In fact, both their minds and consciences are corrupted.*

They were leaving when Laurie heard Mr. Cleaver say something. *Hell is seen?* She stopped and turned back. "I'm sorry?" She cupped her hand to her ear to indicate she hadn't heard him.

"Happy Halloween," Mr. Cleaver said, not smiling or looking friendly in the least.

"Thanks, Mr. Cleaver," Laurie said. "Happy Halloween."

Once again, they were walking away when Mr. Cleaver said something. This time, Laurie heard him perfectly. "Be safe out there, Miss Williams. Your brother is in your charge." Although his words sounded ominous and more than a little judgmental, Laurie assured him that she and James would be careful and thanked him for his concern.

They continued down the block. A few lots beyond the Cleavers', several houses in a row were decorated. James's was immediately drawn to that section. It was only a little after four o' clock, but the sky was already darkening. By the time trick or treat was completed a little less than two hours from now, it would be full dark. That might suffice for children like James but didn't do much for people like Laurie who grew up thinking that trick–or–treat wasn't trick–or–treat unless it was nighttime. They hadn't even started their rounds until the horizon blazed with the brilliant hues of impending evening.

To Laurie, that was the most exciting part of the day regardless of the time of year. It was wondrous, inspiring, mysterious, as if the world is saying it's about to unleash its dirty little secrets. Dusk made an especially exciting time to begin trick–or–treating. The beauty of that sky equated with the start of something kids had been anticipating couldn't be beat.

Walking down the street beneath a stolid line of streetlamps, Laurie and James played a game they played every year. It was inventive, simplistic and fun, and Laurie was always more than happy to go along. They would secretly scan their surroundings, look up and down whichever street they were on, and classify the different costumes people wore into groups: scariest, funniest, neatest, grossest, most original, and so forth.

To Laurie's surprise there was a number of strikingly original costumes this ear. *At least there's no shortage of creativity among the people who get paid to design Halloween costumes.* They reached the end of their block.

"Where next?" Laurie asked. "You want to go up or down?"

"Up."

"Clen–More?"

James nodded rapidly. "Yeah."

Laurie took his hand. "Sure thing, sport. Let's go."

As they were walking, James said, "I think I liked the scarecrow man the best so far. He looked like the evil brother to the scarecrow from Oz."

Laurie laughed. "Yeah, agree with you on that one, buddy."

They passed Richie Almond's luxurious house. "Be careful walking by Mr. Almond's house," Laurie said. *Why do I still refer to him as "Mr."* He was Laurie's former super–intendant, who was forced to quit after charges were filed against him for texting ten–to–twelve–year–old girls. Rumor had it he was very perverted. They also owned at least one German Shephard. This dog was big even by German Shephard standards.

"That dog's nasty," James said. "He's a Cujo." Laurie nodded. Stephen King had managed to create a new dictionary term with his rabid Saint Bernard from the horror novel and subsequent film, *Cujo*. It was supposedly an ancient Indian term meaning "unstoppable force."

The ferns in front of the Almond's house were green and luscious and cast dancing shadows on the red brick in the golden glow of the flood light. Laurie looked to the horizon, which was beginning to come alive with orange and salmon streaks. They would have to head back soon.

She saw something out of the corner of her eye. Not just something but someone. Someone was watching them from the corner of the Almond's yard. But when she turned her head, the figure was no longer there. It made Laurie shudder. Probably Mr. Almond checking out the fresh young tail, strut her stuff on *his* sidewalk. *Oh God, a former student, too.* That was probably a turn on for him.

Whoever it was, he was gone now. Laurie wasn't going to waste any brain energy worrying about it.

They walked out of view of their watcher's keen eyesight, out of the streetlamp's orange glow. Halloween orange. Harvest orange. Their blinking on might have alerted his prey. He ought to curse them, but they were only playing their role.

The stalker worked his way around the back of the house. His breathing sounded loud beneath his mask but in fact would have gone unheard by the untrained ear. His unearthly presence *had* caught another's attention though. A dog barked inside the house. It was loud. The stalker's ears were keener than the average person. The dog's thunderous barking was more like a roar to him. A dinosaur roar powerful enough to vibrate walls.

The animal was causing the stalker pain. This annoyed him tremendously. He began pounding the brick wall. When that didn't silence the animal, his fists moved faster and faster until his gloved hands were a dark blur.

Chunks of brick and mortar flew, creating a gaping hole. Once solid red brick was reduced to powder. At last he stopped, cupped his hands over his ears, and walked casually into the woods behind George Washington Intermediate School.

He let out an animalistic wail that was pained and mournful at the same time. Normally, his movements were fluid, but he was in such pain now that his gait was stumbling.

A human voice echoed from inside the house. It was nearly loud enough to drown out the barking. This combination of noises nearly brought the stalker to his knees. He regained his composure, turned and looked back. He heard the dog's owner hollering at the animal to shut up. He heard him word for word, in fact, tuning in his words despite the dog's barking.

A minute later, the back door opened, and the dog charged out. It made a beeline for the stalker. It resembled a slavering, foaming freight train as it closed the distance. The booming bark that was dreadful enough from inside the house came closer and closer.

The shadowy form stood its ground, not budging. Its hands were even down by its hips, not up or out in front of it to brace for impact. Just as the dog was about to ram its massive dome into him he stepped to the side, sending the huge mass of black and silver hair tumbling head over paws on into a pile of leaves.

The dog regained its footing. Infuriated, the growling, drooling monstrosity of a canine charged again. This time, it was more of a pounce than a charge, but that was a mistake, because the animal left itself susceptible. The stalker seized its throat. The dog planted its real paws and tried to drive the man's arm, but this only caused the grip to tighten.

The barking became high-pitched, almost a yelp, driving spikes of pain through the man's head. He held tight. Goliath thrashed his head from side to side to no avail.

He placed his gloved hand inside dog's mouth and pulled down on the lower jaw so that it couldn't bite his fingers off, if indeed it was capable of doing so. He released the dog's neck and grabbed its upper snout. A slow, agonizing cracking and popping sound filled the air as the strange man with his massive gloved hands pulled the dog's jaws apart.

He released. The canine collapsed into a sorry pile of flesh and fur at the booted feet of its killer. Dark blood puddled from its overextended jaws. The man's shoulders heaved, his barrel chest pushed in and out, as he breathed beneath his glowing yellow–white mask.

The sound of children's laughter and people talking caught his attention, Lights poked through the thin patch of woods behind the Almond's house. He headed toward them.

As he neared the edge of the woods, brief glimpses of trick–or–treating kids and their parents became visible. He pushed down a tree branch that was obscuring his view. His breathing grew more rapid and heavy with excitement as he beheld the people walking up and down the streets. He had a very keen eye. And it wasn't long until he spotted what he wanted.

Clen–More was one of the nicest streets in the city. In fact, it was the second widest. Laurie and James stopped at a house that, every year after Halloween, put up a window display that counted down the days, hours, minutes and seconds until Christmas.

As they worked their way down Clen–More, James wanted to walk around the school and then down Euclid. They went to the house with the white boxer dog with the black spot around its eye. This dog was a female and, when Laurie and her mother went for walks, would usually chase after them to the end of the yard. She wasn't out tonight but was normally contained by an electric fence. Her mother thought the dog was so ugly she was cute.

Then they went to the house of Rosemary Roe, Laurie's eight grade English teacher, who got her interested in Poe.

"Laurie, look at that costume," James whispered as they neared the end of the block.

"Which one?" The was a group of smaller kids ahead of them and James didn't usually care much for bunny and princess costumes. James didn't answer immediately. Laurie looked down to find him staring over his shoulder. She looked too. The figure behind them was tall, over six feet, and what unsettled Laurie most, was that he reminded her of the strange man watching them at the Almond's house. And it wasn't Mr. Almond. He wasn't that tall or broad.

The figure wore a skin–tight leotard beneath a black cutoff vest. The material was blood red and clung tightly to his lean, muscular arms and legs. A thick black belt with overlarge gold buckle crossed his waist and he wore black gloves and pointed flat boots. Laurie thought the outfit was somehow reminiscent of Peter Pan or Robin Hood, though the man in it hardly resembled either. His vest held a red cross with exaggerated points within a circle of gold rope. But it was the mask that Laurie found unsettling. It was the classic drama mask, the grinning one. Whether it was plastic or some other hardened material, Laurie couldn't be sure, but it appeared to be solid. And it seemed to radiate an aura of warm gold light. Every time the mask moved, the expression on the face would change, from grin to frown.

Laurie turned back. The man, whoever he was, was walking by himself, but he was gaining fast. That reminded her of the pickup truck, which sent a shiver down her back.

"That's a pretty neat mask," Laurie said, attempting to mask her fear.

"I'm scared," James said.

"It *is* getting dark," Laurie said. "We should head home."

"Yes," James said, which wasn't like him at all.

She took her brother's hand and walked more quickly. Every third step, she glanced back. The man was still there, still gaining. Nobody else seemed to notice him.

They turned a corner and hit the straight sidewalk in front of George Washington. She looked back, hoping against hope that he hadn't turned, that she was just having a flashback of the pickup incident. Much to her relief, he was gone. A weight fell from her shoulders. *False alarm.*

They continued for a few blocks before turning onto Euclid. There were a lot of houses giving out candy there. James decided it was okay if they spend a little more time collecting candy before heading home. Every now and then, Laurie would do a double take as James was getting his candy, but she wasn't all that concerned.

They continued down Euclid and crossed a dead—end alley, bouncing from one side to the other. When they reached the blue house where a beautiful Labrador retriever was usually chained in front (but not tonight, for obvious reasons), Laurie looked behind the garage. A fence separated the owner's property from the George Washington playground.

The man was there. His masked face pressed against the chain link fence, and his fingers were wrapped through it. He appeared to be looking directly at Laurie. He stomach shrank to a pit.

James didn't notice, and Laurie didn't bring it to his attention. She encouraged him to walk faster so they could hit every house on the street. She didn't see the man again, but it was not because Laurie wasn't looking. Her neck hurt from craning over her shoulder.

They continued hitting streets until the two—hour window was up and it was pitch black out. With only the light from the streetlamps to guide them they made their way home.

"Make sure you remember to check your candy," she said as they went inside. She didn't really have to remind him, but it was sort of a ritual between them. Their mother wouldn't allow him to take one bite without thoroughly inspecting every morsel in his bag. Their mother was good when it came to that. That was one thing about over-worry. It came in useful sometimes, and she couldn't really fault her mother this year after that incident at the Pittsburgh museum.

As Laurie closed the screen door behind them, she scanned up and down the street a final time. Most porch lights were off, and all but one streetlamp was burning strong. Nothing to worry about. Then she saw it, a silhouette of a man standing at the end of their street, motionless and foreboding. Maybe it was the light, but his face seemed to shift and glow.

21

Trick or treat was over in Lawrence County. But Halloween was not, and Laurie and her friends had one last festivity to attend to that would send this most bizarre (even for Halloween) season out with a bang. Laurie had considered blowing off the Haunted House after the Trick–or–Treat incident earlier, but she really couldn't see the point of sitting around the house worrying all night about something her overstressed mind was probably making up in the first place. Plus, she would feel safer with her friends, especially Marshall, or at least more distracted. Still, she would be happy when this night was over. She had had enough of this crazy season.

The six of them made their way to the McGill Library. The library was a favorite sanctuary for Laurie if she had a break in between classes. She loved the quiet, well-lit areas, the orderly rows of books and computers. They walked up the stone steps and through the heavy glass doors before coming to the second set of doors, which was wooden.

"Are you guys ready for this?" Billy joked.

"Ready as I'll ever be," Maggie said.

They opened the doors and walked inside. A sign with an arrow directed them to the right. To the left was the children's section of the library, complete with solid oak tables, Tiffany lamps, and Amish rockers. Straight ahead was a hallway that led to the stairs and a computer lab on the left. There was also a glass case in the middle of the hallway with a sculpture of a patriot riding a horse in it.

They turned right toward the adult section. It was dark in there. Very dark. The only light was silver moonlight which blew up as it hit the stained–glass windows above the study tables. Organ music played. Laurie guessed it was off somebody's iPod plugged into a portable radio.

A thin layer of fog covered the ground up to their ankles, effectively concealing their feet. *So far, so good*, Laurie thought. At the very least, it was atmospheric.

As they worked their way through the adult section, Laurie felt things brushing up against her legs. Whatever it was, it was wispy and wiry.

"Oh!" Maggie said with a hint of startled laughter.

Laurie looked closer. Invisible wire, the kind magicians used to levitate dollar bills, nowhere near strong enough to trip you but would simply break on contact. Although it was simple, it was a very neat effect. Laurie smiled. This was her speed, surprising without the outright terror of demons popping out of nowhere or bats flying into your face.

Just as they were about to enter the neighboring section, was a continuation of the adult book section, but with computers, Rick gave a startled grunt. The group stopped.

"Something grabbed my sleeve." He massaged his elbow. Maggie laughed and touched an animatronic hand affixed to the bottom of a shelf. It jutted toward her. She pretended to shake hands.

"Wow." Rick laughed. "Where in the hell did they get those?"

"Kudos to Jessica," Billy said.

"Yeah, who knew?" Rick said. They hadn't really expected much, so the bar was set pretty low.

"Those hands remind me of the golden coat–hanger–hand–things in *Willy Wonka and The Chocolate Factory*," Marshall said. Laurie nodded and squeezed his arm. So far, everything was good. It didn't even appear amateur.

The group continued to the next room. On the left were more bookshelves, study tables, and the office of Eloise Stevens, the library's resource director. A printout was taped to her door:

Your source for Bigfoot, Moth–Man, and everything mysterious.

There wasn't much to see in this room. Instead, this portion was used as a bridge to the next part of the haunted house. Another sign with an arrow directed them through glass doors at the back of the room and upstairs to the third floor.

They climbed three sets of stairs and pushed through the heavy wooden doors. The third floor was one of the more interesting in the library.

"If Jessica's smart," Darian said, "she'll have the next part in the Samurai Room." The Samurai Room was basically a room filled with novels and textbooks having a Samurai theme. The most prominent feature was a Samurai suit inside a glass case.

Sure enough, another sign with another arrow directed them to the Samurai Room.

Continue if you think you can.

"So, who's going first?" Rick said. It wasn't a question so much as a dare.

"I think maybe you're asking because you don't want to go," Billy said. Most of the group laughed, including Laurie.

"What can I say, brother. You called my bluff."

Maggie wrapped her arm around his. "Don't worry. I'm here for you. You can be the chivalrous knight in shining armor, and I'll—"

"Be the damsel in distress," Rick said drolly.

Maggie laughed and rolled her eyes. "Could you get any more cliché? What I was going to say is that I'll be your brave and courageous woman, who sticks by her heroic man through thick and thin, but I can see that you've already made up your mind. Just don't complain if I'm not there to rescue *you*."

"Excuse me, you guys," Darian said. "I hate to break up this little love fest, but as the two of you are standing there arguing intellectually about clichés and the apparent lack of sensibility that Rick reveals, the rest of us are waiting to go in."

"You're right," Rick said. "Let's get inside so we can get out of here and celebrate Marshall's birthday." He raised his hand as if holding a beer glass and pretended to chug.

They entered the Samurai Room. A howl sounded, followed by hoarse barking sound. It didn't come from just one spot, but several areas at once. Laurie expected a pack of rabid or genetically mutated canines or werewolves, but it was nothing of the sort. Rick brushed his shoulder against a bookshelf as he tried to navigate. A *chi–chang* sound, the sound of an old–time cash register. Suddenly, the Samurai Room was filled with *chi–chang* sounds.

Marshall shined his cellphone onto a shelf and discovered a leather–bound book leaning out. Other books protruded from the shelves ahead, with red, green, or blue covers and no design. As they watched, the books snapped open and shut, displaying triangular silver and gold teeth like mythical man–eating plants or bear traps. The barking came from several of them. Others shot fake nightcrawlers in and out of their mouths. *A very neat touch*, Laurie thought. It was certainly a refreshing twist on bookworms.

This stirred up conversation among the group, especially Rick and Billy, but Laurie couldn't really make out the words. She and Marshall were the caboose of the group and hadn't said much as they tried not to wind up walking down a wrong hall in the darkness.

They were close to the glass case with the samurai suit when something caught Marshall's eye. It had come from the direction of the samurai suit, and since that was something that he wanted to see, he figured he'd kill two birds with one stone and check it out.

Marshall pressed his face close to the glass. The samurai suit wasn't as he had remembered it. Naturally, there was the helmet, the body piece, and the arms and legs, but rather than appearing as parts suspended from a wire form or whatever they used in museums, this suit looked complete. More full and filled out. There was no empty space, no plain old air.

He was looking at a complete silhouette of a solid humanoid being. *It must be part of the haunted house.* It was good that Jessica Hanse's team had neglected this aspect of the library. Blending samurai culture with the themes of All Hallows' Eve made for an interesting scare.

Just as he was about to call his friends over, a face flew up from behind case. A golden–white glow emanated from a grinning visage that seemed to take the horror inside a person and twist it into something darkly humorous. Marshall was captivated.

Laurie also saw the mask, but her reaction was different. Her stomach sank. She recognized that mask. Instinctively, she made her way toward Marshall. She wanted to say shout, but it was too late.

The thin layer of glass that separated Marshall from the glowing face exploded. His eyelids shut by reflex as a diamond–hard fist struck him square between the eyes. Pain flared. His nose snapped. The impact threw him backward. *What is that?* he though just before his head thumped off the ground and he lost consciousness.

Laurie screamed. The assailant stepped down from the case and stripped the Samurai equipment from is body. It was too dark to see exactly what he wore beneath, but Laurie knew by the hulking shape and glowering mask that it was the man who had followed her and James. Although his body was one big silhouette, his mask brilliantly contrasted the blackness of the room. It was so bright, in fact, that it seemed to float through the darkness as he moved toward Laurie.

She could only stare as he came close. He seized her by the throat. His fingers tightened, but not *too* much. Laurie sensed he could easily crush her larynx, yet he did not. She tried to think calming thoughts. If he wanted her dead, he would have killed her. He wanted to scare her, toy with her as a cat might. That gave her, gave them, time.

"Let her go, you psycho!" Rick and Bill pushed their girlfriends aside and bull–rushed the man. Without missing a beat, the masked man drew an object from his belt. It was long and silvery, like a metallic slice of the moon. *The Samurai sword.*

"Look out," Laurie tried to shout, but it turned into a barely audible whisper.

Rick stopped dead in his tracks as he impaled himself on the protruding samurai sword. He grunted softly and looked down. Gasping for breath, he grasped the blade his bare hands and tried to wrench it free. A deep red stain seeped through his shirt. The killer twisted, cutting the meat of Rick's palms. He ripped the weapon free and thrust again, skewering him through the mouth. The blood–stained metallic object made a screeching noise as pushed through the back of his skull. With a quick pull, the killer removed the sword, and Rick collapsed to the floor, dead.

Darian screamed and sank to her knees as Maggie attempted to comfort her. The killer sent Laurie flying head–first into the bookshelf. She slid to the floor. A trickled of warm blood ran down her forehead.

Billy had worked his way around the back of the beast. Now, he seized the hulking figure in a headlock and squeezed as hard as he could. His forearm pressed into the killer's windpipe. He reinforced his hold by pulling on that arm with his other hand. The murderer would pass out any moment. He could *feel* the man losing consciousness. *Then why isn't he struggling?*

The killer wrapped his gloved fingers around Billy's forearm and, with a strength that was shocking, pulled his arm slightly outward and downward, alleviating the pressure. He sent the opposite elbow crashing into Billy's midsection. The elbow wasn't sharp and pointy, but broad and blunt, an instrument to crush rather than to slice. It felt to Billy as if he had been hit a sledgehammer.

Billy grunted. His breath wouldn't come. He tried to hold on, but his grip was weakening. He gasped, choking for air, and let go. He huddled over, nearly dropping to his knees. He breathed in short choppy breaths.

"Billy, look out!" Maggie screamed.

Billy blinked back tears. The killer had turned to face him. Moreover, the sword was poised to strike. With lighting speed, it cut through the air with a swishing sound. Instinctively, Billy raised his hands defensively. The blade cut through his forearm so quickly he barely noticed the pain. His hand and a good six inches of his forearm slapped to the floor. Blood spurted from the stump, spraying the bookshelves, the glass case, even that horrific mask. Screams rang through his ears, including his own.

Suddenly, Darian felt cold, sticky, and soaked with sweat. Her skin turned pale as a ghost, and the dark room seemed much darker. The surroundings seemed to close in around her, getting smaller and smaller. Dizziness overwhelmed her, and she fell face first, spewing chunks of her dinner.

Maggie moved Darian's face from the vomit, so she didn't suffocate and rolled her onto her side. Through her reddened and teary eyes, she turned her attention to poor Billy with one hand wrapped around the base of his gushing forearm. He would soon lose consciousness too. She thought of one of the last things she had said to him— *Just don't complain if I'm not there to rescue* you—and cried.

The killer raised the sword, this time with his arm across his chest and, with a quick, back–hand motion, sliced Billy's throat. The wound bisected his prominent Adam's apple. Blood waterfalled down his shirt, turning the light hoodie a deep black-blue. Billy drew a shuddering gasp and collapsed. His glassy eyes stared at Maggie. Maggie whimpered and cradled Darian. It was too late to save Rick and now it was too late to save Billy. *Soon, it will be too late to save any of us.*

The killer turned his attention to her. She let out a quick, high–pitched warbling scream that synchronized perfectly the mask's changing visage. With both hands, the killer raised the sword above his head and smashed it down. The blade buried a quarter of the way into the floor. He released the hilt and took methodical, plodding steps toward Maggie.

Still clinging to the unconscious Darian, Maggie crawled backward, whimpering and attempting to plead. "Please spare us. You've taken everything. My parents…"

The killer seized Darian's ankles and began to drag her away. Maggie cried hysterically. She wrapped her arms around Darian's waist and held on. The tug–of–war continued for a few heartbeats before the killer ripped

Darian from Maggie's arms and slung her over his shoulder. With a booted foot, he forced Maggie's head onto the ground.

"No…no…no…" Maggie whimpered.

He applied pressure, but just enough. The message was clear. He wanted her to stay put. After a moment, he walked away, disregarding Maggie and Laurie as if they weren't there.

Maggie watched the killer stride away. Darian's limbs dangled like rubber bands, and her body moved up and down with his steps. All of this had happened so fast. Only a matter of seconds. Yet to Maggie, it seemed an eternity.

The killer reached down and grabbed Marshall's collar. *Oh god*, Maggie thought. *He's taking Marshall.* But he wasn't. He dragged Marshall out of his path and continued through the door. The door swung shut behind him. Maggie felt paralyzed for a few seconds. Once her muscles worked again, she crawled to Laurie and tried to wake her.

As she shook her friend, Maggie noticed that something had been scrawled on the wall. A single word written in dark, runny letters.

REDRUM

22

Laurie regained consciousness. "Marshall," she said. "Where's Marshall?" Maggie looked over her shoulder. Tears welled from her eyes and sped down her cheeks.

"Marshall's fine," she said with a quivering lip. "Marshalls' fine. He's knocked out, but I think he'll be waking any minute. You don't have to worry."

Laurie lifted herself up on her elbows and squinted. First, she looked at Marshall. He moaned and lifted a hand to his face.

"Rick, Billy?" Laurie croaked. She remembered them going after her attacker, trying to save her. They were so brave.

Instead of answering Maggie fell back onto her haunches and whimpered. Laurie felt instantly sickened. She turned her and saw their bloody remains. They lay there on the floor, unfeeling, unmoving, as pale as a vampire victim. Their eyes, reflective, soulless marbles, stared into eternally.

Laurie was too sad to cry. She turned away from the awful sight and cradled Maggie in here arms. The tears came then, but bubbling gasps of tears that wouldn't end.

"He took Darian," Maggie mumbled. "She was alive. He took her."

Laurie's cell phone rang. *No Caller ID*.

"Answer it," Maggie urged. "Answer it and tell whoever it is to get help. There's been a murder." She fumbled for her own phone.

Laurie touched the screen. "H–hello." There wasn't an initial response, only the sound of somebody breathing. Then, she heard a voice she recognized.

"Laurie are you there. Hello. Laurie, can you hear me?"

"Oh my god," Laurie said. "Darian. Are you okay? Did he hurt you? Where are you?" Maggie leaned in.

"I'm fine. He wants to talk to you."

"Who?" *The killer of course.* "Where are you? We need to go to the po–"

"No. Not yet, Laurie. He wants to talk to you."

Laure heard a noise that made her heart drop. It was the sound of Darian screaming. But the screaming didn't last long. It was quickly muffled. And then the heavy breathing returned.

"Such a shame is it not?"

The sound of the voice was sickening, terrifying. It made Laurie want to hang up. She couldn't. Darian's life depended upon her. "What…what do you mean?"

"People have shunned the true meaning of the festival of Samhain. Laurie. Is it deliberate or plain old–fashioned ignorance?"

Laurie closed her eyes and inhaled. He knew her name.

"I'm not sure what you mean."

The killer made a noise like a sigh and then something like laughter, but it was so inhuman that Laurie just couldn't be sure.

"So cliché. Do you like that word? I heard one of your friends use it tonight. It is so cliché for you not to know what I'm getting at. I have a sneaking suspicion you do. You know exactly what I mean. I know you, Laurie, and I know you well. Much better than you presume. That's why I've chosen you."

"Chosen me for what?" This was getting creepy even for this catastrophically creepy night.

"In good time. But in order to find out, you'll have to play my game. The rules are simple. In fact, there are no rules. No rules except one. You and your two friends, your two surviving friends, are required to meet me. I'm not going to tell you where. That's the fun part. But it shouldn't be a challenge. In fact, it shouldn't require any thought whatsoever. That's because you already know where. All you have to do is meet me there. There are no time restraints, but I wouldn't take too long if I were you. Oh, and there is one other thing I feel as though I should mention. If you go to the police or make any attempt whatsoever to receive any form of aid or assistance, I will take her apart, piece by piece. Do you understand?"

"Don't hurt her," Laurie sobbed. "We'll do whatever you want. Just, please, don't hurt her."

There was a brief one. "You know what I want. I've made that clear. All you have to do is do it. The rest you'll learn as we go. It isn't complicated, but you have to ask yourself. Is it? With you, Laurie, everything is more complicated than it is. I have the same problem. Do you know what I mean, Laurie? Do you?"

Laurie's head ached. She rubbed her head and crusted blood tumbled down. She felt faint.

"You don't have to answer," the voice said. "I know that you do." The connection ended.

Maggie tugged her arm. "What did he say, Laurie?"

"We have to play a game."

"What kind of game? Laurie, we need to go to the police, we need to get—"

"We can't. If we do, he'll kill Darian. And he'll know if we do. We can't take that risk. We're at his mercy now. It's his game."

Marshall tried to sit but fell back with a thump. He groaned and rubbed his head. Laurie crawled toward him, Maggie at her side. He was still on his back, but his head was raised. His nose was crooked, and blood had clotted on his mouth and chin.

"Marshall, oh my god, are you okay?"

Marshall blinked and worked his mouth. "I'm fine." He shifted his jaw from side to side, stroking it with his fingers and thumb.

"Can you stand?"

Marshall, still squint–eyed and shaky, answered that he could. He had to lean on Laurie and Maggie for support and nearly lost his footing a time or two, but at last, he managed to take a few steps on his own. He looked around the room, the destruction and endless blood.

"He killed them," he said, sounding equally sorrowful and enraged. "That maniac. He killed them."

"Yes," Laurie whispered.

"He killed them," Marshall mumbled. "Why not me? "

"He didn't kill Darian," Maggie said. "He took her with him. She's alive. She called Laurie."

"Why not me?" Marshall pawed at his face with increasing intensity.

Laurie stopped him. She placed her hands on his shoulders and in her shaky, uneven voice said, "Marshall, I need you to look at me. Look at me and focus. He's taken Darian. At the moment, she's alive, but she won't be for long."

Marshall's gaze steadied. "What does he want?"

"We have to go to him. If we go to the police, he'll kill her. Right now, all we can do is play his game, and I think I know the playing field. I need you to come with me. You too, Maggie." Laurie sensed the killer wanted Maggie and Marshall to accompany her. There was some sort of telepathy between her and this strange man, this supernatural killer. *Stop it!* She told herself. He's just a man, a sick, disgusting stalker man. A man with a costume and a knife. And one more thing. He had Darian.

23

The killer walked down a long dark hallway with Darian slung over his marble shoulder. At the end, he made a sharp left, causing Darian to hit her head. He turned as he entered the kitchen, bumping and banging her off just about everything in sight.

This is so dehumanizing, she thought. The killer stomped endlessly around the creaky wooden floorboards of his farmhouse and every time he turned a corner, she banged her head, wrists, forearms, and feet. She was an inanimate object, a ragdoll, a sack of Irish potatoes.

The killer opened a louvered door onto a deep black nothingness. He set Darian on her feet, her back to the abyss and her eyes looking up into the face of a masked madman. It was like a *Choose Your Own Adventure.* Her eyes hurt. She felt the waterworks began to pressurize. What could she say that wouldn't make things worse? *Say nothing.* The thought was quiet, indistinct, not her own.

A shove sent her spiraling down the steps. She hit the dirt floor and rolled to a stop against a wall. Having not broken her neck, she craned her eyes up to the hulking form standing in the impossibly bright doorway. He slammed the door. Sections of louvers clicked closed one by one.

Let there be dark, Darian thought. *Darkness is its own light, is it not?* There was that quiet voice again. Was she going crazy? Already? It had to be the stress getting to her. Trauma. Fear. She shook her head to clear it.

The killer hadn't barricaded the exit, but Darian knew she was not permitted to leave. She could run up those stairs and throw open that old–fashioned louvered door and... the killer would be right there on the other side waiting for her. If not literally right there, then close. He would kill her and that would be that.

"I won't make it that easy," she whispered. The bastard had killed her boyfriend and he was going to pay if she had to sit down here like a mushroom and plot for a hundred years. Another thought tried to come into her. She pushed it down.

What was she going to do? What could she do? At least he wasn't torturing her. Not now anyway. Her only option at this point was to wait. Maybe she would starve to death or die of thirst. That wouldn't be so painful. But it would draw her demise out be more miserable than a novelist could put into words. Perhaps he was going to settle for torture of the mind rather than the body. Mental torture. Mental torture versus physical torture. Which one was worse?

Just stop, she thought. She wasn't helping herself by doing this, and she certainly wasn't going to survive by fixating on torture. She shouldn't sit still. She needed to move. *Just sitting here makes me a sitting duck*, she thought even as the English major in her recoiled. Could she hide? Maybe it would take him a little longer to find her, but that was it.

Mentally, she could not force herself to sit here at the base of the steps and wait for him to come to her. It would be like if a canary whistling away as the cat sneaks up or a gazelle squatting on its haunches while a hungry lioness emerges from the brush. She should at least to get up familiarize herself with her surroundings and possibly, God willing, find a way out.

The cellar was so dark and so damp and so cold that it reminded Darian of the ninth circle of hell in Dante's epic poem. People always tended to think of hell as hot. Fire and brimstone and sulfur, but Darian had formulated a theory after reading *Divine Comedy* in her senior AP English class, that hell was a cold, wet and dark place, dripping and moist and icy. Not a lake of fire, but a lake of ice in which a multiheaded Satan, feasting on Judas Iscariot, was frozen at the center. She hoped that she didn't encounter anything like that down here, but all bets were off at this point.

The cellar wasn't terribly large. Darian couldn't be certain, but she was pretty sure it was divided into two rooms—the room she was now and a back room behind this wooden panel she thought was a door. Her fingers encountered a light switch. She flipped it and light showed around the wooden panel. It was a door, and the switch worked for the room behind it. Unfortunately, there wasn't much to this room she discovered when she opened the unlocked door. It was just a room tucked beneath the staircase and crammed full of junk. No exit, no window.

The most interesting feature was the floor painted pumpkin orange. The pain wasn't uniform but sprinkled with purple as if someone had taken a paintbrush and snapped their wrist back and forth. The purple shimmered the way rocks shimmer.

Shelves and boxes lined the walls. Tucked in a corner beneath the stairs, was what looked like a treasure chest. Upon opening it, she found a couple of old photo albums.

None of the photos were grainy or old. Darian guessed they were taken within the past twenty years or so. Every one depicted a boy of eight or nine and a man who was presumably his father or his grandfather. They showed them doing all sorts of things together, the boy blowing out birthday candles, opening Christmas presents, searching for his Easter basket, and…trick–or–treating. *So much lost. Mine. Ours.*

Darian slammed the cover down. She kept flashing on Rick's body, the blood, the sword protruding from his head. She wanted to throw the album across the small room, rip it to shreds, but what good would it do. This could be her key.

Other pictures depicted the boy and this man, usually dressed in a plaid shirt and coveralls. She extracted a picture of the two of them in front of a house. Not just any house. A farmhouse. Then it clicked. In her hand, she held a picture of the very farmhouse the killer had brought her to tonight.

"Oh my god," Darian whispered. She dropped the photo, then shoved the album off her knee. It was the boy. The boy and his father who went missing Halloween night 1998, the same night four Westminster students were killed. What was the boy's name? What was the farmer's name? Darian thought the farmer's name was John but couldn't be positive.

Darian felt more confident in saying the boy's name was Josh. *Joshua.* Yeah, that sounded right. Darian continued to leaf through the album until eyes were sore. She tossed it into the chest and closed the lid. From what she remembered, the boy and his father lived alone. So, who in the world would have taken these photos?

She opened a couple of crates filled with Christmas ornaments. Artificial trees roped into tight bundles leaned in gaps between some of the shelves. She determined that there were four of them.

She also found Valentines and Saint Patrick's Day ornaments and lights. Easter, Fourth of July, Thanksgiving—and a cardboard box of Halloween lights and decorations. Most were meant to hang on a tree. Darian's grandmother used to have a neighbor that kept a tree up year–round and decorated it on each holiday.

She turned the switch off and went back to the larger room. Now she was back in the dark. She sat against the wall and closed her eyes. A steady beeping noise caught her attention. *Beep. Beep. Beep.*

It was coming from the room she was in now. She must not have heard it earlier. Trauma from her fall, perhaps.

The rhythmic beeping was emanated from the center of the room. It sounded so familiar. Darian racked her brain trying to figure where she knew it from. *EKG machine.* She wasn't positive, but she thought she heard a raspy breathing too. Could it be that she wasn't alone? She moved toward the sound, hands outstretched. A string caught in her fingers. She grasped it firmly and pulled. *Click.* Dull yellow light bathed the room.

She yelped at the sight before her. Strapped to a table was a young man, perhaps a couple of years older than Darian.

Derek stared at the yellow light bulb. It had been days since he'd seen anything as bright as that. Even during the daytime, it was dingy down in the monster's cellar.

Beep. Beep. Beep. His heart rate seemed to be normal, but he couldn't move. The monster had him strapped to this solid mahogany work bench pretty well. His head was tethered with a leather strap, sort of like a weight lifting belt. He was shackled at the wrists and ankles. There was even a lock around his midsection, preventing any part of him from moving. IV lines stuck out of him like quills from a porcupine. The killer had been feeding him intravenously and had inserted a catheter.

200

A figure moved through the light. He clenched, expecting the monster, but this was a girl.

Patricia! You found me! He tried to say these things, but, of course, he was incapable of speech.

Beepbeepbeepbeep

It was too much. His senses spun. He tried to close his eyes but couldn't. *Calm down*, he thought. *Ommmmmmmm. Ommmmmmmm.*

Darian spotted a colostomy bag. Had the killer performed surgery on this poor man? Was he a doctor or a surgeon? Did he go to medical school? How else would he have acquired this equipment?

Is he going to do the same thing to me?

Darian didn't care to explore that question. Right now, she needed to attend to this suffering man. He was stark naked and wasn't in one piece. The skin from his left forearm, along with a layer of fat or muscle had been removed. The rope–like muscles in his forearm looked like a sleeve that terminated neatly at the wrist. A crude stitched–up scar ran the length of his abdomen where the colostomy bag was attached. He was missing several fingers on his right hand. The wounds had been cauterized.

What kind of twisted surgery was this? Darian cupped her hands over her mouth, trying not to scream. She wanted to cry and scream at the same time, but that might just sign their death warrants.

Most of the man's fingers on his right hand were missing or mangled. Not all were completely amputated. His middle finger was gone from the second knuckle, his pinky completely. The index and ring fingers had been hyperextended rather severely. None of the fingers on his left hand, the one attached to the forearm that had been shaved of its meat, had fingernails. What did he use to cut off this guy's fingers? A bolt cutter? Did he pluck the nails off with tweezers? Drive hot needles beneath the beds before doing it?

There was no damage done to the lower half of the man's body. No broken bones, missing toes, his penis and balls were perfectly intact. Darian moved to the head of the table.

"What's your name?" she said. "Can you move? Can you hear me?" She got a good look at his face and let out a yelp before cupping her hands over her mouth again.

His eyelids had been removed with surgical precision. Wide staring eyes gazed upward, so big they were almost comical. The whites were severely reddened. His cheeks were sunken. He had no teeth. Darian didn't want to guess how they were extracted. His toothless and rootless gums glimmered in the yellow light. They seemed overlarge, not only because there were no teeth, but because his lips had been sliced off as well.

A shriveled tongue lolled in his mouth like a fish out of water, and he made a kind of slurping, smacking, sucking noise that made the hair on the back of Darian's neck stand.

She tried to conjure up a way to get this person, this kid who was not much older than herself, unstrapped and off the table. Without a key, it was going to be impossible, not to mention the IV lines running in and out of him like nobody's business. She hoped that Laurie, Maggie, and Marshall hadn't called for help. This guy was serious about killing her, and much worse than that, if they did.

The killer sat alone in his darkened dining room. He had been suffering from the hunger pangs as any normal person would. Just like the normal person that Laurie Williams and her friends thought he was. Except the girl in the basement. She knew. She was beginning to understand. There was a connection. She was resistant, but it was there.

Until the others arrived, he had to do something to occupy his time. And they would come. He was certain of that. Until then, he was hungry. Ravenous in fact. Although it would be easy to assume he ate people, he didn't. The thought of the act didn't revolt him, it was just something he didn't do. Maybe one day he would. Maybe.

With his long hunting knife, he bisected the deer he had killed earlier and bisected. This brought back memories of elementary school, dissecting frogs and earthworms, cats and pigs. His teacher had claimed a worm was stronger than a person and if said worm were the size of said person, it would easily overpower them. This fascinated him.

After splitting the deer, he pushed his gloved hand into the cavity and pulled out a succulent organ. It wasn't just any innard, but the heart.

He set his mask aside and sank his fang–like teeth into the red–black flesh of the heart. His teeth weren't exactly fangs, but fang–like, and not just the canines, but the incisors as well. Certainly, more pointed than an average human, maybe any human. But they could still be considered human, right?

Blood squeezed between his fingers and oozed, from his paper–thin lips. The deer hadn't been difficult to kill. It was easy prey. No weapons required. He had taken down the animal with his bare hands.

He didn't usually like to run, but tonight was different. The events of the evening had amped him up and he'd had no problem catching the deer. It helped that he was stealthy enough to sneak up on it before it bolted, but that didn't really give him the credit he deserved. He had outrun the animal for a short distance at least. Once he caught it, he wrestled it to the ground, grabbed its antlers, and twisted its head off, or close enough. He loved the pop of bones twisting out of joint almost as he loved bones breaking.

And thus, supper. Most people nowadays preferred to call it dinner, but Pops had said supper, so for him, it always was and will be supper. Even with little things like that he relished going against the grain. Anything associated with them, people, he hated by default.

He sat there tearing at the heart until there was nearly nothing left. The tube–like arteries, the atrias and aortas were perfectly delicious fodder. The pieces he chewed usually made snapping or tearing sounds as they ripped free. He found that satisfying too.

As he was finishing the first course of his supper, a flood of red and blue and white lights strobed through the window. The tell–tale lights of the police. With one sleeve, he wiped his mouth, then put his mask on and walked to the dining room window.

A police cruiser that had pulled to the end of his long dirt driveway. The driver's side door read Canterbury Township Police, so he knew that the girl, his favorite girl, the one that he had chosen because she reminded him of himself as a boy, hadn't contacted them. That would have caused a Willoughby "Falls" dispatch.

He released the curtain and backed from the window so as not to be seen. Although it was dark inside, the glowing of his mask might give him away. It wasn't that an officer frightened him. Far from it. He just wanted to play the role of the hunter not the hunted. It was more fun.

A voice sounded from the cellar. "Help! Help! Help! Help us! Oh please, God, help us! We're down here!"

The killer grunted softly. As the cop approached the porch, he realized that he was going to have to take care of the situation. So much for a pleasant supper.

Sherriff Gram had hardly gotten any sleep since Deputy Flynn was discovered scalped and floating in Lake Britain. Unable to sleep tonight, he had decided to investigate Old Man John's farm for himself.

Seventeen years ago, six people went missing here and then the cop who investigated turns up brutally murdered. That didn't sit well with him. Never had. He didn't care how many investigations had been done, how many departments had taken jurisdiction only to let the case fester. It was his turn now. And what about those rolls of film stuffed in that boy's eye sockets? He wasn't trying to play hero. All he wanted was an answer. One that would hopefully make the worry lines in his forehead go away.

As he was aiming his flashlight around the grounds, he heard screaming. It sounded faint but close at the same time. A female voice, maybe coming from cellar?

Sherriff Gram drew his gun, dashed up the porch steps, and kicked the door in. He went in head first, not stopping to look back or reconsider. He made his way forward through what seemed like the most maddening, longest, darkest stretch of hallway he had ever seen. His gun was drawn, flashlight beaming. Ready for anything.

The voice was directly beneath him now. He just needed to find the door. He sure felt sorry for anyone who got in his way. The big man was so hyped up he felt as if he could go through anybody.

Suddenly and without warning a dark shape exploded from a side door. It was a massive form at least as big as him and it drove him into the wall like he was a powder puff. His ribs and right arm took the brunt of it, but he was not hurt bad. He did lose his gun. He dropped to his knees and sprawled for it.

The figure kicked the weapon down the dark hallway. On his hands and knees, the sheriff reached for his lapel mic, but the figure grabbed the back of his neck and pulled him upright. The killer worked his gloved hand around the sheriff's thick neck and quickly added his other hand so that both massive mitts were wrapped securely around the officer's throat.

Gram grabbed the killer's wrists, trying with all his might to break his grip. The killer lifted Gram off his feet. Wind milling his long solid arms, Gram attempted to knock batter his assailant, but the force of his blows had little effect. He noticed that the side and back of his attacker's head was covered in a red spandex material that would not cushion a punch.

He kicked. His toe connected with a groin. The killer flinched, and Gram landed a considerable powerful blow above the killer's ear. The killer shook his head slowly from side to side, but it had no other effect.

The killer's grip tightened further. Gram couldn't breathe. He fumbled for his belt and managed to pull his nightstick from its holder. He swung for the fences, again connecting with the killer's head, just above the ear. The blow had no effect. Gram couldn't believe what he was seeing. The madman had to be on crystal meth or PCP.

The killer let go. The sheriff fell back and slumped against the wall. He wheezed, drawing air through his distressed airway. He coughed and adjusted his collar, before trying again. Starting from his toes, he began to deliver a blow that the mask–wearing freak couldn't possibly survive, let alone shake off.

With a quickness that was almost comical, the killer caught the nightstick in his left hand and kicked the sheriff's knee, bending it backward. Gram dropped with a grunt. The killer ripped the club from his hand. As Gram was in this submissive position, the killer grabbed his hair and pulled his head back.

"Ah," Gram groaned.

The killer shoved the nightstick down his throat. Gram gagged and clutched at his neck as his trusty club was jammed past his uvula and stretched the esophagus. He attempted to remove the stick gullet, further exacerbating the stabbing pains in his ruptured trachea.

The killer grabbed either side of his head and squeezed. Gram's eyes wide. He removed his hands from the baton and grabbed the killer's wrists. He tried with everything he had left to pull those hands apart, but it was to no avail.

The pressure was beyond incredible. Gram began having flashbacks to eighth–grade woodshop when he and his friends splintered blocks of wood between the table vices for fun. That's what his skull felt like. It was splintering. A deafening crack and crunching sound filled the hallway, the sound of teeth grinding down to nubs inside your head.

Gram's eyes bulged. As blood vessels ruptured, the whites transitioned from soft pink to severe allergy red to blood itself. Scarlet tears burst free. His nostrils and mouth began to leak. Both sides of the sheriff's skull gave simultaneously. A final *crack-squish* and his carcass accordioned down.

The killer wiped his hands on Gram's jacket, and went to the kitchen to finish his supper.

Downstairs, Darian heard the struggle. She might have been able to escape during the fight, but she couldn't leave the young man behind. She had made her decision, and she was going to stick by it. She thought about Laurie and Maggie and Marshall. *Wherever you guys are, you better get here quick.*

24

History was repeating itself. Maybe events weren't exactly unfolding as they had on Halloween night, 1998, but Laurie guessed there were some very strong correlations. Four boys had disappeared, but had they really disappeared, or were they murdered? That seem like a good guarantee.

Laurie, Marshall, and Maggie walked the same trail that the four friends, had traversed seventeen years earlier. The night was dark and cold. The dirt road was uneven, not to mention narrow and winding. There was a full moon in the sky. This time it was a blood moon. Laurie remembered hearing stories about the blood moon when she was a kid.

Supposedly, the blood moon was a precursor to the four horsemen of the apocalypse. This, from fellow students in Catholic Sunday school. Other students claimed it signaled the gates of hell to open on Earth and spill demons, beasts and leviathans upon the world. The ones she remembered most were not religious but concerned monsters. Monsters of all sorts coming out to eat children, sneak around gardens at dusk, tap on their bedroom windows while they were asleep, etcetera.

"What are we going to do once we get there?" Maggie asked.

Laurie had already told them they were going to the farm. Why the killer wanted Laurie and her friends to return to the scene of his first crime, she wasn't sure. Maybe Farmer John's farm was a sentimental spot for his sick and twisted heart.

"I don't know," she said. "If we want to keep Darian alive, we're probably going to have to do whatever he tells us."

Maggie cried. "I don't like this, Laurie. How are we going to come out of this alive? What if Darian's already dead?"

Marshall pushed between them. "Don't think like that, Maggie. We're going to be fine. Darian too. We just have to stay strong. Take all that sorrow and remorse and fear and throw it away. Keep the hate and the rage. Those emotions will benefit us the most."

They happened upon a sign, a crudely constructed sign post that almost resembled a picket sign. It was fashioned out of splintery oak and sported an extremely faded white coat of paint. In melting letters that looked like their dead friends' blood were the words:

Haunted House

An arrow below it pointed the direction they were heading.

"Is this some a trap?" Maggie asked. "Is he trying to lead us into—"

"No," Laurie said. "This is no trap. The only surprise we can expect is him. And we already know he's going to be there."

The three exchanged glances. Their walk was concluding. Soon they would be reliving the horror of the Samurai Room, the same horror that so many people had experienced but not lived through this Halloween season.

Laurie wondered if the victims were fortunate in a sense, considering that they didn't have to live with the memories that she and her friends would. *Provided, we survive.*

They came to the blue two–story farmhouse, complete with chimney and weather vane at the end of a long dirt driveway. Tangled masses of growth surrounded the porch steps. The rich blue paint had faded and peeled. A lot of the windows were boarded, but not the ones in front.

The house was done up in rather fine fashion, just as it had been on Halloween nights past. The front lawn was covered in a thin coat of fog. Jutting up from the fog were prop tombstones.

They knew what they had to do. As they started down the driveway, Marshall said, "Whatever happens, we're going to face this together."

Strobe lights lit the fog green—boogeyman green—and blue—death blue. Christmas bulbs of various hues decorated the eaves. Somehow, the color scheme, which should have been pleasing to look at, was menacing when attached to the devil house. The house that Laurie was starting to think might be an entrance to hell.

They were being watched from the windows, two on both sides of the door and three above the porch roof, but not by anything living. Not yet, anyway. On the front porch, the two windows that were on either side of the front door were occupied.

To the right of the door, a very tall and broad figure with skin stitched together glared from the window. The skin, which was in patches, was purplish black and blue in some spots and yellow in others, the colors of differently–aged bruises. Its lips looked like shiny black lipstick against a mouthful of impeccable pearly whites. The eyes were different colors, one green and one blue. It wasn't the creature so commonly mistaken as Frankenstein from the classic Universal horror pictures, but Frankenstein's creature from Mary Shelley's classic work of literature and one of Laurie's favorite novels. She would never be able to read that book again.

In the opposite window the Count from Bram Stoker's seminal vampire tale watched warily. He looked like he had just fed—cheeks flushed and rosy, lips full and blood–red. Even his eyes burned red. Two vulpine canines descended from his trim black mustache. His hideously long fingers with were propped so that they looked like those twisted fingernails were rapping the glass.

On the second floor, directly above Dracula, was the Gill–Man in all his green, scaly splendor. His amphibian skin carried a viscous layer of slime, the kind that Lovecraft seemed particularly preoccupied with. His eyes bulged out of their sockets. Shark gills on the side of its neck expanded and contracted as its mouth repeatedly opened and closed. Its webbed talons were clearly visible.

In the middle window, was Brundlefly, the hideous mutation that Jeff Goldblum morphed into in David Cronenberg's 1986 classic. Laurie considered that film a great example of bodily horror, but she felt more repulsed by this life–sized prop than she ever had watching the film. Even the maggot–child birth scene paled next to this. Brundlefly's bulbous blue eyes seemed to stare right through her as its mouth feelers twitched in strange, contorted patterns. Its crab–like claw contracted and its wiry insect hairs stood littered its body like erect pricks.

Directly above Frankenstein's monster, was yet another ghoulish figure, a clown in a silver suit. The material seemed to be metallic, the kind that spacemen wore on the moon. A line of blue pompoms ran down the clown's chest and stomach. His collar and sleeves were ruffled, and his head featured big poof hair and a blue rubber ball nose. Even his cruel contorted lips were painted with blue greasepaint, exposing a mouthful of needle–like fangs. Instead of hands, it had a pair of reptilian claws. *Pennywise the Dancing Clown.* Whether it was intended to be Tim Curry's version from the TV miniseries or Robert Grey from Stephen King's epic novel was anybody's guess.

They walked up the porch steps. The treads were fittingly creaky, almost as if the house were crying out with each step they took. The columns supporting the roof looked as though they might give out at any moment. It was as if the house's mass had become so great that its anatomical structure could no longer support it.

The front door hung crooked from one hinge. It was closed though it no longer fit the frame. Fresh splinters showed along its edge.

"What next?" Maggie said.

Marshall swallowed hard. It was a surprising amount of spittle that had accumulated since he had arrived at the farm, considering how dry he had been on the walk over. He wasn't sure how to answer Maggie, so he stood there for a moment to think it over. But he knew he had to think fast since every moment that passed was a moment that moved the killer closer to killing Darian.

Laurie touched his forearm. It was like an injection of courage. He stepped forward and pushed the door. It fell inward with a crash.

"Wait, what are you doing?" Maggie said.

"We have to go in," Marshall said firmly. "That's what he brought us here for. That's what he wants. I'll lead the way. You two stay behind me."

The moment had arrived. The one they dreaded. Marshall turned away from his girlfriend and her friend. He felt as if his heart was a drum being violently beaten. With a deep breath, he stepped over the threshold.

25

Darian made another discovery. There was another room in the basement behind the jury-rigged operating table. The door was short and narrow like a secret compartment or maybe a dungeon trap. A disgusting sour stale smell wafted through the doorway. As she bent down to enter it, she promised the semi–conscious man she wouldn't leave him behind.

"I *will* be back." She didn't know if he really heard or understood, but she needed him to know.

A twin mattress lay on the floor. It was old and stained. Darian couldn't tell if those were piss stains or cum stains. Maybe both. Maybe neither. A stiff sheet, withered and yellowed, covered a portion of it. Old newspaper articles were scattered haphazardly around it. *This must be his den. His man cave where he's been living for...years?*

She turned her head from the disgusting disease–ridden mattress, only to find more newspaper clippings thumb–tacked to the wall. One that caught her eye was dated November 1, 1998. FOUR WESTMINSTER STUDENTS MISSING. Darian briefly scanned the article.

> Four Westminster students never returned home after leaving a fraternity party. Friends of the four have expressed their concern. Police do not suspect foul play. The search continues. If you have any information about the whereabouts of these young men, please contact...

Another headline read, LOCAL FARMER AND SON MISSING.

> Local Farmer John Moran, 61, and his son, Joshua, 8, have gone missing on the night of October 31. The farmer and his son lived at 1857 Darden Lane. Suspiciously enough, the father–son pair went missing on the same night as four Westminster college students. Farmer John was known for his annual haunted house display that he would set up at his home and charge visitors a minor fee to visit.

There was a door on the far back wall. It was a hinged door, the wood was rough and splintery, and the light blue paint rather faded. Darian walked over and opened it. A creak sounded, so bone chilling that she felt as if her skeleton had turned to ice. *Seeeeeee?* the door whispered to her soul. *Open your senses and seeeeee.*

This room was small and dark, the air so thick that Darian nearly choked. She covered her mouth. This room, this basement, this whole farm, had to be riddled with asbestos and lead paint. She expected corn whiskey, Irish whiskey, Wild Turkey, and various other bottles of rare vintage alcohol with sparkling amber tones like butterscotch or liquefied lion's eyes. Or a wine cellar with dusty bottles stored for generations.

She pulled the light string. It wasn't a wine cellar, but a small rectangle lined with shelves holding paint cans, some empty, some not. Articles of clothing, most of them torn and blood spattered, were scattered about the floor. Darian stepped over them as if walking on eggshells. She came to a pile of wallets and ID's—driver's license, student identification cards, and more. Darian recognized the names of some of the victims.

Darian nearly dropped everything when she found the student Id's and driver's licenses of Jack Sayer and Julia Wrightson. The killer was taking trophies. *We...* Something opened within her, a budding warmth.

"No," she muttered. She focused on the task at hand. The wallets were empty. Either they had been empty to begin with, or the killer discarded the money. She doubted he had much use for the stuff.

She heard steps. A jolt shot through her. He was coming. She dropped the wallets and identification cards and ran back to the main room, closing doors behind her. She wanted him in the open where at least she had a fighting chance.

The light was still on above the young man. Ever so faint, ever so dull, but still making things visible. As she neared the table where he was strapped, she heard the steps again. They *were* footsteps, but from upstairs. It didn't sound like killer's heavy plodding, but like more than one pair of feet. At least two, maybe three pair. It had to be Laurie, Marshall and, Maggie.

Darian's heart fluttered. Should she scream up the stairs, or would that be setting them up? Either way it was a lose–lose situation. If she stayed here and was silent, he would pick off her friends one by one. If she hollered up to them, he would still pick them off, maybe all three at once, before coming down to finish his work on her and the young man strapped to the table. She was caught between a rock and a hard place. She had to do something.

"I'll be back," she whispered to the young man. *If I can*, she thought. She crept upstairs. *There is no return*, the voice whispered. *Once you understand what has been lost. Soon...*

Marshall led the way through the stygian hallway. The first door led to the old dining room. After determining that neither Darian nor the killer, was in that room, Marshall closed the door and moved on.

"Darian," Laurie called in a hushed tone. "Darian are you here?"

Marshall stopped abruptly, nearly causing Laurie and Maggie to bump into him. Pressing his ear against the nearest door, he listened.

"Marshall, what is it?" Laurie said.

"Shhh!" He motioned with his hand. "I hear something." *Sawing*, he thought. The sound of a blade being drawn back and forth over wood. It seemed ludicrous, but that's what he heard.

"Stand back." Marshall took a deep breath, feeling as if he'd just swallowed his heart, and gripped the door handle in his sweaty palm. A twist and a push, and the door opened. The sawing sound intensified. His eye was drawn to the center of the room. Pretty much right at his feet, only a few inches away. Body parts. Lots and lots of body parts scattered across floor. Hands and forearms, amputated feet. And blood. There was blood everywhere.

The killer, hacksaw in his hand, was sawing through the neck of a law enforcement officer. Marshall's gag reflex kicked in. He jammed one hand over his open mouth and the other hand over his stomach. The rusty serrated blade slid back and forth across bone.

"Marshall?" Laurie said. "Is everything okay?"

"Stay out," he said louder than intended.

The killer looked up, mask shifting from frown to smile. With a final thrust and a wet pop, the head came free. The killer lifted it for Marshalls' approval. Tendrils of flesh and tendon draped from what was left of the crushed skull. An eye stared blindly from ruptured flesh.

"God," Marshall whispered.

The killer turned the head until it looked directly into his eyes. He admired his handiwork before turning his attention to Marshall. Slowly, he got to his feet. First, he dropped the hacksaw. The bloody tool of metal and wood clattered down. The killer stepped toward the door. Marshall retreated to the hall and nudged Laurie and Maggie back. Should they run?

The killer tossed the severed head behind him. It thumped as it hit the floor and began to roll. He withdrew a gleaming metal instrument from his wide belt. It was an exceptionally large hunting knife.

"Oh man. Run, run, run!" Marshall shouted. He didn't want to turn his back on the killer but would be able to move faster if he did.

He didn't get far anyway. With a quick burst of speed, the killer caught up and plunged the knife into Marshall's lower back. Marshall skidded face first into the wall and slid down. He tried to push himself up, but the killer stepped on his back. With one hand the killer withdrew the deeply embedded blade from Marshall's back. Luckily, it hadn't hit his spine.

The sour taste of warm blood filled his mouth. Maggie and Laurie stopped and turned.

"Go!" he shouted, blood spattering the wall.

The killer raised the blade high over his head and paused dramatically. Marshall closed his eyes.

Maggie got to him first. She tackled the killer, completely blindsided him, not quite knocking him off his feet but coming close. He stumbled into a door with Maggie's arms wrapped around his torso. The blade descended.

Maggie wrapped both hands around his forearm in a valiant attempt to stop the killing stroke. His arm was so solid that it felt as if it was carved from wood. With all her might, she worked against his downward moving arm. His arm slowed but didn't stop. He was too strong.

The blade slowly slid into her shoulder. It was painful as hell, but at least it wasn't fatal. The killer withdrew it, and Maggie collapsed to the floor. Laurie tried to jump on his back, but with a swift backhand, he knocked aside and gave her a bloody nose in the process.

Maggie scrabbled further down the hall. Laurie glimpsed something on the floor near her. A gun. *Hallelujah*, she thought. She kicked at the killer's leg, hoping to distract him. He looked down. She saw amusement in the eyes behind the mask.

Maggie turned and aimed the .38 Smith and Wesson. The killer reacted instantly, leaping and kicking in the same motion. He booted her directly in the mouth, busting open her lip and sending her onto her back. The gun spun on the floor. She managed to shove it toward Laurie. Laurie dove to retrieve it. She flipped onto her back and aimed the weapon at the killer, praying the safety was off.

With one arm extended, the killer leaned toward her. The blade was raised high in his other hand. Laurie pulled the trigger. The chamber rotated, and the tip of the barrel exploded in a flash of light. Recoil drove her arm into her chest.

The bullet struck the killer's shoulder. The impact was so great that it jerked him halfway around, nearly screwing him onto the floor. Dark blood spurted from the wound. The sound was deafening, and for several seconds after, the only thing Laurie could hear was a ringing in her ears.

The killer clutched at his shoulder with his knife hand. Laurie climbed to her feet. She aimed again. He dropped his hand from the wound and stood there facing her. It might have been a classic Western standoff, except that one of the participants had brought a knife to a gun fight.

Laurie pulled the trigger again and again and again. Rounds fired in rapid succession, pounding the killer's chest and torso one right after the other. *Splat. Splash. Crack.*

The killer slumped back, grasping the door frame for balance. *How is he still on his feet?* There had been six bullets in the gun. Even through the ringing in her ears, Laurie heard labored breathing from behind the mask. He dropped the massive hunting knife and stumbled into the room.

Laurie hurried to the doorway, intent on finishing the job. Somehow. She stopped at the threshold and watched the killer lurch across the room and run into a bookshelf. He grasped the wood frame. As he collapsed, dozens of leather–bound books tumbled down, effectively burying him.

Laurie dropped the gun. A heavy copper smell pushed at her. Blood and body parts coated the floor. And books. Her gaze fell on a deformed human head. It single eye glared at the killer. Laurie felt for a moment like she would retch. The moment passed. Relief sagged through her tired muscles. She backed into the hallway. After more than a month of this madness, it was over. She had stopped it. The killer was dead.

26

Maggie's entire sleeve was stained red, but she was on her feet.

"Hey," she said with a tired smile. She nodded toward Marshall a few strides away, sitting with his back against the wall. He coughed, and a fine spray of blood spewed from his mouth.

"Oh my god." Laurie knelt beside him. Tears steamed in her eyes. "We have to get you to a hospital." They couldn't call for help. None of their cell phones had reception in this dead zone.

She helped him stand.

"We have to find Darian," Maggie said.

But she was already there. Darian stood quietly in the doorway between the hallway and kitchen.

"You guys came for me," she said. There was something odd about her eyes, her lack of expression, that held Laurie back.

"What happened to you?" she said. "Are you all right?"

"There's a man down there," Darian said, finger pointing at the floor. "He's strapped to a table. He won't make it much longer."

"Why are we standing around?" Marshall said. "We should leap into action." He took a tentative step, then grabbed for Laurie's shoulder. With Laurie on one side and Maggie on the other, they made halting progress to the kitchen.

"Can this man walk?" Laurie asked. How would they deal with another wounded man? They couldn't possibly support all that weight. Maggie and Marshall might bleed out in the process. Then again, she couldn't live with herself if she left a helpless person down there and he died before they could send help. Even dead, the killer was a Mephistopheles, causing her moral dilemmas.

"I didn't tell you something," Darian said. "The straps are padlocked."

"No problem," Marshall grunted. "We'll be fine." He glanced at Maggie.

She nodded back. "Let's rescue the guy and get the hell out of here."

The louvered door was open. They navigated down the steps, Darian leading the way, followed by Laurie and Marshall and Maggie wrapped arm in arm. When they finally reached the bottom, they had to deal with yet another horrific sight. The young man lay on a table, naked and mangled, lidless eyes staring helplessly at the ceiling. His arm was a mess and his hands. Tubes draped all over him.

Maggie went to help Darian. The two of them began to unhook the IV lines. Laurie hung back with Marshall, who was still leaning on her heavily.

"We're going to need something to cut these shackles," Maggie said.

"There's a toolbox in the back room," Darian said.

"This room behind me?" She pointed at the small door to the paint can and trophy closet.

"The other one." She nodded across the basement.

Maggie stood there for a moment.

"What's wrong?" Darian said.

"Wouldn't it be better if you went for the toolbox?" She indicated the bleeding arm clutched to her chest. "I mean I can pull out IV tubes, but I'm not sure I can carry a toolbox."

"Really?" Darian said. "Here, let me help you." With that, she withdrew a .45 Magnum from her pants, aimed at Maggie's head, and pulled the trigger.

27

Laurie and Marshall saw it coming too late. Even if they had screamed for Maggie to watch out, there was no chance she would have gotten out of the way. Darian's finger was already squeezing the trigger by the time the gun was visible to them.

The entry wound in her back was small and much larger coming out. Blood splattered the wall behind the sink adjacent to the table the man was strapped to. Streaks of gray matter mixed with the blood. Bits of brain and bone decorated the floor. Laurie could barely bring herself to look at Maggie. The gaping hole in her head wasn't a perfectly neat circle. The edge was jagged and rough.

Laurie directed her attention to Darian. The gun aimed at them. Laurie clutched Marshall.

Darian made the revolver click and seemed ready to pull the trigger again. She let out a laugh. It was her normal laugh. The laugh Laurie had grown so accustomed to.

How can this be? Laurie thought. How could it be that the girl she grew up with was a killer?

"Darian," she said.

"Shut up!" The demand was so harsh it made Laurie want to backtrack even further upstairs.

"So which one of you two wants to be next?" Darian waved the gun back and forth. "No wait. Don't answer that. It's no fun if I let you decide. That would mean your fate is still in your control, and it's not. If I'm the decider, I have total power. Complete control over life and death. And being in charge of the fate of two star–crossed lovers, well, that just really tickles my fancy. Makes me a little moist to tell you the truth. Right now, I just want to drop my pants and finger myself."

"That's what this is all about?" Laurie said. "Killing people gives you a sense of power? That's why you murdered your best friend?"

Darian cackled. "Oh, Laurie. Always the analyst. You think you're so smart, don't you? Miss I–Always Have–an–Answer–for–Everything. Miss thinker. Well, I got news for you, sweetheart. You are nothing more than a dot on a dot on a black canvas. You know about one–eighteenth of what you think you know. Power? Well, that may be part of it, but it isn't the whole picture, dear. You want to know the truth? The real truth?"

"Yes," Laurie screamed. "Yes, I want the truth!"

Darian wiped her jaw with the sleeve of her forearm. "You know what the strongest and oldest emotion known to mankind is? Fear. And do you want to know what the strongest and oldest type of fear is? The fear of the unknown."

"Lovecraft," Laurie said. That quote came directly from Lovecraft's essay, 'Supernatural Horror in Literature." Darian knew it inside and out, just as Darian knew that Laurie knew it inside and out. Although neither of them had been big Lovecraft readers, it wasn't an alien topic.

"Are you saying you didn't have a motivation to be that killer's accomplice? And dress up like him and go around to those haunted houses and kill people?"

"Who says I did any of that?"

Laurie was dumbfounded. "You mean you weren't his accomplice? Why in the hell did you kill Maggie?"

"Laurie, Laurie, Laurie. What am I going to do with you? You just don't get it. I'm starting to think you never will."

"Then enlighten me, Darian. Please, tell me what is going on!"

"I believe in his cause. I believe in what he stands for."

Laurie looked to Marshall, who looked back to her.

Then he spoke the inevitable question arose. "Who's 'he'?"

"Joshua. Upstairs. The person that you, trying to play hero, killed."

"Joshua?" Laurie said. "The boy from—"

"Yes, the boy who disappeared seventeen years ago. Do you even know what happened that night?"

Laurie shook her head.

"I didn't think you would. Well, here, I'll give it to you. Those boys, the four college boys. They murdered Joshua's father. That's right. They murdered him. Sure, they claimed it was an accident, but instead of doing the right thing, they concoct this scheme to bury the body in the woods."

"How do you know this?" Marshall said.

"Because I do. Don't interrupt again! Where was I? You made me lose my train of thought. Oh yes. They murdered him. They took his corpse tried to hide it, but he took care of them."

"You mean Joshua?" Laurie said.

"Yes, of course, Joshua."

Laurie was starting to see the larger picture. "So that's what this is about. His father gets murdered, he takes care of the killers, and then how many years later, he decides to dress up and go around to haunted attractions killing people as part of some sort of revenge. How do you fit into this?"

"Laurie, you're still not grasping. Joshua didn't kill four college kids. He was just a boy; how could he have?"

"With a knife," Laurie answered snidely, disregarding the .45 Magnum pointed at her.

"Listen, smartass. Now's not the time to be messing with me."

Laurie was starting to think of a way that a young boy could kill four grown men. He was supernatural. Not paranormal. Paranormal can be explained through science. Supernatural can't. At least that was how Dr. Mitchell had explained it in Film Criticism.

Darian smirked. "The spirit of Halloween killed them. Have you never noticed the streetlamps in this town? The orange glow, the otherworldly orange? Isn't it so creepy?"

Laurie stared. Of course, streetlamps glowed.

"The reason they glow like that—that shade of orange—is because that's not the light, no, not the light, but the energy. A disembodied energy field belonging to the spirit of Halloween resides in the streetlamps. We're its agents."

Laurie thought of the classic film, *The Quartermass Xperiment*, starring a disembodied energy field as an alternative lifeform. It was a classic example of the cosmic indifference that permeated Lovecraft's writing. Its organic form was the result of the absorption of a representative range of plant and animal life, and the entity itself was teratologically Lovecraftian, a giant eyeball with multitentacles.

"What does the spirit of Halloween look like?" Laurie said, attempting to engage Darian's sick brain. "Have you actually met him?"

Darian chuckled. "Well, that's the thing. 'Him' is not the proper pronoun. It's not a he or a she, it is an 'it.' Are you familiar with M'Nagalah? The postulating cancer god of cosmic scope?"

Laurie was shocked. Darian apparently believed that she and the killer were agents of an elder god from Lovecraft's mythos, or something very similar.

"What exactly did Joshua tell you?"

Darian smirked. "Joshua? He doesn't talk much, hardly a word in years. When he does talk, it's on his own terms. Are you presuming that I'm somehow brain–washed, a groupie of the Joshua cult? Oh, Laurie, you don't honestly think I would be susceptible to that, do you?"

Darian took a step. Laurie and Marshall moved backward.

"You need to stop and think about what you're doing here," Marshall said. "Even if there is a spirit of Halloween—"

Darian screamed, "There is!"

"Okay, okay, but that doesn't mean you have to do what you're thinking about doing. We're friends."

Darian's laugh was hysterical. "I've known you for a month. I would hardly consider us friends."

"Okay. But you and Laure *are* friends. If you're going to shoot someone, shoot me." Marshall moved in front of Laurie.

A shuffling sound came from upstairs. Something was being pushed or slid across the floor. Laurie's heart pounded double-time. *The bookcase. He's still alive.* Heavy plodding footsteps echoed down the stairwell.

Darian's eyes grew round. Shaking her head and blinking her eyes, she dropped the weapon. When she saw Maggie's body, she began to scream and cry, before dropping to her knees. "Oh my god. No. Maggie baby. What have I done?"

Laurie felt a moment of compassion. Darian was not herself when she shot Maggie and turned the gun on them. She was sick. What Laurie couldn't figure out was how she could have known Darian so well and not even guess she suffered from a severe mental condition.

Darian crawled to Marshall. "Oh God, you guys. I need help. Please help me. Please. He's in my head."

"Joshua?" Marshall said.

Mind control? Laurie thought. Impossible. But if that was so impossible, how was he was still alive after Laurie fired six shots into him?

As Laurie was trying to convince herself that it had to have been a bullet–proof vest, the louver door pulled open forcefully. In the opening stood Joshua. The hulking frame and glowering mask was a terrifying sight. It was like an upward shot in a movie that makes characters seem larger than life.

Joshua began to descend.

Darian groveled and tugged at Marshall's pant leg. "Please, guys. Don't let him take me again."

Laurie stared at the six dark bullet holes in Joshua's body. One in his shoulder, five scattered across his torso. A scarlet smear marked each one, blood glistening in the room's light. He couldn't be wearing a bulletproof vest.

Marshall burst toward him but was stopped in his tracks when Joshua brought a knee right into his abdomen. Marshall gasped. Joshua threw him face first into the stairs. Laurie backed away. Her whole body went cold.

Joshua started toward Darian. Laurie, who always tried to give people the benefit of the doubt and see the good in everyone, wanted to protect her friend, but how could she trust the woman who had shot Maggie point-blank?

As Joshua closed in, Laurie screamed. "Joshua!"

He stopped immediately and stared right through her soul. It was the strangest sensation.

"Joshua. I'm sorry about what happened to your father. But please understand. My friends and I had nothing to do with it. Please, let us go. Stop punishing innocent people."

Joshua moved toward Darian.

"Joshua!" This caused him not only to stop but take a few steps back. "Joshua," Laurie said. She pointed to Joshua's mask. "Take it off. Let me see…" She pointed to her face.

Joshua's shoulders heaved up and down. Slowly, his arms lifted. His ungentle fingers interlocked across the holographic mask, and he pulled it off, as well as the red spandex covered his head and neck. The sight that that revealed was enough to make Laurie want to ask him to put the mask back on.

He wasn't burned or deformed. In fact, his features were human, but only barely. His forehead was a thick bony ridge. His jaw was prognathous, his nose and cheekbones exaggerated. Dark hair matted his squarish skull, sweat–soaked strands clinging to his brow. Even his orbital bones seemed thick, reinforced. The skull structure was almost primitive.

There was almost no coloring to his skin except around his eye sockets, which were a deep purple, almost black, as if he was wearing mascara. Vulpine teeth overlapped his thin lips. They looked so sharp, like cannibalistic needles.

His face had human features, maybe scary, maybe exaggerated, but human. He stared at Laurie through his dark eyes. A thick tongue ran over his fangs.

"What are you waiting for?" he said to Darian. "Why haven't you dispatched her?" His voice was also monstrous, but human. That was the key word, the word Laurie kept trying to tell herself. He was human. *Then how is he still alive?*

"I'm not going to kill my best friend. Stay the hell out of my head."

Joshua laughed. To Laurie, it sounded more like choking. She wanted to cover her ears.

"Insubordination?" Joshua gestured toward Maggie. "Haven't you already killed your best friend?" Tears streamed down Darian's cheek.

"You're insane," Laurie said. She looked to Darian. "Don't let him manipulate you. Listen to me. We have to get out of here." Darian seemed to understand. She seemed to be herself, the Darian that Laurie had known for fourteen years.

Joshua smiled. It was a calm and patient smile. Laurie thought of the devil's smile in the short story "The Man in the Black Suit." He gazed upon Darian. Darian gazed back.

"Look away," Laurie said. "He's trying to control you."

Darian nodded, then shakily raised the gun and aimed it at Laurie. Her lip quivered. "I'm sorry, Laurie." Joshua's grin grew broader, one of the evilest sights Laurie had beheld. Darian's finger tightened on the trigger.

"Darian," Laurie whispered, "you have to be strong. Fight him."

Trembling, Darian turned her attention to Joshua. His diabolical grin vanished like a magician's prop. If looks could kill, Laurie imagined that Darian would have dropped dead on the spot.

"Come on, Darian. Fight it. Fight him."

Darian nodded. Slowly, she diverted the gun from Laurie to Joshua. Her hand trembled violently. She braced the gun with her other hand, but it didn't help. Both hands shook.

Biting her lower lip, she screamed, "Screw you!" The magnum was aimed directly at Joshua's head. There was no way he could survive that. As Darian's finger tightened, he attacked.

A lightning–fast swipe of his hand batted the gun away. As soon as it hit the floor, he kicked it into the darkened back room, the one with the photo album and crates and boxes filled with holiday decorations. The gun went off. Nobody was hit, but Laurie screamed and took a huge leap backward.

Joshua seized Darian's throat and pulled her to her feet. He dragged her to one of the two pipes that connected from the floor to the ceiling between the operating table and sink. Violently, he began to bash her head and face off the pipe. *Bang! Bang! Bang!* The sound was sickening. Blood and teeth and shards of bone exploded in all directions.

Laurie attacked, punching and smacking and clawing him from behind. It had no effect. Joshua pulled Darian's head back and deliberately showed it to Laurie. Darian gasped for her last breaths of life. Her face was a pulp of bloody flesh. Joshua discarded her like a slab of meat. Her head and smashed face bounced off the floor with a wet smack, and she was gone.

"No!" Laurie screamed.

The man on the table began to moan. Joshua snapped his head toward him and back to Laurie. The look on his face told her he had something to attend to before murdering them all. He disappeared into the back room.

Laurie rushed to Marshall, who was starting to come around. "Can you get to your feet?" she whispered.

"Yeah, I think so." Laurie wanted to tell him that he didn't have a choice. It was either get to his feet or die.

Joshua emerged from the darkness holding a wooden shaft with a gleaming half-moon of metal lashed to its end. A scythe. He was very much the Grim Reaper in that moment, the angel of death that the devil himself fears.

He darted across the room and with a *whoosh*, swung at Laurie. The blade grazed her leg, splitting her jeans and leaving a gash.

Laurie yelped. Joshua raised the scythe and swung it at her head. Marshall pulled her up the steps, just out of harm's way. The scythe's breeze brushed her throat. Marshall and Laurie stumbled upstairs.

Joshua turned his attention to young man, still strapped down, still helpless. He raised the scythe and buried it between the man's thigh and pubic area. The blade punctured his groin, severed the femoral artery. Blood splattered onto the floor, mixing with the Darian's blood and brain and teeth and bone.

Deathblow dealt, Joshua withdrew the blade and made for the stairs.

28

The door was in sight. Thank God. Marshall limped. He was still bleeding internally and growing weaker by the moment. Just as he thought they were going to reach the safe haven, something grabbed his ankle. It was the blood–covered scythe. Joshua had caught them. Marshall tripped, nearly taking Laurie down too. He summoned the will to roll over and look up at the harbinger of death whose weapon was about to descend.

With a strength that Laurie never knew she had, she pulled Marshall out of the way as the scythe embedded into the floor. Joshua tried to extract it, but the blade was too deeply embedded. He grabbed Marshall's ankle and yanked him free of Laurie with such ease it reminded her of a video she'd watched of a mountain gorilla dragging a researcher away.

Laurie kicked. She imagined she was trying the break the hang time record for an NFL punt. Her shoe clipped Joshua's elbow and continued to his chin. His grip on Marshall's ankle released. He jerked halfway around and went to one knee.

Marshall crawled sluggishly to his feet. There was virtually no chance they would make it out the front door before Joshua recovered. *Up*, Laurie thought. Find somewhere to barricade or at least hide.

As they ascended, Laurie kept thinking of horror films. When the camera ascended the staircase it never meant anything good. They reached the top of the staircase and Marshall went straight for the attic door. Laurie heard Joshua's heavy footsteps pounding up the stairs.

The attic steps were very narrow and cluttered. Crates, bed comforters, bushel baskets overflowing with clothes. Laurie yanked the items aside and squeezed past, tugging Marshall behind her. If felt as if someone or something was trying to prevent their escape. Crude illustrations of cartoon characters were scrawled on the walls.

Laurie began to wonder Marshall had come this way. Other than gaining a little extra time, they seemed to be leaving themselves with no way out. *No. There must be something up here. Something we can use to fight back.* They reached the landing and a tiny window that overlooked the backyard. A small stand with a lamp stood in the corner. Boots pounded the floor behind them.

"Hurry," Laurie mouthed. Only four steps remained between them and the open attic. They may have ascended them in a single bound.

The attic was exactly as Deputy Flynn had witnessed—four skeletons on the couch, the eerily preserved corpse of Joshua's father in the casket, the antique embalming machine complete with wires, an old–fashioned wheel handle, and two glass cylinders, one labeled *ether*, the other *suction*. Laurie cupped her hands over her mouth. Marshall, who was leaning most of his weight on her for support, gaped in disbelief.

Sounds of clutter tumbling and thudding footsteps brought them back to their senses. Joshua was coming quickly. They only had a matter of seconds. Even if he was unarmed, even if he had not been able to free the scythe, it would be no contest. In their weakened state, neither Laurie nor Marshall stood a chance against the larger, quicker man. Death by bare hands would simply be slower.

They moved to the end of the attic filled with file cabinets, sculptures, and crates of children's books, coloring books, and old drawings and hid as best they could in shadow.

Joshua appeared at the head of the steps. His bug eyes turned to them as if he knew exactly where they were. His scowl became a hostile grin, fangs gleaming dully.

He didn't advance, but just stood there, apparently relishing the moment.

"Tell us why," Laurie said. "Why did our friend help you kill those people?"

"The first act of murder that your friend committed was the one right in front of you, the one you witnessed yourself, the murder of your friend Margaret. I simply provided her the means." Laurie knew that he was referring to the 45 Magnum.

"How did you make her pull the trigger?" She was surprised by Joshua's articulate speech. He was not some mindless demon, which only made the situation worse, really.

Joshua laughed. "You already know the answer."

Mind control? Telepathy? Laurie didn't want to believe that. It was impossible. But if it was impossible, how did he survive the gun shots? Laurie's eyes fixed on Joshua's monstrously humanoid features. He was more than just Joshua. He was the fiend that brought harm to the creatures of the earth, soiled their crops, the bane of all mankind. The poisoner, destroyer, bringer of sickness and death.

He had to be more than the boy with the vendetta against mankind for what they'd done to his father. Maybe he had started as that boy, but there had to have been a transition point. She couldn't accept that Darian had aided him in the haunted house murders. But why would Joshua lie to her? And Darian *had* killed Maggie right in front of Laurie.

Flashbacks poured into Laurie. Her conversations with James, trying to reassure him and set her younger brother's mind at ease. If she knew then that she would come face–to–face with the killer, she might have taken a different tone. *The world is not a safe place after all, James.* She gazed into Joshua's insectoid eyes, the sunken sockets that looked like he was wearing an excessive amount of mascara, the sandy blond hair, matted and stringy and caked to his reinforced forehead.

"Don't blame me," Joshua said with a growling chuckle. "I may have coaxed your friend once, but she was quite the little murderess, once unleashed."

"I don't believe you," Laurie shouted.

Joshua shrugged. "She may have had a hand in the trio of murders at Ghoul Mansion, as well as the execution at the Fortress of Fear. But then again, maybe not, huh? Maybe she *was* the sweet little slut you imagined. Oh, and how can we forget about the tampered candy?"

"What kind of monster are you?" Laurie screamed. He was playing mind games. *He* had made Darian kill Maggie. Whether it was supernatural was up for debate, but Darian couldn't have had anything to do with the other deaths. Could she?

Joshua stepped forward, causing Laurie and Marshall to back as far as they could. "Do you really want to know what I am? Wouldn't it be so much more delicious to finally discover what *you* are?"

Laurie didn't know what to say.

Marshall scanned his surroundings, using his periphery to search for a weapon of any kind.

"Extinction is inevitable," Joshua said. "Nature eventually selects every species for extinction. It is a frozen, immutable truth. Extinction is necessary. Without extinction, other species cannot ecologically flourish and diversify. Imagine a world where the dinosaurs had not gone extinct. No Tertiary era, no rise of mammals, and therefore, no you or him."

Marshall's squeezed Laurie's hand. He might not be good for much, but he was here. Her skin was slick, pulse pounding.

"I am an agent of extinction," Joshua boomed. "Armageddon. Apocalypse. I serve it, it serves me. We operate on mutual parasitism."

Marshall barely had the strength to stand, but he did the best he could to draw himself up. "Shut up, you sick creep." He found a broken pencil atop a filing cabinet. It was less than ideal, but better than nothing.

Joshua's expression didn't change. "I have been given a mission to kill every human being on the face of the earth. To usher in the end of times."

Did he think he was one of the four horsemen of the apocalypse? Marshall leaned away from Laurie and gathered himself. How do you reason with a mind–set like that?

"I'm not a monster," Joshua said. "Nor am I insane. It is simply inevitable for all species, including humans to become extinct. I'm expediting the process. And you, Ms. Williams, do you want to know why?"

"Because of what happened to your father," Laurie said.

"Oh, Laurie. Always the thinker. But sometimes you produce such shallow results." Joshua's scowl reappeared. "When I bore witness to my father's demise, I did declare war on them, all of them. I swore eternal vengeance, eternal hatred. I vowed that from that day forward, I would no longer be a boy. I had to become something…more."

"That's when you met the spirit of Halloween, right?"

Joshua nodded. Some invisible force seemed to beam from his shadow eyes. Her head snapped back nearly hard enough to cause whiplash.

A vision came to her. College boys, four of them, Shawn, Randolph, Earl, Donald, alone in the deep, dark woods with Farmer John's corpse. Joshua was nowhere, but Laurie could *feel* him watching.

Violence gushed from nowhere, an invisible claw that tore at the back of the boy carrying Farmer John's feet. Blood sprayed. The others dropped the body, eyes jumping from one dark place to another.

A fine red mist settled. A second attack tore the young man's spine from its fleshy abode. Friends screamed as the dead body collapsed in on itself. A high–pitched roar came from the forest as some sort of demonic dragon tore from the void.

The remaining three were gashed, disemboweled, and torn to ribbons. Entrails dangled from dissected torsos. Blood seeped from every orifice— *drip, drip drip*—onto the leaf-strewn forest floor. Laurie heard the pounding of her own heart in the silence that followed. Was Joshua showing her the truth or manipulating her with a lie?

Laurie willed herself away from terrible scene. A garish orange light blinded her temporarily—a fade–to–white screenshot—and the vision was over.

She looked to Joshua, who was once again grinning broadly, making a seemingly deliberate effort to show off his teeth. Laurie thought of mandrills, baboons. A lion.

Joshua began to close the distance between them.

"So what," Laurie said frantically. "The spirit of Halloween killed the four boys who killed your father? Then what? Did it possess you or something?"

Marshall's knees buckled. For a split second, Laurie had to pull against him, using her strength to keep him on his feet. Sharp pains shot down her back. She prayed that she could hold out long enough. *For what?* She saw the pencil clutched in Marshall's hand like a child's pretend knife. It seemed so hopeless.

Joshua looked on with an unchanging grin. "Or something," he said.

Laurie wanted to ask if she was speaking to Joshua or the spirit of Halloween operating through Joshua. She didn't. Delving deeper into Joshua's madness was exactly what he wanted. It only lessened her odds for survival and threatened to crack her sanity at a moment's notice. She knew in her heart that Joshua was Joshua. He operated out of his own mind, and his actions were his own.

Joshua began to click and grind his teeth, a grating sound that sent chills down her spine. "The druids used to hold sacrificial rituals. Great fires were lit. People from across the land dressed in costumes to ward off evil spirits and dance around those fires. There were banquets and all manner of festivities. The Celtic people were in awe of time and believed that on the festival of Samhain, time lost its meaning. Past, present, future converged, until the celebrators existed beyond the space–time continuum. The dead and denizens of the other worlds were free to walk among the living. It was a time of fairies, ghosts, demons, witches. Winter–time became the season of ghosts, Samhain a celebration of their release from the underworld." Joshua shivered, an entire-body vibration like a dog after its bath.

"It was a magical time," he said. "You people have forgotten such details, and yet you are so quick to celebrate what you don't understand, aren't you? Partake in festivities pertaining to the unknown rather than fear it the way nature intended."

"Not everyone," Laurie murmured. If only Joshua's father had not died.

"My father was the tip of the iceberg," Joshua said. "Pardon the cliché. The truth is that human beings like to operate from an anthropocentric mind–set. Monsters and gods become the stuff of fantasy. Why is that, Laurie? You know a *little* history, right?"

"I... don't... tell me, Joshua." *Keep him talking. We need more time.* She glanced at Marshall, now leaning against a file cabinet. The pencil shard was still gripped in his white-knuckled fist, but he looked entirely incapable of wielding even that.

Joshua laughed. "You begin to appreciate how small your brain has become through atrophy, don't you, Laurie. It must be very humbling." He spread his arms. "When polytheism was common and there was a deity for every act of nature, every element, earth, wind, water, fire, monsters were more simplified and traditional. Nowadays, the notion of gods, is laughable to most and culture is more dependent upon more and more complex monsters. Monsters begin to resemble gods."

"You put supernatural figures on a pedestal, Laurie. You worship the antithesis of the Great Creator. The spirit of Halloween opened my eyes. There's more to Samhain than costumes and candy. I've come to understand that, and soon the world will too.

"My mission is to restore balance to the natural order. Then, although no human will live to see it, the laws of the natural world will repair. The world of the living will merge periodically with the world of the dead as in ages past. The living who are soon to be the dead will become part of a new and blossoming species. Time will muddle as the universe speaks, and the Great Creator will be appeased as he witnesses the unification of heaven and hell and earth. Imagine it, Laurie. Weakness and sickness abolished, no more innocent people victimized. People will learn their place in the universe after the hills run red with blood, and at last you will see nature the way God intended it."

A sudden rage steamed through Laurie. She thought of Jesus on the cross, the crucifix in her Grandmother's living room. "Are you out of your mind? This is not what God wants."

Joshua's arms lowered to his sides. For a second, he stood stock still, as if considering the possibility, she raised.

Then came at them.

Laurie screamed. She clawed at Marshall's arm, his fist, the pencil. *Pathetic.* The thought came from nowhere and everywhere.

Joshua knocked Marshall aside and wrapped his fingers around her throat. "I hardly think you're in a position to speak for God," he said. "But you are correct. It's what *I* want."

Marshall lay like a ragdoll on the attic floor. He wasn't going to make it much longer. Joshua lifted Laurie by her throat. She choked and thrashed violently. She gouged his eye. Joshua growled, more rage than pain, but there was a *hint* of pain in there somewhere, wasn't there?

Laurie pushed her thumb into the socket until something gave. As Joshua released his grip, she saw that the eye was swelled shut and a deeper black–blue than it had been. She fell to the floor and stumbled back into the wall. A massive pressure developed behind her eyes and pounded through her forehead. Her face tingled.

Joshua wiped blood from his cheek. A dark red rivulet trickled from his deformed eye. Marshall groaned. His hands moved into position to do a pushup but splayed out at his first effort. He fell flat with a quiet grunt. *We have to get out of here*, Laurie thought. *Please God, we need a miracle.*

An inhuman growl came from Joshua. Laurie felt an indentation in the wall behind her. She moved sideways and backed into a tiny back room. Just how invulnerable was Joshua? His skin seemed tougher than a normal person's, much tougher, but it was penetrable as was evidenced by the six bullets she had put into him. But that had only slowed him down rather than stopping him dead. Exactly how that was, she couldn't answer. There was a chance she hadn't hit any vital areas, but six slugs should have taken him down, regardless.

No, she forced herself to think. *It's not hopeless. If it bleeds, we can kill it. If he bleeds, he can die.*

"Believe whatever you want," Joshua said as he squeezed through the doorway. Laurie thought of Cthulhu squeezing through the doorway of his underwater tomb in the monstrous city of R'lyeh. There was only one option. Fight. She would fight harder than she had ever fought before. Laurie had heard of ninety–pound women fending off fifteen–hundred–

pound polar bears when their central nervous system stopped regulating the percentage of muscle fibers used for a given task, and they tapped into their hidden, hysterical strength.

"You're too cerebral for that," Joshua said. "You know, I really am disappointed in you, Laurie. I thought you'd put up a better struggle."

Laurie trembled. She couldn't even raise her hands defensively. *No hint of hidden strength here.*

"Hey, Joshua," Marshall called from the attic.

Joshua turned slowly. Laurie saw Marshall through the doorway. He had crawled to the casket and lifted himself to his feet.

"What do you think of this?" he said. He leaned his full weight into the casket until it toppled sideways, scattering a portion of the copious candles that surrounded it. Farmer John's body spilled onto the floor. Flickering flames licked the curtains. Wax formed pools and spouted dancing fire of varying hues—red and orange and yellow, green and blue.

Joshua let out a growl so riddled with hatred and unadulterated rage that it sounded even more removed from humanity than before. He advanced on Marshall.

That's it, Marshall thought. *Keep coming. I got a present for you. Come here and see what I got for you, you maniac.*

Behind his back, Marshall held a sickle in his trembling hand. It had been hanging on the wall behind the casket like a Christmas present just begging to be opened. The sight had inspired Marshall to new effort. Hidden reserves had opened to him.

When Joshua was within striking range, Marshall swung. Joshua caught his wrist and twisted. With a sick snapping sound, Marshall's arm bent, then cracked, a jagged bone shard pushing through the shiny skin of his inner wrist. The sickle clattered to the floor.

Joshua punched Marshall, splitting his lip. He drove Marshall backward over the burning casket, sending him headfirst into a tiny window. Fresh pains lanced Marshall's face.

Joshua hauled him back by his belt and flung him onto the burning floor. Marshall's head smacked the burning coffin. The strength went out of him a final time. He had no further reserves.

Joshua pulled his father's body into the coffin and heaved the entire thing across the attic. Flames sprouted from the coffin's lining and lid and spread to the wall. He turned his attention to Marshall. With his boot, he forced Marshall's head sideways onto the hard floor.

At least I gave Laurie a chance to escape, Marshall thought. He tried to look for her, hoping she *wasn't* there. He saw a quick movement but couldn't focus.

As Joshua hovered above Marshall, Laurie scampered to the neglected sickle. She seized it firmly in both hands.

"Joshua," she yelled.

Joshua grunted primitively and turned to face her. This time even his cat–like reflexes could not prevent the attack. The blade sliced through his throat. The cut was so broad and deep it appeared his entire head would peel off. Joshua gripped the wound with both hands. His carotid artery and jugular vein had been severed. That much Laurie could tell. She had nearly decapitated him.

Joshua dropped to his knees as blood welled between his fingers, down his Halloween costume, and onto the burning floor. Joshua choked for breath. Laurie felt a tad bit sadistic. She *liked* the sound coming from him.

Joshua's mouth opened and closed. His remaining eye, that bulging, black window of evil, looked up to Laurie. The hands holding his neck together, she thought, are the same ones he used to strangle and stab all many people. She'd felt that grip on her own throat. *I'm not sorry,* she thought. *I have no reason to regret.* His hands formed somewhat of a tourniquet, but even his strength could not stop blood from spurting out. What little color that he did have in his face was draining into his core.

Suddenly, Joshua stopped gasping. Still staring up at Laurie, he slumped onto his side. His hands let go of his throat and, with a loud thump, he was nothing more than a mass of dead flesh. Dead. His glassy black eye stared into the eternal abyss that it had once invoked in Laurie. At last it was over. After a month of terror and death and brutality, the nightmare was over. Joshua was dead.

Laurie dropped the sickle. She knelt beside Marshall and helped him to his feet. Carrying most of his weight, Laurie limped for the stairs.

Before she knew it, they were on the front lawn. They had passed all those colorful and frightening rooms filled with Halloween props without a second glance.

Marshall sagged onto the grass. Lauri let herself go down beside him. They sat there on the front lawn and watched the farm go up in flames. Windows exploded, ceiling collapsed, billows of black smoke spiraled up. The crisp October air became redolent with the scent of burning wood, like a giant bonfire…or a druid fire. Sirens sounded in the distance. Lauri imagined she could hear the wails and laughter and agonizing screams from the Halloween props as they burned to cinder.

Skeletal beams gave way, tossing flurries of embers into the night sky. Laurie saw two things. A couplet of images, one followed by the other, men in Halloween costumes. The first wore a velociraptor mask, beige, with chocolate–brown stripes and eyes like Green Lantern, and a blue– and–green–striped sweater. The second was dressed in a bisected costume reminiscent of Harvey "Two–Face" Dent from the Batman comics, a plaid sweater and a face that was half werewolf and half burlap sack.

As quickly as the figures appeared, they were gone. Laurie recalled Joshua's description of time converging. Was that what she saw? An omen? A vision of the future? She grasped her knees. She was tired of thinking. She would need to see a shrink when this was done. She had lost four of her best friends. Nearly five. She nudged Marshall. He tilted sideways, then back against her shoulder. His eyelids fluttered.

29

Marshall lay on a stretcher in the ambulance. A breathing mask covered his lower face and he was hooked up to more tubes and IV's than Laurie could comprehend, but they said his condition was stabilized.

"That's one tough man you've got there," a paramedic said. "I wouldn't worry if I were you, hon. He's going to pull through just fine." A weight lifted from Laurie's shoulders. She touched Marshall's unresponsive hand. She recalled the commotion that ensued as the press descended upon the crime scene. Authorities hadn't yet taken full control. The yellow tape had just started to unwind.

Laurie was bombarded by voices. It was a mangled and confused mass of words, but the one question that she had actually picked up on was "How does it feel now that's it finally over?" Police and paramedics had gotten to them before Laurie could answer. She mumbled to herself as the crowd was being driven back. "What makes you think it's over?"

One of the reporters, a woman with crinkled brown hair ducked under the chain of interlocked arms. A microphone jutted from her clenched hand. "Ms. Williams, what was that? Could you please—" A detective shoved her back. "Show some respect. Leave the girl alone, she's been through a lot."

Beyond the heaving crowed, Farmer John's house was reduced to a smoldering heap of blackened beams. Firefighters continued to spray the area in crisscrossing patterns. Laurie wondered if the water would run out. She swallowed thickly and squeezed Marshalls fingers. They were safe for now.

Brilliant lights flooded the ambulance. Laurie's eyes welled as she thought of Rick and Billy and Maggie and even Darian.

"Hey," Marshall's groggy voice whispered. "We made it."

Laurie sniffled and wiped her tears. She gripped Marshall's hand even tighter. She didn't say anything because there was nothing more to be said.

They *had* made it. They survived this long ordeal. Next came the hard part. Surviving its memory.

As if closing the door on this chapter of their lives, the ambulance doors clapped shut, sealing them from the remnants of Halloween night. Laurie wept. She wept because she had to, because it was the only thing she could do. For the sake of her lost friends. She would survive. She and Marshall. It would take time, but they had all the time in the universe. As she thought these thoughts and clung to Marshall, paramedics and drivers loaded themselves into the vehicle. Sirens wailed. They jolted toward the road that would take them home.

Epilogue

Like a phoenix Joshua's roasted corpse rose from the smoldering remnants of his childhood. The gaping wound in his neck had been cauterized and more than 90 percent of his body was covered in third–degree burns. Charred skin smoked. Patches of muscle, tendon, and ligament showed through his blackened body. Tufts of singed hair jutted from his malformed skull.

A firefighter unfortunate enough to encounter the burned figure had received a red–hot rusted nail through his eyeball for his troubles. Joshua was safely concealed in the woods behind what was once his house. Not that it mattered. Nobody could stop him. He had overcome everything they'd thrown at him.

Calmly, he watched the commotion of unwelcome visitors on his property. Gleaming white fang–teeth contrasted sharply against his lipless black mouth. The whites of his eyes stood out in the darkness that he now called home. There was a nostalgia in this. He recalled the skinless and burnt figure that had watched the four boys years ago. There were patterns in life and death. He lifted a linen pillowcase from the ground near his feat. It contained a couple of costumes miraculously preserved from the flames by the wooden box that had held them. The box was ash now, a sacrifice to the inferno.

Clutching his meager possessions, he turned and proceeded into the woods. He was going away for a while. After a time, his sensitive ears and eyes and tongue and nostrils were safely away from the scents and sights and sounds of the battle. He could relax here. His broken body would heal. Plans would congeal. He had as much time as he needed, and he was going to take advantage of it.

But not too long.

Afterward

I must begin by saying thank you to my two uncles—Danny and EJ Ryan—and a good friend of ours, Shawn Bullisco, for giving me the idea for this book. Even though I wrote this four–hundred–plus–page beast, without the late nights those guys stayed up way back in 2002, brainstorming different plotlines for what would make an intriguing haunted house/murder mystery/Halloween–themed story, I would've had nowhere to start. Thank you all, and I'm sure the three of you are glad, at least as much as I am, to see that all those years of us sitting around and coming back to this has finally led to something in the form of a published horror novel. Now the next step is for us to get this tale adapted into a movie, and the dream will finally come full circle.

Haunted Farm formerly published as *Haunted Revengeance* (and I need to give a shout out to Stephen Ramey and Sue Linville for suggesting a much less confusing title) is more or less my love letter to the horror genre. Whenever I sit down to watch a movie, I always gravitate towards those types of films. That's how it's always been and, I assume, how it will remain. There are numerous references to slasher films throughout the book, and I drew a lot of inspiration, naturally, from the *Halloween* series of films and lesser–known novelizations, particularly of the first, second and fourth entries. A lot of the supernatural undertones in this work come from those, including a line of tie–in comics of the franchise published by Chaos Comics and a wonderful line written by Stefan Hutchinson that was beautifully written and illustrated and ran from 2003–2008. Of course, there are a lot of nods to Poe, Lovecraft and Stephen King, as well as the holiday and traditions themselves. My goal was to make the book as laden with rich detail as possible, and I can only hope, as you read by candlelight, that you can smell the crisp air and taste sweet things. Hope you're not too scared. It is just a book, after all.

Preview for *Mediums*

It is where all points converge—life, reality, heaven, hell, thought, imagination—that therein lies the answer. It is here, you see, wherein a governing instability, a kind of hideous, unquantifiable destruction, ever–presently lurks. At this spot, I'm afraid you'll learn, in ways you've never known you were capable, that Titanos reigns at The Throne of Ultimate Chaos.

Don't try to understand it, you can't. And don't try to think about it either. You're already happier than you know that you lack that capability as well without even being aware of it. Just settle on this for now. This is whatever you sense around you, regardless of your condition. Just never lead yourself into believing that there isn't an off switch for the universe, for the heavens, for the underworld, and all of that conjoined and augmented past the invention of numbers, because what breathes life into all grows stressed, trembles with each titanic function. All you need know is that The Throne of Ultimate Chaos weighs it all down, creating hells out of heavens and hells out of hells. This, my tender ear, is the ultimate reign of Titanos.